"*The Consequence of Loving Colton* is a must-read friends-to-lovers story that's as passionate and sexy as it is hilarious!"

—Melissa Foster, *New York Times* bestselling author

"Just when you think Van Dyken can't possibly get any better, she goes and delivers *The Consequence of Loving Colton*. Full of longing and breathless moments, this is what romance is about."

—Lauren Layne, *USA Today* bestselling author

"The tension between Milo and Colton made this story impossible to put down. Quick, sexy, witty—easily one of my favorite books from Rachel Van Dyken."

—R. S. Grey, *USA Today* bestselling author

"Hot, funny . . . will leave you wishing you could get marked by one of the immortals!"

—Molly McAdams, *New York Times* bestselling author, on *The Dark Ones*

"Laugh-out-loud fun! Rachel Van Dyken is on my auto-buy list."

—Jill Shalvis, *New York Times* bestselling author, on *The Wager*

"*The Dare* is a laugh-out-loud read that I could not put down. Brilliant. Just brilliant."

—Cathryn Fox, *New York Times* bestselling author

Risky Play

The Seaside Series

Tear
Pull
Shatter
Forever
Fall
Eternal
Strung
Capture

The Renwick House Series

The Ugly Duckling Debutante
The Seduction of Sebastian St. James
An Unlikely Alliance
The Redemption of Lord Rawlings
The Devil Duke Takes a Bride

The London Fairy Tales Series

Upon a Midnight Dream
Whispered Music
The Wolf's Pursuit
When Ash Falls

The Seasons of Paleo Series

Savage Winter
Feral Spring

The Wallflower Series (with Leah Sanders)

Waltzing with the Wallflower
Beguiling Bridget
Taming Wilde

The Dark Ones Saga

The Dark Ones
Untouchable Darkness
Dark Surrender
Darkest Temptation

Stand-Alones

Hurt: A Collection (with Kristin Vayden and Elyse Faber)
Rip
Compromising Kessen
Every Girl Does It
The Parting Gift (with Leah Sanders)
Divine Uprising

Risky Play

Red Card, Book One

RACHEL VAN DYKEN

SKYSCAPE

SKYSCAPE

Published by Skyscape, New York

www.apub.com

Amazon, the Amazon logo, and Skyscape are trademarks of Amazon.com, Inc., or its affiliates.

ISBN-13: 9781542043724
ISBN-10: 1542043727

Cover design by Letitia Hasser

Cover photography by Wander Aguiar Photography

Printed in the United States of America

*To Tracey and Krista, I'll never
be able to express how much your
feedback means to me on a daily
basis. This one's for you.*

Prologue

MACKENZIE

"Mackenzie Allistar DuPont." Alton drew out my name like it was part of me, the most important part. My gut twisted as he held my hands between his, squeezing my fingers so tightly they lost feeling, all before he leaned over my hand and whispered, "I can't do this." A sense of foreboding trickled down my spine. I swayed on my feet. It was wrong, the way he said my name like I was a thing and not a person. The way he looked at me like I was a stranger.

Blood rushed to my face as a choking sensation wrapped around my neck until I was afraid something was going to pop. I must have heard him wrong.

My head began pounding as whispers of outrage floated around the winery.

The very exclusive Prosser Winery.

The chocolate-brown hair that I'd so often run my fingers through at the nape of his neck provided no comfort like it used to. My eyes soaked in his features, his dark eyebrows looked like angry slashes across his forehead as he looked down at our hands in confusion like he wasn't sure how we got to this point, but I knew. We were here because of our parents' expectations. This moment had been bred into us since we could talk. It was a foregone conclusion.

He gave his head a shake and stood to his full height, released my hands, and simply turned around and began walking. My jaw dropped. He was walking away.

From me.

One step. Two.

My breath caught. The choking sensation around my throat worsened to a painful degree.

His sigh had said more than it should. It said all the things that hadn't been spoken about. It said this was wrong. It said we were wrong.

My eyes filled with tears as my bridesmaids huddled around me in a flurry of swear words and cryptic comments like "I knew he would do this."

Guests stood.

Dad started yelling obscenities.

His groomsman Jagger ran after him, most likely to punch him then talk some sense into what used to be his close friend.

But I was frozen.

Because I had done this to myself.

We'd done it to ourselves.

Partners. We were supposed to be partners.

And even though I hadn't loved him the way I knew I should.

It still felt *right*.

Didn't it?

My bouquet seemed to fall apart in slow motion as it hit the floor. The petals scattered around my perfectly pink pedicured feet, and I wondered if this was the ending I deserved after doing everything right. After being the perfect daughter. Perfect student. Perfect fiancée.

I started walking along the same aisle I'd just marched down seconds earlier with a bright smile and a wink in Alton's direction.

I squeezed my eyes shut as my feet carried me farther away from the beckoning calls of my parents and the people that called themselves my friends. I knew the truth, though. Alton had been my best friend, my only friend, my one ally within the circle of people who wanted me only for my name, for my money. Friends? Now I had none.

I walked.

And wondered why my tears weren't spilling onto my cheeks as I finally made my way to the first car I could find, hopped in the passenger side, and said, "Drive."

Chapter One

MACKENZIE

Six months later

"What do you mean you're on a plane?" Mom's worried tone only made my decision more resolute. I chugged the first-class champagne like water and held out my glass for more, hands shaking around the tiny stem.

"Mom, I need a break from all of this. From everything . . ." My throat squeezed so tight I almost broke down and burst into tears. I hadn't shed one yet, and I wasn't about to now that I was sitting in first class on my way to Puerto Vallarta all by myself.

On the honeymoon I'd purchased as a surprise for Alton.

The bright-red reminder was on my calendar. It had been staring me down for months. I'd picked up the phone to cancel a dozen times, only to hang up. Was it because it was the last remaining thing that connected me to the life I thought we were going to have? Was I still holding out hope? After seeing him at work and being on the receiving end of more than one of his "bless your heart" smiles, I'd decided to use the trip as a show of independence and a "my life isn't over, it's just begun" sort of thing. Only now? Now I was clearly realizing I wasn't okay, not by a long shot. When you're okay you don't chug champagne and hold tears back in first class.

It wasn't just that I missed us.

I missed him.

My best friend.

We'd been inseparable since birth.

Our first baths had been side by side, as awkward and weird as that sounds, and our moms had been best friends.

We belonged to the same country club.

We attended the same high school, where as a cheerleader, I cheered for him. Alton Davis, star quarterback and the hottest guy to ever hit West Valley High. God, I could still see my dad's face after Alton proposed, it was like the son he'd always wanted was finally going to become part of our family. I'd been so proud to flash that ring to anyone who asked. I'd finally succeeded in having it all, right? I was finally worthy of my parents' dynasty.

I had said yes to the man I'd been glued to since I could talk.

The man who took me to prom every year.

The man who waited to sleep with me out of respect.

The man who had it all.

The man who was supposed to take over my father's empire at my side.

So why had I felt empty on my wedding day even before he turned his back on me? I swiped a tear from my cheek.

"Honey." Mom's voice softened. "I'm worried about you. You rarely come to family dinners, I haven't seen you at the club since—" She didn't have to say it. Since I was left at the altar.

Since my marriage bust had become national news.

After all, it wasn't every day an heiress to one of the largest and most sought-after wine brands was left at the altar. "Used Wine Back on the Market."

Yeah, that had been a fun one.

With lots of memes.

Involving, you guessed it, fruit.

"One Cherry Less Popped." That had been a personal favorite, since my dad also owned enough cherry farms to put any farmer in the nation to shame.

"I know." I didn't let her finish. I shuddered a bit as the captain came over the loudspeaker. I normally had Alton with me on every business trip. I wasn't necessarily scared to fly, I was just . . . alone. So damn alone. "I promise I'll call you when I land. I need this, though, I just need—" *To breathe.* I needed air. I needed to find out who I was without him. And if that woman even existed, since I couldn't remember a time when I wasn't by his side.

Thirty years I'd been part of a duo.

And now, now I was just . . . me.

It was depressing.

And six months ago when he'd walked out of my life.

I'd cut him out of mine.

It hurt too much, even if he was right in doing what he did.

Alton was always stronger than me.

I was a total people pleaser and he was the schmoozer who always had people eating out of the palm of his hand. He took charge, and oftentimes when I tried he told me he'd handle the situation. And he did. I frowned. Was that right? Was my future really that of a trophy wife with no thoughts of her own? No. No, that wouldn't . . . I always thought he was similar to me, just wanting to please his parents, until finally, he didn't. In the end he pleased himself and told everyone else to go to hell.

I hung up the phone to my mom's murmured "I love you."

And stared straight ahead as more champagne was poured into my glass. I tilted it back without a second thought, gulping the entire contents and then wiping the liquid from my lips with the back of my hand.

"Scared of flying?" came a cultured Spanish accent from next to me. It was barely noticeable, but I traveled enough to catch it. I slowly turned my attention to the guy who'd just sat down in the aisle seat.

Black Bose headphones hung around his neck, and he wore a tight Under Armour hoodie and a denim jacket, which indicated he was a guy who knew how to make comfortable look fashionable. He had this cool personal style that made me look. My eyes took in his burgundy skinny jeans and gray high-tops. I almost gave him a nod of approval for doing his own thing, when he turned a golden-eyed gaze to me and winked.

Caught. So embarrassingly caught checking him out.

Oh.

Oh.

I jerked my gaze away.

Like a kid caught stealing a piece of candy.

"No." I finally found my voice. What had he asked? Oh right, flying. "I travel all the time, it's just been a rough . . . day." Or year. Yeah, let's go with day, though. Don't want to sound too pathetic.

"I'm sorry to hear that," he said smoothly with another wink before ordering a glass of Merlot that I knew by heart. I'd tasted the first barrel. My mouth watered.

It was a good choice.

Damn him.

Men who knew wine were my weakness.

Alton had always—

Stop. I needed to stop.

Alton was gone.

Gone.

I cleared my throat. "Good choice, that's one of my favorites."

"Other than champagne?" He grinned, showing straight, white teeth that almost blinded me against his smooth, tanned skin.

"Other than champagne," I agreed, still a bit tongue-tied as the flight attendant brought his drink in a stemless glass. He swirled the wine around, examined the legs, sniffed.

My jaw almost came unhinged as I watched him test it.

I waited on pins and needles for approval, not even realizing how much I needed it until he sipped the wine.

God, was I that ridiculous?

Needing a stranger to tell me I had good taste in my own father's wine?

I really did need a vacation.

"It's good," he finally said.

"Good," I repeated. "Good?"

He smirked at me. "Emotionally invested in wine, then? Just had a desire for champagne instead?"

I narrowed my eyes. "What about the aroma of cherries? I think if you take another sip you'll also notice the robust—"

He placed a finger to my lips and whispered, "I said it was good, are you trying to change my opinion, then?"

My lips parted.

"Folks, looks like we're first for takeoff. Flight attendants, please prepare the cabin."

I watched in shock as he didn't finish his wine but handed it off to the flight attendant. Annoyed, I decided not to speak to him the rest of the flight.

Great, now I was punishing a stranger because of his taste in wine.

I was going to die alone.

Damn it, Alton.

If he'd been there he'd have held my hand, rubbed his thumb lightly over my skin, and then later told me something like the guy was beneath us. Which wasn't true. He had a very low opinion of anyone who wasn't in his circle, which had always bothered me. Now I was nervous that the one thing I'd despised about him was rubbing off on me.

My chest tightened.

That's why I needed this vacation.

I needed to decide who I was.

Because at thirty years old, when I looked in the mirror I didn't see just me, I saw the man who was supposed to be by my side, along with all the flaws that somehow pushed him away. My need to please, my need for my parents' approval, pushing my girlfriends away because I had him, because they made me lose focus on the prize—running the family business. Thirty years old and I had no life to speak of and now no fiancé.

Chapter Two

Vacation had been the only option after getting offered one of the highest salaries in US soccer. They needed a face to sell . . . and I wanted to get away from my old team.

Not to mention my old co-captain and former best friend.

I jerked my headphones over my ears and closed my eyes. I was so damn jetlagged I could sleep for years. The wine had tasted phenomenal, but I was too exhausted to finish it, and I wasn't an animal.

One never chugged wine.

Or champagne for that matter.

The woman next to me started reading a gossip magazine. The faces staring at me from the cover belonged to me and my ex-girlfriend, and I cringed.

Thank God I was wearing my hair down around my ears so I wasn't immediately recognizable.

The black beanie helped.

But there was nothing I could do about my golden eyes.

People typically saw what they wanted, though, and according to the world I was still hiding out in my flat licking my wounds.

I squeezed my eyes shut.

From Premier league to the United States.

From Chelsea.

To Seattle.

It was career suicide.

But I'd wanted to be as far away as possible.

And since my mom was American, it made sense.

At least to me.

My former teammates had something else to say about their number-one striker running away.

I snorted. Let their girls get knocked up by a teammate and get back to me.

Shit.

Music pounded in my ears, lulling me to sleep. A few days away before the chaos started, and I'd be good as new.

I licked my lips, still tasting the wine on them, and closed my eyes, letting sleep take me.

◆ ◆ ◆

"WAKE UP!" a voice screeched next to me.

I jerked to attention as the woman tugged down my headphones and reached for my hand. "Engine failure!"

"Stop yelling." I pressed a hand to my temple as I looked around the cabin. Everyone seemed to be panicked and staring at the flight attendant like she was going to somehow fix this or hand out parachutes.

"This is your captain," crackled a reasonably calm voice over the loudspeaker. "We've lost one engine, but luckily we're a few miles out from the Puerto Vallarta airport. Just hang tight and try to relax. We'll be making an emergency landing in the next ten minutes." Oxygen masks tumbled from the panel above us. The captain came back on. "Flight attendants, prepare the cabin, and buckle up."

The woman next to me was pale as a ghost. "This!" She held her head in her hands. "It can't end like this! I'm not ready, you hear me, universe!" She clenched her fists. "I was left at the altar, this is unfair! Completely unfair!"

"Uh, can I get you something?" I whispered to her in an effort to both calm her and try to get her to put the mask over her nose and mouth. "To help you calm down and stop talking to yourself?"

"One thing." Her light-blue eyes met mine as an electrical charge pulsed between our bodies.

The plane shook and dove a few hundred feet. I grabbed her hand and rubbed it with my thumb.

She shrieked and reached for my shirt, gripping it with both hands while her eyes frantically searched mine for confirmation everything was going to be okay.

The plane plummeted again.

I gripped her hands, needing the distraction just as much, as a loud noise filled the cabin.

"Answer this question: What one thing do you regret?" she said in a voice that sounded like failure, like giving up, like the world was against her in every single way.

"Just one?" I tried to make light of the conversation even though my adrenaline was spiking like I'd just started the championship match. The plane kept diving at rapid speeds, causing my stomach to lurch. We needed to get our masks on, but getting them on seemed like it would only make her more frantic, and I needed her calm. I wasn't sure why—I just did. Maybe because her touch was calming me. Maybe because it was the first time I'd touched another woman since being betrayed by the one I thought I loved.

"One." She nodded more calmly now.

I kept my eyes locked on hers. "I would have drunk all the wine. You were right, it deserved more than a 'good.'"

Her eyes lit up like I'd just told her she was the most beautiful woman I'd ever seen, which wasn't too far off the mark. From her caramel-colored hair to her almost too-big eyes to the wide smile on her pillow-like lips, I could imagine many things I'd rather be doing with her than talking.

"Really?"

"Really." I nodded. "Your turn."

The plane dipped, and she sent a worried glance toward the cockpit.

"Hey." I grabbed her chin. "It's going to be fine, pilots are trained for this. Just focus on me, on my voice. Can you do that?"

She swallowed, closed her eyes, then nodded. "Yes, I can do that."

"Good." I dropped my hand as an alarm sounded around the plane. The flight attendants ran to their spots as we lost more elevation. I could see the mountains in the window right along with civilization; we were at least ten thousand feet, maybe lower. The airport must be nearby.

"I would have said no," she finally answered.

"Said no?" I repeated, confused.

"To Alton, when he asked me if I loved him. I would have said no. I would have said not the way you deserve, and I would have walked away."

Heavy.

My eyes briefly scanned her left hand. No ring.

"And then"—she kept talking—"I think I would have kissed you."

My eyebrows shot up as a smile spread across my face despite my growing anxiety over how fast the plane was traveling and how close we were getting to the ground. "Oh? You often kiss strangers?"

"Only ones from Spain." So she'd nailed my heritage without even asking. Which seemed impossible, I was mostly half Spanish and German with a whole bunch of other things my mom couldn't seem to remember.

"Spain is for lovers," I found myself saying like an idiot.

She smiled, though.

And I wanted to think it was because of me, not because of who I was, or what I did.

"My favorite place in the world," she said in a faraway voice as the plane bounced lower, making her shriek as she clutched both my hands in hers. "Are we going to die?"

"Absolutely not," I lied. I wasn't sure what was going to happen, but I couldn't die, not when I finally had a fresh start. "We'll be just fine."

"Okay." She nodded a few times and gulped. "But just in case, I think I'll do this—"

Her mouth was on mine before I could protest.

And then any argument I would have had died on my lips at the first taste of her tongue. Her hands tugged on my hair as my arms wrapped around her warm body.

The plane made a screeching sound and then slammed against the runway, pulling us apart amidst sirens and cheers from the other passengers.

I stared at a pair of lips I wanted to taste again.

And when she said, "I'm Ashley, what's your name?"

I did the dumbest thing to date and lied. "I'm Hugo. Nice to meet you."

Chapter Three

MACKENZIE

I just mauled a nice stranger with my tongue.

And gave him a fake name.

All within the span of five minutes.

This was not normal behavior.

But he'd been there.

And those eyes.

Paired with my absolute panic that we were about to die, I just . . . I reacted.

And it felt good.

So.

Good.

The last time I'd reacted to something without thinking, it had been with hives after eating too much peanut butter. Well, that and this vacation. Two instances.

I wasn't reactive.

I was a planner.

Which was probably why my parents were so concerned about my impromptu trip. I was the girl that had a wedding book at age five and had picked out my colors and flowers at six.

"Where are you staying, Ashley?" Hugo asked.

Oh duh, me. He was talking to me. I was Ashley, not Mackenzie. "Um, the Secrets resort, something . . ." I frowned. All I could remember was that I'd booked the penthouse with a swim-out because Alton said he'd want his own private pool for us since we wouldn't be leaving the room at all.

I blushed at the thought.

Funny, since the guy had never passed third base the entire time we were together.

Saving it for later, he said.

Making it special, he said.

He respected my father too much, he said.

Hugo handed me my bag. "Me too."

"You too?" I said in a confused voice as we were shuffled out of the plane by security and enough police officers to make my head dizzy.

"Secrets," he said slowly. "It was one of the first ones to pop up on my search engine. I booked it and didn't look back."

"Oh." My head felt warm as I followed him off the plane and toward customs. He went into a different line, not that I was watching.

By the time my passport was stamped and I found my luggage, he was nowhere to be found.

I tried not to be disappointed.

After all, this vacation was about me.

Not the handsome stranger I'd kissed in first class when I thought I was about to die.

"You ready?" Hugo said from behind.

I jerked and then turned as he dangled the keys to what looked like a Ferrari—the rearing horse emblem was a dead giveaway—in front of my face.

I was used to money.

But my family didn't spend it if it wasn't necessary.

So renting an expensive foreign car?

Not necessary when you could invest!

Who was this guy?

"You're not one of those people that kidnap Americans and then get a ransom, are you?" I asked stupidly.

He bit down on his lip. "Do I look like a kidnapper?"

"Well . . ." I narrowed my eyes and studied him. "No. Yes. I'm not sure."

He leaned in until we were chest to chest. "Trust me."

I sucked in a breath, he was so close, and the gold flecks in his eyes were so hypnotic I didn't even blink. "Can I?"

He shrugged. "Who knows? You're being spontaneous, you're the one with all the regrets."

"Not true—" I started to argue.

He silenced me with a brief kiss that left me shocked, aroused, and my heart pounding. "Then why the question? The one thing you ask before you plummet to your death is what you would do different, which makes me assume you would do a lot of things different, and you don't look like the type of girl who gets into cars with strange men."

"That's because I listened about stranger danger in school." I smirked.

He barked out a laugh. "I must have missed that lesson." One side of his mouth lifted in a cocky half smile. "I skipped a lot of school . . ."

"Shocking." I crossed my arms.

"Get in."

"But—"

"Send a text to your mom, dad, best friend."

I tried not to cringe at the words *best friend.*

"Let them know where you are and where you're going just in case you really don't trust me, then get in the damn car."

He was already taking my bags when I texted my mom my location and turned on my GPS.

And then I was suddenly sitting with a complete stranger in a sexy electric-blue Ferrari that roared to life so hard and fast I almost felt sorry that we couldn't just take it out for a few hours. Then again, he was a stranger. Would it be weird to ask for a joyride? Something told me that's how good girls get kidnapped or end up pregnant, sports cars and guys who look like that.

Hugo put on a pair of black Ray-Bans and grinned over at me. "You ready for vacation?"

"Ready." I wasn't ready. I so wasn't ready. This wasn't me. This behavior. But something was building in my chest, something exciting, something that felt both wrong and right at the same time.

He hit the accelerator.

I let out a scream as we flew out of the airport and down the streets of Puerto Vallarta. We passed malls, restaurants, car dealerships, and finally about ten minutes into our trip he turned right then left, and there we were.

Secrets.

The guard at the gate asked for our passports, then widened his eyes for a brief minute before Hugo slipped something into his hand and fired off something in Spanish.

The man grinned and held out his phone.

Hugo turned to me. "He wants to take a picture of us on our first day. I may have lied and said we were married . . ."

My face fell.

"It will be quick, promise. No worries."

Before I knew what was happening, I was leaning in and taking a picture with Hugo, and then I was being helped out of the car and handed a glass of champagne.

The staff seemed a little eager to see us arrive.

Maybe it was the car?

Hugo seemed to calm everyone down with a few gorgeous words in Spanish. I even found myself nodding, though I couldn't understand a word because he was talking so fast. I could only catch enough to know he was discussing his stay and something else about a newspaper.

I'd stupidly studied French all through college.

That, I was fluent in. But Spanish? Nada.

Okay, so I knew nothing.

Literally.

In seconds, I was swept away to registration. Across the room, Hugo was making sweeping motions with his hands while a little kid ran up and tossed him a soccer ball.

I frowned.

The ladies at registration kept pointing and covering their mouths with their hands while they giggled.

Yeah, I got it, I did.

The man was gorgeous.

Not merely "Oh look, he has nice eyes and a body that could run for days without breaking a sweat," but really just . . . beautiful to look at.

All smooth skin, rippling forearm muscles, and bracelets—how did a guy get away with wearing so many different rope bracelets without looking stupid?

I blinked and looked closer. Did he have a braid in his hair too?

Huh.

The same silky hair I'd tugged on.

I shivered.

"Welcome home!" Marta said with a grin. "You've booked the penthouse suite for four days. Anything you need at all, and we'll have a butler personally see to it, Miss—" I grabbed my key cards before she could say my name.

"Thank you!" I interrupted and stood. "I'm tired, I think I'll just go—" I did a 360. "Where's the elevator?"

"I'll go with you." Hugo flashed me his key card.

"Hmm, you following me now?" I teased.

"Apparently we both have good taste." There were two penthouse suites per floor.

Side by freaking side.

I was P601.

And he was P602.

I shook my head; it was ridiculous, wasn't it?

These things didn't really happen, did they?

The elevator dinged at our level, and we stepped off. "I'm just going to . . ." I pointed to my door.

"Nap? Relax? Drink?" he offered.

"Yeah, all of the above," I admitted.

"See you around, then." I felt his smile make its way down my body like a caress and then experienced extreme disappointment after I slid my key card and was met with emptiness when the door opened.

This was supposed to be our room.

Our honeymoon.

Filled with champagne and sex, that was what you did on a honeymoon, right?

Like I would even know.

I walked out to the balcony and swim-out pool as the sound of waves crashing against the sand filled my ears.

A chilled bottle of champagne waited with chocolate covered strawberries.

"Congratulations, Mr. and Mrs. Davis!"

I ripped the card in half, then in thirds, then momentarily lost my mind and imagined setting it on fire, when a voice called out. "Great view, huh?"

Hugo was literally my neighbor except for a partition that blocked him from seeing my pool and into my room.

I gulped and looked out at the ocean. "Yeah, it is."

"More champagne?" He pointed to my hand still clutching the champagne with a viselike grip.

"Yeah," I croaked.

"Are you by yourself?" he asked a few seconds later.

"Yes." Don't cry. Don't cry. Don't cry.

"Do you want to be?" he asked softly.

I shook my head, no . . .

Just then he hopped over the partition, swept me into his arms, and lowered his head. His mouth was searing hot, his grip tender like he knew my shame, my sadness, and wanted to make them go away the only way he knew how. I clung to that kiss like a lifeline and promised myself I'd do whatever it took to forget Alton—and be the girl of adventure I'd always wanted to be.

I was going to start with Hugo.

Chapter Four

I was kissing her again.

Maybe it was because it had been months since I'd had a decent kiss, since I'd jumped into the arms of anyone who didn't know me by name.

I could be Hugo for a few days.

Hugo seemed spontaneous.

Hugo seemed relaxed.

Hugo seemed fun.

I sure as hell needed some fun.

I broke away from her kiss and trailed my fingertips down her chin. "So, now that we've established the plane didn't crash and we're here side by side, what did you have in mind?"

Ashley grinned up at me, her eyes a bit hesitant as she looked from me to the ocean. "Well, I've never gone cliff diving, I heard there's a great place close by."

My eyebrows shot up. "No offense, but you don't seem like a thrill seeker."

She laughed. I decided I liked the way her laugh relaxed me, made me respond with a smile and a need to kiss her again. "I'm not, trust me." She sobered a bit. Her lips turned down.

I wanted nothing more than to press a soft kiss to the corner of her mouth just to see if it would make her decide to smile in my direction again.

"But it would be fun, I need fun."

I sighed heavily and looked at my feet. When the hell had I ever looked away like that? "That makes both of us."

"Great!" She walked ahead of me into her penthouse suite, which matched mine even in color. I suddenly wondered what she did for a living. I mean I could afford it because I had been the highest paid soccer star in Europe for the last ten years. I could literally wipe my ass with hundred-dollar bills on a daily basis and still have money to burn.

The place was around three grand a day.

I eyed the large master suite as she ran around and then held up her hand. "One sec, I'm going to change into a suit, alright?"

"Great." I smiled reassuringly. It would give me time to look around, not that I was stalking her, but I could never be too careful. I was still surprised she didn't recognize me. And I knew when she did, this little facade, this freedom I felt in my chest, the easy way she let me breathe around her? It would go to hell, and I'd need another escape.

I thumbed through a few of the magazines on the table, and dropped the last one down just in time to hear the sliding bathroom door open and see a goddess emerge.

A one-piece swimsuit covered her body. It had a plunging neckline that showed off two generously sized breasts, and I immediately regretted not telling her who I was.

Because clothing tended to get pulled off, not put on, when I was in the room.

I eyed the scrap of material she called a swimsuit, my eyes raking over her muscular legs, her curvy body.

"Unless you're jumping naked, you should change too," she pointed out, then cleared her throat and looked away like she was insecure. Damn, the woman could make a man cut his own heart out for a taste of her special brand of sin.

I peeled my shirt off over my body and shrugged. "Ready."

Her eyes went so wide I had to fight not to laugh.

I knew what she saw.

I had fucking Instagram pages dedicated to my eyes alone, don't even get me started on my abs.

Eight.

Tight, packed abs, all tanned and golden like I was the sun god himself.

"Uh, right." Her cheeks brightened as she clasped her hands together. "Let's go!"

I checked her ass out the entire time she walked ahead of me, and when she caught me staring I just shrugged and said, "Next time wear more clothes if you don't want me to look."

"You should talk," she fired back.

"Misunderstanding." I grinned. "I wanted you to look."

She slapped a hand against my bare chest.

I laughed, and then grabbed her hand and kissed her fingertips. "You ready to jump off a cliff with a stranger you've kissed three times?"

"Once," she corrected with a whisper. "I kissed you, you kissed me, we're even."

The doors to the elevator opened as I whispered under my breath while her ass swayed back and forth. "Not for fucking long."

◆ ◆ ◆

"Are you sure this is safe?" Ashley squeezed my hand and peeked over the edge.

My gaze followed hers. Below, sparkling blue-green water beckoned. The target area reflected darkly, but nearby, dark-gray rocks dotted the surface, their presence giving a bit of an ominous feel.

"Hell no, you're the one who suggested it!" I hated heights. Fucking hated them, but she'd suggested the jump, and I wanted to spend time with her. There was something magnetic about her, something that made me want more even though I knew anything short term was crazy, especially for a guy like me. I loved her strange mannerisms that didn't match her words at times. Like she was an old soul trapped inside a younger, hotter body. I peered over the edge again. "Hell, that's forty feet."

"Are you sweating?" She laughed.

"It's forty feet!" I repeated. "I'd be concerned if I *wasn't* sweating over this. That's high. Shit, I think I'm seeing double."

Her laugh carried through the breeze.

I closed my eyes and inhaled the way it wrapped around me, the way that her presence took away every ache and pain, every worry I'd had these past few weeks, and just silenced them all.

"Hey." She grabbed my hand. "We jump together."

"Deal." I squeezed her palm. "And if we die, at least it wasn't in a crash."

"And when we live . . ." She leaned in, her lips tasted like bubblegum as they covered my mouth in a slow, sensual kiss that drew out every primal instinct in me to lay her across the cliff and claim her.

"If we live, what?"

She winked. "Jump and find out."

"Tease."

"Hah, I don't think anyone's ever called me that."

Impossible. The woman was a walking hard-on—I would know.

"Jump on three?" I offered.

She nodded. "One."

"Uno," I added.

She just laughed harder as I counted in Spanish.

On three, we jumped.

The wind caught us as we gained velocity, and I wasn't sure which one of us was screaming louder.

But once I hit the warm water—felt it close over my head—and survived, I surfaced and caught the look of joy on her face. In that moment, I realized I would do anything to make this stranger smile at me like that again.

One. Day. In.

Chapter Five

I found a part of myself in that jump. I experienced so many things simultaneously.

The freedom of being alive.

The terror of still not knowing who I was without Alton.

Feeling okay to do something spontaneous because of the man holding my hand.

I knew it was stupid . . . to fall for someone I barely knew, especially so soon after Alton, but part of me wanted to just jump in with both feet and see what happened, and being around Hugo had me laughing and smiling nonstop.

Add that to his devastating good looks, and I was ready to grab his phone number, email, Instagram account, and beg him to move closer to me.

See? I wasn't ready to date if I was turning into a stalker so soon.

"So, was it everything you thought it would be?" he asked, swimming over to me. He ducked his head under and shook off as he came up, then ran his hands through his choppy long hair, which had darkened, reminding me of rich Colombian coffee.

If this was what Spanish pirates used to look like, no wonder they had all the gold.

"Everything and more." I splashed him. "I'm curious, though . . ."

"What?" He spit out some salt water.

"Was that high-pitched scream that sounded like a goat getting sacrificed coming from you or did we actually hit a goat on the way down?"

He threw his head back and laughed. "Very funny, I guess I deserved that. I hate heights."

I frowned. "Then why did you say yes?"

"Because," he said, pressing his hands on either side of my face, "any man would be insane to say no to you."

I fell a little harder as he pulled me into his arms, his lips teased mine in a way that made me breathless, made my chest ache, like he was afraid I was a mermaid that was going to disappear into the deep-blue depths of the ocean. He tugged my lower lip with his teeth, then deepened the kiss as we treaded water. I gripped his biceps, letting myself drown in his embrace. If this was what attraction was supposed to feel like . . .

Then I was completely out of my element for once in my life.

Out of control.

And in such need of more of his warmth, his taste, that I found myself whimpering when one of his hands brushed across my breast. My body jolted against his in response.

He chuckled darkly against my mouth. "I knew you'd taste like this. Everything about you is . . . on fire."

I opened my eyes.

His intense gold orbs seemed to swirl before me.

A wave crashed over us and against the rock wall, ruining the moment as he grabbed my hand and dove under water.

I followed him.

And swam to the nearby beach.

By the time I made it to the shore, I was exhausted. I lay back against the warm sand and looked up at the clear blue sky as the sound of waves crashing against the shore filled me with peace.

And then Hugo was blocking the sun with his body as he hovered over me. "This is crazy, right?"

"Crazy," I agreed.

"Tell me to go back to the hotel. Make me go back to my room— anything, Ashley—"

It wasn't my name.

I almost winced.

Instead, I kissed him again, and with a hungry growl, he pressed me down against the sand. I could feel his arousal press against my thigh.

I wanted more.

I wanted him.

I wanted to be the woman I saw reflected in his eyes.

Our mouths met in a frenzy as he pulled the string to my one-piece and shoved it down to expose my breasts, his mouth hot, punishing, as he sucked one nipple, then grazed his teeth across it.

Anyone could see us.

And for once, I didn't care about what people thought.

All I cared about were the sensations he awakened within me.

And the way he made me feel in his arms.

His wet hair slid against his forehead as he moved his mouth, and then kissed up my neck to my jawline. I reached for the string on his shorts . . .

And then he broke the kiss.

We stared at one another.

I was being impulsive.

And stupid.

I didn't even know him.

I'd known Alton my entire life, and he'd touched my boobs maybe a dozen times.

But this guy? This guy I was ready to just strip and lie down for?

He bit back a curse and blew out a rough exhale. "We should get back."

Disappointed, I quickly tied my suit back up and nodded.

I could still see how painfully aroused he was.

How much he wanted me.

And I knew it wasn't a lack of attraction that had him stopping.

But probably because he had more self-respect than I did.

Which seemed to be the problem with the men in my life.

Not that I was complaining.

It was chivalrous.

But sometimes, a girl just wants wild.

Chapter Six

SLADE

Self-control was not something I lacked. It had been an essential part of my training since I was a child. My father, a soccer coach, now retired, thanked God when he discovered my skill with the ball.

And ever since then.

It's been soccer above all else, even family.

It was everything.

Until it stopped making me happy.

Until it became a job.

Until the money became meaningless.

Until I was betrayed by those closest to me.

So maybe my self-control was frayed and well on its way to snapping, and at the worst possible moment in time, alone, on a beach with the most tempting woman I'd ever met.

I don't know how I stopped.

I just knew I needed to.

Because I was seconds away from being the guy that has random unprotected sex in Mexico like every spring break gone wrong.

And she didn't deserve that.

Even though I was in physical pain as I pried my body away from her.

By the time we made it back to the resort, night had fallen. I walked her to her door and leaned against the frame. "Dinner?"

She tapped her chin. "Dinner, hmm?"

"Dinner and drinks."

"In an hour?"

"Of course." I kissed each of her cheeks, wanting to do more, then pulled away and made sure she made it safely into her room.

When I opened my own door, loneliness descended.

I hadn't planned on this.

To be thirty and without a wife, kids. Family was important to me. The only thing that rivaled that was soccer, and that was because my father had made it so.

I took a quick shower then checked my cell.

Ten missed calls.

All from my mother, who had been expecting me this week in the States, and one from my dad.

She was worried.

And lonely now that she and my dad were separated and living in different countries.

I was supposed to be in Seattle by now, relaxing before the season.

Instead, I escaped to the first place that caught my eye on the search engine. Maybe it was fate?

I sent off a text. I'm fine, something came up, I'll see you in a few days.

The next phone call was from my father; he'd left a voice mail. "Look, I know this decision did not come lightly, you love soccer, I love soccer. I don't want to see you throw your life away, but you're old enough to make your own choices. I talked with Philamena, and we decided that I will visit for the holidays, but I'll do the cooking, God knows that woman burns rice because she knows it drives me crazy." I snickered and kept listening. "I just want you to be happy."

The voice mail finished.

And the guilt descended.

He wanted me to be happy, and he'd sacrificed everything in order for me to get it, and even though I took care of him financially, I still felt like I'd abandoned him when I took the job with the Seattle team.

I brushed the thoughts away and quickly dressed in a pair of white linen pants and a button-down blue linen shirt.

With five minutes to spare I was knocking on Ashley's door. She opened on the third knock. "Ready?"

"Is it on purpose?" I asked, casually eying her tight white dress and the way the straps disappeared in a crisscross pattern down the small of her back as she did a little turn. Her tanned skin was like a homing beacon, I couldn't look away.

"What?" Her lips were brushed with something shiny that my mouth decided it was going to sample later.

"Did you dress like that to torture me?" I hit the elevator button. "You look . . ." I shook my head and exhaled. "Like cake."

"Cake?"

"Before you get offended, I want to make you aware of the very serious relationship I have with cake. Get between me and cake and you're taking your life into your hands. And you?" I leaned in and sniffed her neck, then pressed an open-mouthed kiss below her ear. "You'd be chocolate sin filled with molten lava spilling out onto the plate, waiting to be slowly licked up. I think I'd savor you for hours, days . . ."

She shivered.

I almost hit the up button to take us back to our suites and our two empty beds.

And I knew how to make use of both of them with finesse.

Instead, we walked to dinner. Her blushing, me lusting.

Football was huge in Mexico so I wasn't sure if I would be recognized. I'd seen posters of myself on the streets on the way in. So the minute we were seated, I excused myself and sought out our server. I took out my wallet, grabbed a few hundreds, and handed them to the surprised young man. "Make sure nobody disturbs us or recognizes me. If people want autographs, I'll sign everything later."

"Sí, senor." He shook my hand.

By the time I returned to the table, Ashley had ordered wine and was giddily pointing to my glass. "Okay, honest opinion, go!"

"Something of a wine connoisseur?" I asked her.

"Something like that." She glowed, her confidence in her own skills was sexy as hell.

I sniffed, swirled, and then tasted as the dry Cab ran down my throat and exploded into a sensation of blueberries and something tart. "That's . . . perfect."

She did a little mock bow. "My calling in life."

"Drinking?"

She laughed then shrugged. "Cheers, I guess?"

Our glasses clinked together. "So what is it you do, then? You've got me curious."

"Oh, um . . ." She shifted in her seat. "I actually used to work for a wine company, I was a sommelier. In layman's terms, a wine taster."

"You need to have the perfect palate for that." No wonder she had such a perfect mouth.

"Yup."

"What do you mean was?"

She looked away. "Long story, let's just say I'm taking a much needed break from life. And you? What do you do?"

"Ah." Her job explained her extravagant spending, tasters were paid well. I suddenly felt comfortable sharing more. "I'm an athlete."

"No shock there." She smiled sweetly. "What kind of athlete?"

"The kind that gets paid." I shrugged the question off. "Nothing too exciting, trust me."

Her voice lowered. "Would people here recognize you? Are you that kind of athlete?"

I grinned and whispered back, "Do you see people rushing our table?"

She scrunched up her nose. "I guess not. But still, professional, that's huge. I bet your family's proud."

"Yeah." I started to feel more guilty that I hadn't yet called my father back. "They're very supportive. Family is everything, you know?"

A shadow crossed her face.

I knew there was a story there.

But I didn't push.

Because I still didn't know how to define what was happening.

"Are you ready to order?" Our server arrived. And all thoughts of sharing our pasts vanished between bottles of wine and savory food, and when we made it back to her room four hours later, a bit drunk, and laughing, I swept in and kissed her again.

This time, she clung to my shirt with her hands like I was her lifeline. I didn't realize how long it had been since I'd been truly wanted.

For me.

Not for what I did.

How much money I made.

Or how many Olympic medals I had.

Her tongue tasted like wine and the chocolate soufflé we'd shared for dessert. I slid her key card against her door and we stumbled through. I slammed it behind me as I pulled her into my arms and then slowly lowered her dress over her breasts, down her stomach, and off her curvy hips.

She was completely naked underneath.

"Fuck . . ." I captured her mouth again as she kicked off her heels and pulled the string to my linen pants. They fell to the carpet, exposing me completely. Apparently we'd both had sex on the mind, sex and the least amount of clothing possible between our sweltering bodies.

I leaned down and grabbed a condom from my pocket. I wasn't wearing briefs but I'd at least come prepared.

"Presumptuous?" she said against my mouth.

"Absolutely," I said honestly as she ground her hips eagerly against me. I groaned when she raked her hands down my chest, her fingernails leaving trails of red all the way to where our bodies were about to join. I hissed in pleasure and grabbed her hair, pulling her body closer to me with one hand, the other placed on her hip.

"This is crazy," she whispered.

"I love crazy," I said back.

And our eyes locked again with something I didn't fully understand, something that told me the universe was giving us a chance, a moment in time, to come clean, to confess before it was too late.

And then the moment shifted.

And she was shifting beneath me.

And I was inside her.

Wondering where she'd been my entire life.

"Oh wow, okay . . ." She gripped my biceps like she was either in extreme pleasure or extreme pain. I stopped moving, letting her body adjust, letting mine slow the hell down.

I slowed my movements, I felt her everywhere, her body sang to me with each pump. I was drunk on her feel, the way she clenched onto me each time I tried to push or pull—she was everywhere and everything. "Hugo . . . faster . . ."

I hated Hugo.

Was gonna kill him off soon.

But not now.

Not when she was clenching tight around me.

Not when she was crying out with each thrust.

Not when my own control finally snapped as I sang praises to Ashley and her quirky mouth and her impulsive kiss.

The high that followed was unparalleled, I reached heaven in her arms, and I vowed to visit again and again and again.

Chapter Seven

MACKENZIE

"You should have told me," Hugo said in that delicious accent as he stood from the bed and walked naked into the bathroom. I wasn't a prude, but the fact that he was so free with his body shocked me a bit, even though I'd just touched every inch of it. Even though he'd literally been inside me seconds ago.

The bathroom light illuminated his path back to the bed as he grabbed a warm cloth and rubbed it down my legs. I clenched them together and squeezed my eyes shut only to be on the receiving end of another wonderful kiss that tasted like the Mexican heat with a heavy dose of wine. I licked his lips and relaxed as his hands moved between my thighs.

"Stop clenching," he whispered against my mouth. "Had I known you were a virgin, I would have . . ."

"You wouldn't have," I said softly. "And it's a long story."

"A long story that makes absolutely"—he rubbed the cloth between my thighs and then lay down next to me, propping a pillow beneath his head—"no sense."

I leaned on my elbow, wincing as my fingers caught in my hair, which was a tangled mess. I didn't even want to know how horrible I looked, but the feeling in my soul? Hot. So hot. I was ready to jump all over his olive skin and kiss my way down his body. "How about I just had a very . . . careful . . . boyfriend?"

"Are you asking me?"

I laughed. "No, I'm telling. It's not important, though."

It was important, but something about sharing those intimate details felt far riskier than sex. Maybe I had it all backward, but I wasn't ready to go there, not yet.

"Hmm." He flicked my lips with his fingers and then pulled me against his chest until I was on top of him, skin against skin, straddling his legs. "I guess his loss is my gain."

"Glass half full." I winked.

He ran a calloused hand over my ass and squeezed. "Absolutely."

Suddenly nervous, I cleared my throat and waited. I was in completely unfamiliar territory with this stranger. Six months ago I wouldn't even go on a vacation by myself let alone jump into bed with a guy who could be a potential serial killer.

"What are you thinking about?" His grin was both gorgeous and teasing all at the same time. Where did they make guys like this? Clearly not in the US, but still. His beanie was off, allowing me access to his hair. I tugged a few pieces and then leaned down and brushed a kiss across his lips.

"You know." I kissed him again. "You should model."

His lips twitched. "Is that so?"

"Yeah." I ran my fingers through his hair again and locked onto his golden eyes. "You'd make millions, though you're clearly not struggling if you booked the penthouse, hmm."

"Fishing for information?"

"Yeah, but in a passive-aggressive way that sounds more cute than stalker."

"Or more stalker than cute?" he teased, nipping at my lower lip before bringing it into his mouth and sucking. "How about we kiss . . . we make love—"

He just said *make love*.

My heart thudded against my chest then started skipping.

"And then we'll just do it over again . . ." he whispered in my ear. "That is, if you aren't too sore and tired."

"I'm ready." I said it so fast I nearly crawled under the bed and disappeared.

His eyes almost closed completely as he slid a hand down my ass and then found my core. I jerked in surprise.

Hugo grinned. "Just making sure."

"Oh yeah? And what's your vote?"

He sucked on two of his fingers, the ones that had touched me, and whispered in a gravelly voice. "Ready."

Chapter Eight

SLADE

For a virgin, she sure was insatiable.

She was lying naked next to me, all soft curves and long brown hair with strands of gold that looked like they'd been naturally highlighted by the sun. Just beautiful.

I was often surrounded by beauty.

And I appreciated it.

But it paled in comparison to her.

I got up and stretched. My phone said three a.m., and she'd just fallen asleep a half hour ago, but I'd lain awake worrying.

Worrying about my old reputation.

Worrying about my new one.

The team.

The relocation.

And what the media was saying about my leaving my old team. I'd left to get away, but they twisted things to sell stories. And according to everyone else in the world, my ego couldn't take the obvious pay cut I was going to be getting after not winning the cup last year.

Like one man was responsible for that. Besides, my mind had been on other things, and soccer, it doesn't allow you to be human and have emotions, not during a game. No. Winning is all that matters.

The more I thought about it, the more my chest tightened until I was trying to breathe deep just to get my anxiety under control.

I clutched my phone in my hand and walked out to the balcony as a warm breeze filled the air.

Maybe this woman would be the start of something different for me.

Maybe this would go beyond vacation.

I looked over my shoulder as she rolled to her side and made a mewling noise in her sleep.

Grinning, I turned back toward the ocean and straightened my shoulders.

"I'm going to keep you," I said to myself, my voice carrying across the wind like the universe heard my promise and was going to help me keep it no matter what.

I felt it in my soul.

There was more here in this moment. More than sex, more than coincidence. Maybe I'd finally found my other half, halfway across the world.

I leaned against the wall and thought about the possibilities as my phone started buzzing in my hand.

Mom?

It was late.

I answered quickly. "Everything okay?"

Silence, and then, "No, no, Slade, no." She hiccupped. "Your father—"

I sighed. "I know, he's worried. Things will be fine."

"No." She started to sob softly into the phone. "Slade, your father is—"

"Don't say it." My breathing turned shallow as I gripped the phone tighter, her sobs making my stomach sick, my heart fearful. "He's fine, he just left a message today, I was going to call him back, he's fine, he's probably just not answering his phone, he's—"

"Slade!" she interrupted with a wail. "Your father is dead."

Your. Father. Is. Dead.

I swayed on my feet. "No, no, I don't . . . I can't." I ran my hands through my hair.

"His heart just . . . the doctor said it stopped before the paramedics got there . . . he was going to surprise you . . . for your first practice, he was packing—"

I couldn't listen anymore.

I squeezed my eyes shut as a tear ran down my cheek. My stomach roiled while my heart slowed in my chest and then, as if it no longer wanted to pump, almost completely stilled.

Gone. He was gone.

My biggest supporter.

My best friend.

The only person who had ever truly understood me.

"Slade, are you there?"

"Yeah," I croaked. "I'll be on the first flight out. I love you."

"I love you." She sobbed. "I'll see you soon. Everything's going to be fine, everything's going to be fine . . ."

She didn't believe it.

And neither did I.

My father was the glue.

He was the leader.

He was everything.

And now?

He was gone.

I walked on hollow legs back to the small wall dividing the penthouses. Numbness settling in, I jumped over, grabbed my bag, and threw things in, not caring if I left anything.

I didn't care.

I just didn't care.

And when I thought about the girl next door, still sleeping, I couldn't bring myself to do anything except touch the wall dividing us and cast blame.

She was the reason I was so distracted.

The reason I hadn't called him back.

Women.

I thought my ex had cost me everything.

But the stranger sleeping in that bed—had cost me the most.

Chapter Nine

MACKENZIE

Cold silky sheets wrapped around my legs as I stretched my arms overhead and felt the spot next to me. The pillows were gone. And the space was empty. I opened my eyes and yawned. My body hurt in the worst and best way possible as I slowly moved my feet to the floor, grabbed the sheet, wrapped it around my body, and walked around the room.

The sliding glass door was open. I frowned. I hadn't opened it last night. Maybe Hugo went to his room to shower? I didn't really think anything of it.

Until I heard a vacuum.

Frowning, I peeked over the divider between our two penthouses. Two maids were working tirelessly around the patio, while another was inside vacuuming the living room.

Panic seized my chest. "Um, hola!" I called like the idiot American I was.

One of the ladies turned to me and grinned. "We speak English, miss."

I mentally rolled my eyes at myself, of course they did, this was Puerto Vallarta. It wasn't like we were in the heart of Mexico, and even then. I gave my head a shake.

"Sorry." I finally found my voice. "The man, staying here? Do you know where he went?"

She gave me a curious look and then her eyes roamed over my naked body, the sheet barely covered anything. Understanding dawned on her face. "I'm so sorry, he's no longer here."

"He died!" I yelled and covered my mouth with my hands. I'd heard about Americans getting killed by drug cartels in Mexico, but I didn't know it was true! "Did anyone else get taken?" I gulped as panic seized my lungs. Where the hell was Liam Neeson when you needed him?

She smiled softly. "No, no, you misunderstand, he checked out of the hotel. We were told to get the room ready for the next guest. That's all I know."

"Oh." My stomach sank while my heart thundered in my chest. "Right, I must have gotten my days confused too, I thought he was leaving . . . umm, tomorrow."

She just smiled like she knew I was lying.

"Thank you." I forced a smile as my heart lodged in my throat. I stumbled back to my room and sat on the bed, putting my head in my hands. I would not cry. I'd cried too many times over men.

Too many times to count.

It had just been a one-night stand.

Best sex of my life—not that I had anything to measure it against.

Kisses shared with someone that I'd compare every single man to for as long as I lived.

I'd never been a risk taker.

And the minute I decided to live on the wild side, I'd slept with a complete stranger, who'd taken my virginity and then bailed.

Why the hell hadn't I just bought a lottery ticket?

I let out a laugh.

The laugh lasted two seconds before it turned into weeping as I lay down across the bed and pressed my face against the place he'd been snuggled up next to me.

Men.

All they did was hurt me.

And I truly didn't think his was intentional.

He'd just seen someone who wanted a good time.

And gave it.

So. Stupid.

Stupid girl.

I wiped the mascara from under my eyes, slowly rose to my feet, and made my way into the bathroom.

When I looked at the floor there was a pool of linen. His clothes from last night.

I kicked them in disgust.

Then picked up the shirt and inhaled.

My body rocked with memories of his mouth, his hands.

I had been left at the altar.

If I could get through that, I could get through anything.

Except my treacherous heart kept demanding that the universe answer the one question I'd been asking for years.

Why was I never enough to fight for?

Chapter Ten

SLADE

Two weeks later

I fucking hate funerals almost as much as I hate traveling coach. The only seat I was able to get was on a plane with over three hundred passengers and a high school dance squad who had more pep than normal teenage girls should have. A headache pulsed between my ears as the plane took off for the States.

I put on my noise-canceling headphones, pulled my beanie over my head, and closed my eyes.

I hadn't slept in days.

And every time I closed my eyes I saw his body.

His calm face.

The casket.

The tears in my mother's eyes.

And the pathetic condolences from teammates who suddenly gave a shit about me because my father died.

I didn't remember what I said. I only remembered standing in front of a room full of strangers who wore smiles of pity and telling them how incredible my father was, and they pretended to understand, they pretended to care with their nice words and side hugs, but I knew the truth.

I was alone.

Mom was trying to be strong for me.

And I was trying to be strong for her.

But two broken pieces can't be strong for each other when they don't even know how to heal themselves.

Someone kicked my seat.

My eyes slammed open as kick after kick maimed my back, forcing my body to jerk toward the seat in front of me.

I tore off my headphones and turned around. "Do you mind?"

I'd been groomed from a young age to be careful in public, someone always has a phone, someone is always watching. My father had drilled it into me so much that I was afraid to piss at restaurants.

But at that moment, I had no more fucks to give.

I had just buried him.

I'd buried him!

Tears burned my eyes as the gaping teen narrowed his eyes and then kicked again.

"That's it." I stood, hovering over him.

He started choking. Little shit probably accidentally swallowed that wad of gum he'd been blowing and popping endlessly while kicking my chair.

"Sir?" One of the flight attendants approached. "The seat belt sign is still on." She pointed to the light above my head while I continued my stare-down with the punk kid.

"Fine," I said through gritted teeth. "But can you please tell this little jackass not to kick my seat anymore?"

"Hey now." His dad finally spoke up. He had a brown mustache and a Yankees hat on backward, and I could smell the faint aroma of weed on his clothes. "He's not hurting anybody."

"Really?" I crossed my arms.

"Sir." The flight attendant flashed me a dazzling smile. "Why don't you take a seat, and I'll see if I can move you elsewhere."

"Fine." I sat down, and then finally looked around the cabin. Several phones were directed at me.

"Fuck." I put a blanket over my head and stayed that way the rest of the flight. And when paparazzi met me at the airport asking why I was yelling at an innocent kid and if I would ever play again.

I snapped.

And hit a photographer.

So far? My continuing soccer career in the States?

Not going well.

Chapter Eleven

MACKENZIE

Four weeks after Puerto Vallarta

The country club was the same.

I was the one that was different.

Changed for better or for worse.

I squeezed my eyes shut as laughter and chatter filled the large dining room. The scents of perfume and steak filled the air.

It was all the same.

I felt altered.

"Are you sure you're not coming back?" Dad slid a glass of wine toward me. It was fresh hell not grabbing the perfect crystal stem, lifting the red liquid to my lips, and tasting.

It was my passion.

But if working with my passion meant I had to see Alton's face day in and day out with his brand-new girlfriend who had been hired to work on the marketing team, well, hard pass.

"I'm sure." I gulped some water then reached for my wineglass only to remember it was empty. I begrudgingly grabbed the one he'd slid to me and took a small sip. Flavor burst in my mouth. I would miss this.

Dad sighed. "What are you going to do, then? Just sit around, watch Netflix? You need to do something or you're just going to stay . . ." He stopped himself. I knew what he was going to say. Stay sad. I would just stay sad.

I cleared my throat and stared into the salad I hadn't touched. "What about the Blue Service Assistant Company? Since Aunt Shelby's pregnant, I know they need people."

He touched his fingers to his chin like he always did when he was thinking. "Isn't that a bit . . . beneath you?"

I rolled my eyes. "I'd be an errand girl to rich cranky customers with too much money and not enough time on their hands." I spread my arms wide as we took in the country club around us. "Yeah, I think I'll be okay."

He just chuckled. "Well, if anyone can handle rich people with too much money . . ."

"Exactly." I beamed.

"I'll give them a call, let them know to expect you in the morning, the caseload has been pretty crazy since some of the local athletes have started using them. Half the Bellevue Bucks football team signed up the minute they discovered someone would run errands for them and sign ironclad NDAs."

I shrugged, even though inwardly I was rolling the word *athlete* around in my head like a bowling ball. *He'd* been an athlete. Or was that a lie too?

Not the point. The point I needed to focus on was that I had a job lined up. It wasn't glamorous, but it would keep me away from Alton.

He'd moved on.

And every single time I saw him, he tried to force his friendship on me like the lady at the perfume counter with a bottle of spray in one hand and a sample in the other.

I wanted no part of it.

But he just wouldn't stop spraying.

Apologizing.

Sending texts.

Telling me that he was sorry but that I would really, really love Joanna!

Yeah, he even sent me a text with a winking emoji.

Hell. No.

I didn't want to like the new girlfriend.

I didn't want to see the place she took in his life, the place where I was supposed to be standing, however unhappy I would have been.

I just wanted my life back.

Or some semblance of it.

I wanted . . .

My mind flashed back to Mexico.

Adventure.

I wanted Hugo.

Ugh, it had been a month, and I still woke up in a lust-filled sweat thinking he was in my room, his mouth on mine, my fingers digging into his tanned skin, squeezing his biceps while he chuckled against my neck.

I shivered.

"Cold?" Dad asked, concern laced in his drawn-up brows.

"No." I offered him a small smile. "I just need more time."

"It's been seven months since—"

"Yeah, I know," I interrupted. Not like I had a calendar with giant red X's crossing out every day since being jilted at the altar or anything, but a woman doesn't exactly forget that sort of thing. "More time, please."

He sighed and stared into his wineglass. It was a table red, a mixture of Cab Franc and a Cab Sauvignon. One of my favorites. My mouth watered for more. The faint taste of cherries lingered on my tongue along with an aftertaste of blackberries.

"Fine," Dad finally said. "You get two more months before I want you back here tasting. I'll need you during Spring Barrel, and you're the best we have. It's not just about having my daughter around me." His eyes filled with tears. "But you're so damn good at what you do, and you love it, I know you do. I just hate that it's been tainted by—"

"Mack?" Alton stopped at our table with a fresh bottle. "How are you?" He leaned down until we were at eye level. It made me feel like a child. Had he always talked to me like that? Like I was the kid and he was the adult?

"I'm . . . just leaving." I forced a smile and glanced at his perfectly tailored suit. It fit his arms like a glove, but something was missing.

Biceps?

Actual muscle?

Had he always been that lean? Where had all those football muscles gone?

I mean he'd always been a runner, but . . .

I jerked my gaze away from his lean arms when my dad cleared his throat and stood. "I love you, Mack, be safe."

"I live in a penthouse apartment overlooking the Sound, with a bellman and full security," I reminded him with a wink. "I think I'll be okay."

I sidestepped Alton, still smiling so hard it hurt my face, and then walked away from everything yet again.

I kept my head high until I got into my Lexus SUV and started the engine.

The AC pumped through the vents as my eyes watered with unshed tears, and in a complete moment of weakness, I reached into the console, pulled out a linen shirt, and inhaled.

Chapter Twelve

SLADE

I had holed up in my house on Lake Washington for a good two days after the video from the flight went viral. I'd been known as the golden boy of soccer.

Now?

Now I was the bad-boy European football star who'd lost his shit on an airplane and was just waiting to infect the American population with my dirty ways. It didn't help that every damn article featured a picture of my father and speculation that I was losing my shit because of his death.

There were rumors of drug use. False.

Public drunkenness. Also false.

Oh, and a personal favorite? An ex had come forward and said that I used to mentally abuse her. She asked for a million dollars in restitution.

I told her to go to hell.

That, also, made the news.

So to say I was in a bad place since my father died? That was an understatement.

It didn't help that my house was a mess, and I was due at practice the next day. I hadn't done laundry in I don't even know how long. I hadn't even gone out to buy dog food in two weeks out of fear that someone would take a picture and I'd lash out again.

Amazon delivery was my new best friend.

And every fucking time my mom called, it was to say she was worried.

I rubbed my eyes with my palms and grabbed another bottle of beer from the table before seeing my phone buzz, the vibration causing it to fall from the couch onto the floor.

With a curse I picked it up. "What?"

"Well, you're an absolute joy today, aren't you?" My agent laughed on the other end while I gave him a mental middle finger. "Let me guess, you're watching TV by yourself and having one last beer before practice in the morning?"

I growled. "You know me too well."

"We've been friends since we were sixteen, I know you better than you know yourself."

"Oh yeah? What am I thinking?"

"Easy, you think you're finished, you're depressed as hell, and you think moving was a mistake."

I didn't say anything, and my throat closed up as I looked away from the TV to the lake in front of my property. "Maybe it was."

He sighed. "Signing with the Sounders was the right thing to do. They're going to honor the rest of your fifty-two-million-dollar contract—"

"Which I only had eight left to pay out from Chelsea, maybe I should have just . . . retired."

"Bullshit, you're thirty, you don't just retire at thirty. Plus you're one of my favorite people."

"Fifty-two million US dollars, I can't imagine why." Matt and I had met during one of the summers I spent with my mom in Seattle, and we had been inseparable ever since. We even went to college together. The guy was as smooth as they came. The bastard made money like a silver-tongued devil.

"I keep you around for more than the money." He chuckled. "You're the best wingman a guy could ask for."

"So true," I grumbled. I'd been in relationship after relationship until my last ended in tatters, so my wingman status had been on hiatus.

A fresh breeze drifted in from the open window. It was cooler than the one in Mexico, but it reminded me so much of my day spent there—my night in her bed—that my chest hurt.

Her fault.

She'd caused all of this.

I needed someone to blame.

And I couldn't blame myself, I just couldn't.

"Alright, so I hope you got all that."

"What? You were speaking still?"

He just laughed. "Do me a favor, don't be an ass. She'll be at the house at eight in the morning. I gave her the code to the gate. Her background is solid and the NDA is ironclad, you're welcome."

I frowned. "Wait, why are you sending me a woman again?"

"Were you listening to anything I said?"

"Not really, no. My life's a bit of a mess, so forgive me if I mope around in misery a while longer."

"Wipe that moping ass with a few hundreds and get your head back in the game. You have practice in the morning, and I can't believe I'm actually saying this to someone who used to donate half his earnings to the cancer charities in London, but be nice, alright?"

"I'm nice!" I roared.

He sighed. "You're . . ." His voice lowered. "Never mind."

I knew what he was going to say.

I was sad.

Angry.

Confused.

I ran a hand through my long hair. "I won't yell at her. Happy?"

"Thrilled," he said in a dry tone. "See you at practice."

"Shit, you're coming?"

"Someone has to make sure you play nice."

"I've never had a problem before," I pointed out.

Another long sigh. "Slade . . . if you need someone to talk to . . ."

"I don't want to talk," I said through clenched teeth.

"Yeah, that's what I thought, man."

Silence crackled over the phone.

"I gotta get some sleep," I rasped.

"Yeah."

"Night." I hung up before I spilled my guts, before I burst into tears and told him every fucking regret I had. I'd never told my dad I loved him. I never got to tell him how much he meant to me.

I never got to say those words.

Because there would always be another time.

Another day.

And now, he was gone. There would never be another day again.

I reached for the beer and slammed it against the wall.

Chapter Thirteen

MACKENZIE

I pulled my Lexus up to the keypad and typed in the code. The black iron gate made a dinging noise and then whined a bit as it opened wide, revealing a three-story mansion. A fountain complete with statue sat in the middle of the circular driveway.

I tilted my head and examined my surroundings as I pulled to the front. A red Ferrari was parked outside and running like the owner was warming it up before taking off. The garage attached to the house probably held enough cars for half the human population.

My aunt hadn't said anything other than this guy was big-time. And by the time I passed the background check and talked with the guy's agent, he was so thankful that I wasn't crazy and could start right away that I wondered how horrible his client really was.

I typically worked for rich clients who needed me to walk their dogs or water their plants. The job was mindless, but it kept me away from Alton.

It kept me away from my old life, and for some stupid reason it made me feel invisible, for once I wasn't the one getting my picture taken.

I wasn't at some society event being asked if I was going to hop back on the horse or if I was sad that Alton was already dating.

I shuddered.

No. That would come soon enough.

My dad gave me two months to get my head straight.

What better way than feeding some rich guy's dog and making sure he had groceries and clean clothes?

"Well, here goes nothing." I killed the engine, grabbed the small bag of dog food I'd been instructed to bring, and got out of my SUV.

The stairs leading up to the house were a black marble that looked expensive, giving me no clue as to what this guy played.

Was he a football player? Basketball?

What athlete had a house like this? Maybe he played for the NBA? Mariners? Hawks?

I was told not to ask too many questions and to make myself as invisible as possible.

No problem. That was part of this job, gain trust and become nonexistent. Rich people were almost too trusting when they let strangers into their homes. I was told I'd see my fair share of tax papers, social security numbers, text messages from mistresses on phones and computers—and that at the end of the day it didn't matter. It was their business, and I was just there to do a job.

If I knew how to write a book on all the scandal I had access to without getting sued—I would. It was fascinating, to say the least.

I lifted my hand to ring the doorbell just as the door jerked open.

I noticed the Sounders gear right away.

Black Adidas joggers paired with tall Adidas socks and sliders.

I slowly looked up.

Gray jacket with the green insignia of the Space Needle.

And then.

Lethal, caramel, almost golden eyes.

I jolted backward so hard that I tripped on my heel and broke it.

I stumbled to the side, gathered myself, and blurted, "Is this a joke?"

At the same time he snarled, "Are you fucking stalking me?"

Tears welled in my eyes as I stared down at the phone that was given to me and the address.

My hand shook as I glanced back up into Hugo's eyes. "No, I'm not stalking you, I must have the wrong—" Oh God, this was not happening. I felt the back of my neck heat. I had his linen shirt in my car. Mere feet away from me. I closed my eyes in embarrassment while anger replaced my hurt. "I'm sure there's an explanation."

"Really?" He crossed his bulky arms. A pair of black Bose headphones were wrapped around his neck, and pieces of his golden-brown hair were hanging loose by his chin. He looked different. Harsher somehow. His dark eyebrows slanted in an almost-V above his eyes, and his lips curved downward like he'd forgotten how to smile. "So you didn't find out who I was and just show up? Fuck, how much money do you even want? So we had sex—that doesn't mean you get to write a tell-all story about the one night you got Slade Rodriguez to fuck you."

I flinched.

A slap would have been preferable to what he'd just said.

The fantasy that I'd been holding in my heart came crashing down at those words.

I never wanted to believe my gut instinct.

That I was nothing to him.

I wanted to believe that it had meant something.

It had to.

It was too good not to.

Too perfect.

I was wrong.

About everything.

His name wasn't even Hugo.

Slade Rodriguez.

Slade Rodriguez.

I took in his outfit again.

Why did that sound so familiar?

I felt my eyes widen as tears threatened to pour over. Oh, I'd been a one-night stand alright, with none other than soccer's newest European transfer.

I should have seen it.

The money.

Good looks.

I'm sure he thought he could just screw anything with heels.

Anger replaced all the sadness, all the insecurity. I was ready to bang him over the head with my phone when it started to ring.

It was Matt.

Unable to speak, I shoved the phone in Slade's direction.

"Shit." He cursed at the screen, slid his finger across it. "Seriously, Matt?"

They talked.

He stared me down with that empty golden gaze I'd once found alluring, beautiful. But those eyes, they were just like every other pair of eyes that had looked at me and found me wanting.

They looked their fill.

They walked away.

Slade handed the phone back to me. Matt was gone.

I cleared my throat. "I have dog food, for your . . . dog."

His eyebrows shot up. "Really, Ashley? Is that what you feed them?"

"Mackenzie," I said in a low voice. "My name is Mackenzie."

He gave his head a shake of disgust. "Wow."

I glared. "Really, Hugo." I drew out his name with malicious purpose.

He stared at my mouth, shook his head, and looked away. "Just don't steal anything."

I'd never been so insulted and embarrassed all at once. "Oh, you mean don't take pictures and upload them to eBay? I'll try to control my poor unfortunate self."

He leaned down. I could smell him. It still made my knees weak, but I was too angry to recognize the feeling as lust when all I wanted to do was hold onto the rage. "Yes. Try to control yourself."

My eyes narrowed.

He stepped around me and called over his shoulder. "And feed Alfie."

"Alfie," I repeated just as a fat bulldog came scurrying toward the door barking.

Slade didn't even turn around, just hopped into his ridiculous sports car and sped through the gate, leaving me a complete mess with a dog that was snarling and tearing into the food I'd dropped by my feet when I saw Slade's eyes.

With shaking hands, I grabbed the food and walked as best I could with a broken heel into the house. "Come on, boy."

He licked the side of my leg, getting nothing but black skinny jeans and the smell of Escada perfume.

The hall was clean.

The kitchen was gorgeous, but a complete mess, like he hadn't done a dish since he'd moved in.

With a grumble, I found a bowl, cleaned it out, dumped some dog food inside, and then started working with the dishes.

Chapter Fourteen

SLADE

I pulled up to the stadium and tried not to throw my bag at the ground and jump on top of it with my cleats.

What the hell?

Matt was waiting by the door. "You look . . . rough."

The same couldn't be said of Matt. Every hair was in place. His suit belonged in a boardroom full of millionaires with too much time on their hands, and yet there he was, perfectly poised and polished with his blond hair swept back and his designer suit making everything around him seem cheap in comparison. The only thing standing out was the toothpick between his teeth. The guy had a thing about sucking. And let's just leave it there.

I glanced down. Adidas cleats.

At least he came prepared to chase me out of there, if need be.

He used to play for an American soccer team in LA before an injury led him to switch to the business side of things, and now he managed everyone from bands to athletes.

"She was late," I said, sweeping by him and heaving my duffel over my back. "And she was rude. You should fire her."

"After ten minutes in your company?" He gasped. "Rude, you say? Color me shocked."

I flipped him off.

He swatted my hand away, and his blue eyes searched mine. "I could have been partying on a yacht with Tom Brady and Ben Affleck right now." He gripped me by the shoulders. "But I'm in Seattle, midwinter, it's bloody cold, and I'm staring at your ugly mug instead of drinking champagne with supermodels."

"Sacrificed a lot, have you?"

"Super. Models," he felt the need to say again. "Don't fuck this up, not if you want to keep playing. They'll just bench you and pay out your contract. This team is different from Chelsea. They need a leader, alright? That's what they're paying you to be. The leader, the co-captain. They want a cup. You're here to give it to them. So bury all that shit inside, and play like the Fifty-Two Million Dollar Man, got it?"

I bit down on my lip until I tasted blood. "Got it."

He slapped my ass. "That's the spirit, now get in there and change, you're almost late and Coach Mesinger said warm-up starts in five minutes. They'll want you leading some of the drills, Mr. Number-One Striker."

I was tempted to flip him off again as I made my way into the locker room and pulled off my warm-ups. At least the stadium was new and covered so I wouldn't be freezing my ass off on the field.

The locker room was already empty. I pulled off my sliders and grabbed my cleats like I had so many times over the last decade. Only this time my hands were shaking.

This time I was walking out there without my dad.

Shit.

I inhaled deeply, put on the cleats, and slowly stood.

I took the walk down a long hall, and when I pushed the door open, all of the guys were already out on the field with the coaching staff.

Silence blanketed the field as I approached, and with each step against the turf, I felt more and more angry. Angry that I'd been forced away from a team I used to love.

To a new team that was going to expect fucking miracles from one human being.

I stopped at the edge of the group as Coach Mesinger gave me a quick nod. "Let's all give a warm welcome to the number-one striker in the world—"

I hated it when they announced me like that, like I was important when I was just coordinated and hardworking.

"Slade Rodriguez."

I pulled a confident smile out of my ass.

I could almost feel Matt breathe a sigh of relief from across the field.

"Mile run," Coach called. "Then Rodriguez is going to run you through the warm-up. He's your new co-captain, treat him that way."

Most men met my gaze and nodded.

Most.

Save. One.

Jagger Komokov.

The other captain.

The goalie.

My nemesis.

We'd been at each other's throats for years. It didn't help that Matt represented us both—nor did it help that we had history that went beyond our game. Just seeing him reminded me of mistakes.

Besides, he would rather run me over with my own car than shake my hand. We'd gotten into it at finals last year. Penalty cards were thrown. Punches followed. We're both lucky as hell we didn't get kicked out of the game.

Finally, he met my gaze, his icy blue stare boring right through me. No acknowledgment, just hate.

So it was going to be like that?

I turned on my heel and started to run around the stadium, and the rest of the players followed like I knew they would. I was a born leader.

I just didn't feel like one anymore.

Instead, I felt like a giant fake.

Who was one mistake away from never feeling normal again.

Chapter Fifteen

MACKENZIE

The guy was an animal!

He ate more takeout than a college student, and his poor dog was so hungry I had to give him three more helpings of food.

It was starting to get dark by the time I heard the car pull up.

And it was impossible not to hear that engine.

I had turned a few lights off, made sure the oven was off, and left a note, but there would be no escape. Not tonight.

My heart clenched when the door opened.

I busied myself with wiping the counter.

"Shit, you're still here?" His raspy voice sounded tired. The slight Spanish accent I'd once found sexy now made my heart hurt and my embarrassment fan to life as I remembered the way his mouth had nibbled and nipped trails inside my thighs.

So. Stupid.

I'd trusted too easily.

Never again.

Well, I'd done what I had set out to do! I'd lived on the wild side and got my heart broken in the process. Well. Done.

"Yeah," I responded, dumping the paper towel in the trash as he made his way into the dimly lit kitchen. "Dinner's in the oven, already finished, I reorganized your dishes because they were everywhere. Alfie's been fed a few times, since he's clearly not eaten in a month, but you should have enough dog food to hold you over until I get back in the morning."

I tried walking by him, but he caught me by the elbow. I thought maybe he'd say thank you or even apologize. Instead, he stared me down with hatred. "Never. Ever. Touch my shit again." He jerked his hand away.

My lips parted as I stepped back slowly and accidentally said out loud, "Who are you?"

His eyes flickered with something before he sneered. "If I never told you my real name, do you really think you knew me at all?"

Getting punched in the gut would feel better than this. "No. You're . . . right." I ducked my head and walked by him. With as much dignity as I could summon, I grabbed my purse, leaned down and kissed Alfie on his fur, and then stalked out, slamming the door as hard as I could behind me. I prayed pictures would fall from the wall and create such a mess of glass he'd cut up his perfect soccer feet.

Tears streamed down my cheeks as I made my way to the first Central Market I could find. I cut the engine, ran inside, grabbed two bottles of my favorite blend, and waited in line.

Only to suffer through more torture.

His face was everywhere.

US Weekly. In Touch. People.

They all had him featured.

European bad boy.

Downward spiral since his father's death.

I frowned.

Then grabbed every last magazine I could, and dumped them on the belt, brain spinning.

I was losing it.

Was I really going to be that person? The one who believed everything I read in the tabloids when I'd been on the receiving end of their hatred more times than I could count?

I looked back down—one had him shirtless in Mexico.

My skin flushed.

Yes. Yes, I was.

Because behind him, in that very same picture, was a girl I no longer recognized.

A girl who looked like she'd just tasted freedom and never wanted to go back.

"Ah." The checker scanned the magazines. "I get it, he's smokin' hot, but I bet he's got a small thing. Most of the good-looking ones do."

"Thing?" I squinted at her, seeking clarification.

"Peter." The woman was in her fifties at least, with salt-and-pepper hair and purple lipstick. "All the good ones do."

He doesn't, I wanted to say.

Maybe it would be easier to forget him if everything about those moments in his arms had been a letdown.

But he'd been . . . everything.

He'd been gentle, tender. Well, if soccer stopped paying him millions he could probably win Oscars for his performance, because for a hot minute I had believed he actually wanted me as much as I wanted him.

And needed me—maybe even a little bit more.

Chapter Sixteen

SLADE

I woke up to a loud banging on the door followed by Alfie's howling and then my fucking doorbell going off like the apocalypse was coming.

"Shit!" I jumped out of bed, heart pounding. I hopped across the room, pulling on my sweatpants one leg at a time, then stumbled down the hall.

I yanked open the door.

Her.

It hurt to look at her.

Mackenzie held out Starbucks and sighed. "You're supposed to take it."

"Did you poison it?" I crossed my arms.

"Did you want me to?" she countered with a saucy smile that made me want to shove her against the wall and taste the bitterness of whatever she was drinking.

I looked away. "It's Tuesday."

"You have practice every day, which means Alfie needs a walk every day, and from the looks of your kitchen I figured I could get you some groceries. Want me to just pick up some—"

"Look," I growled. "I don't need your help. You're here to make sure that I have no more added stress beyond my daily practices. That includes taking care of Alfie, not playing house. Whatever you think is going to happen between us—won't. Just drop it. I'm not going to marry you just because I saw your pussy."

I wasn't prepared for her to slap me so hard that I stumbled against the doorframe.

Tears filled her eyes. "Listen up, you piece of shit. I'm here because it's my job. I can get insulted by plenty of people who haven't seen me naked, thank you very much."

I didn't know why, but my lips twitched at that.

"I don't want you to marry me, you narcissistic prick!" Her voice rose, and she gritted her teeth. "You're a job. A nice-paying one. One that means I don't have to go back to my old life for two full months. And as shocking as it sounds, I'd rather be here in hell with you than there." She ducked under my arm and put the coffee on the counter, then grabbed the leash from the door and hooked it on Alfie's collar.

"Let's go, buddy," she said in a sweeter tone and pulled him down the stairs. He followed with a lopsided grin and stared at her tight ass for a few seconds, the dirty bastard.

"Traitor," I whispered under my breath when she bent down and he licked her face.

"Oh!" She turned. "And you're welcome for the coffee and the gluten-free muffin with the breakfast burrito, and for cleaning up all your shitty, moldy takeout, and for the pot roast I left in the oven. Really, it was a pleasure serving you." Her words sliced through the air like the perfect swordplay.

And I was left defenseless and feeling like the biggest ass in the world when I shut the door behind me and leaned against it.

This wasn't me.

My mother would slap me.

My father would take me out back and make me dig a hole until he was satisfied with its depth.

But my mom was hurting.

And he was gone.

I shoved away from the door, marched into the kitchen, dumped the coffee down the drain, and put the muffin in the garbage, only to search for it five minutes later when my stomach growled. Then I hopped in my car and sped past her as she walked my dog.

I refused to feel guilty for not trusting anyone around me. Not after what I'd been through, not after being alone in this world without my one pillar.

I sped like hell the entire way to the stadium and momentarily toyed with the idea of hitting Jagger on his way across the parking lot.

I hit the accelerator and the car lurched forward a couple of feet. He jumped and shot me a venomous stare, so I gave him an innocent shrug before I pulled into a parking spot and followed him in.

As luck would have it, we were both late, which left the two of us in the locker room in edgy silence.

The sound of us both putting on our gear was more intense than a United Nations meeting.

Cleats tied so tight my feet hurt.

Shin guards squeezing the life out of my sore-as-hell legs.

And then Jagger opened his fat mouth, and his irritating voice pierced the tension. "You're not gonna last, pretty boy."

I grinned at that. His Russian accent was barely noticeable now that he'd been in the States for the last few years.

I stood and crossed my arms. "Thanks, man, I've always wanted another player to call me pretty. Life made."

He glared.

"Oh, and maybe next time you compliment my good looks, make sure it's around other dudes so I don't assume you want to see me naked, yeah?"

He lunged for me, but I was already jogging out onto the turf. Coach stared me down, then nodded while I started the mile run to loosen up my muscles. Jagger fell into place beside me and what started as a jog ended as a fucking sprint. My legs burned once we circled around to stretch.

"Rodriguez, Komokov, try not to be competitive assholes . . . you're on the same team now. Act like it."

"Yes, sir," I said quickly.

Jagger grumbled, "Sure, Coach."

Lying through his ass, that guy.

We didn't speak the rest of the day, and when we broke apart for drills, I purposely stood on the opposite end of the field so I wouldn't have to look at him. We might be on the same team, but there was no chance in hell we would ever be mates.

Chapter Seventeen

MACKENZIE

It wasn't in my nature to sit and stew over things out of my control. Like the situation with Alton? I'd like to think I did something a bit crazy, made a few bad choices, and now avoided him like the plague.

But with Slade? I was stewing.

I analyzed every single piece of furniture. Every stupid coffee mug, and even his choice in dog.

"What do you think, Alfie?" I yawned and reached into my purse. I had a few of the magazines stashed for my lunch break later. I never realized how much help the guy needed. My job was to water plants, feed the dog, clean up.

How Slade managed to live in his own chaos like this and sleep at night, well, I had no clue. He'd managed to keep the kitchen clean, and the living room looked fine, but when I finally made it upstairs all I saw were boxes.

Frowning, I sent a text to his manager.

Me: Hey, this is Mack. Am I helping your client unpack as well?

Matt: Ha, be my guest. Just make sure you check the labels beforehand, some shit he won't want you to see.

Me: Hey whatever I see I forget immediately, that's part of the contract.

I could tell he was typing.

What could I possibly see that I hadn't seen before? I tried not to think about seeing him naked, and what that did to me. Okay, so I hadn't seen a man like that before, but that was different than unpacking boxes.

My insecurity chose that horrible moment in time to come flooding back, filling my cheeks with heat while I thought about the things I let him do to me, and the words he threw at my face earlier today. "Just because I saw your pus—"

A text came in.

Matt: If it's labeled family, father, or anything related, don't open. Anything else is fair game.

I was both curious and ashamed that I was spending time being angry with him when he'd just lost his father.

Was it crossing a line if I probed a bit about that? I chewed on the thought and typed back.

Me: Got it. I'm sure he's still struggling with losing his father.

Matt: If struggling means nearly losing your shit every day since, then yes, he's struggling. I hope he's being nice to you.

I rolled my eyes.

Me: The nicest.

Matt: Bullshit, but thanks for putting up with it.

I didn't respond, just shoved my phone back into my jeans pocket and made my way into the large master bedroom. With a sigh, I knelt down and patted Alfie on the head. He snuggled against my hand and let out a whine.

"I know, buddy . . . it's a lot of boxes."

He whined again, took off toward a stack of boxes, and ran headfirst into it.

"Alfie!" I yelled, leaping after him. "Bad dog! No, no, no, we don't make a mess like that!"

He whined again and hit the tower of boxes.

Before I could reach the top box it fell over. The crunching sound of glass made me cringe.

"Please don't let that be a picture. Please don't let that be a picture." I gently picked up the box, flipped it, and opened.

"Pictures." I sighed. "Crap."

Alfie whined some more and then turned around in a small circle before sitting right in front of the box.

I pulled out the first wrapped picture. It wasn't broken. It was a family photo from the looks of it.

The next was a team picture.

I sighed in relief when each picture I pulled out was in perfect condition.

The sound must have been the pictures hitting each other? I reached in and jerked my hand back as a piece of glass sliced my two fingers.

I sucked the blood and then winced as more blood poured down my palm.

With a curse I jumped to my feet and turned blindly toward the hall to run to the bathroom.

"Doing some recon?" Slade tilted his head, his eyebrows shoved together in an angry slant while he put his hands on his hips like he was guarding me from leaving the room.

I gritted my teeth. "No, actually. Matt said to help you unpack the less personal boxes and your possessed dog made a run for the tower and it fell and—"

"Are you this competent at all your jobs?"

I glared. "I'm competent at everything."

"Are you, though?" he hissed.

I took a step back.

How dare he!

He actually smiled like it was funny.

FUNNY that we'd had sex.

Funny that I hadn't known what I was doing.

Comical.

I looked away, my fingers throbbing as I collected blood in my palm. "I'll just finish up tomorrow."

"Finish up tonight," he said with a shrug. "Just don't break anything you can't afford to replace."

I bit my tongue.

It stung hard enough to remind me not to mouth off.

Not to tell him I had a sixty-million-dollar trust fund from my grandfather. That I was a socialite. That before his face graced covers of magazines—it had been mine.

Granted, it was a horrible picture of me crying at the altar, but still.

I checked my watch.

"Am I boring you?" He wiped his face with his hands. That was when I noticed the exhaustion, the dirt covering his cheeks, and the flash of anger in his eyes that hadn't been there before. As if I was the reason he was upset.

I frowned and then shook my head. "No, sorry. I have dinner plans, so I'll go ahead and unpack a few boxes, and then I'll be on my way."

His jaw tensed.

How had that made him even more pissed?

"I, um, made you a casserole, but if you want to go to a boring dinner with great wine, you're more than welcome to come with me." I was waving the white flag, being generous. Maybe he just needed to get out, needed friends, laughter.

I couldn't believe this was the same man I had met.

I refused to believe it.

He let out a humorless laugh. "You know? I have to admit that's clever. And I'm so tired it's almost tempting to say yes. We'd go to an expensive restaurant where you'd most likely be seen, get your picture taken, the friends you invited suddenly can't make it—perfect plan, right?"

I frowned. "No, actually, that's not what—" I bit my tongue again, then sighed. "You know what? Never mind. Invitation taken back." I turned around, completely forgetting about my injured hand before reaching for a box and jerking my hand back as the cuts reminded me with burning intensity that they were still there.

"Why the hell are you bleeding?" His hands were on my hips before I could say anything, and then he was turning me in his arms, pulling my injured hand away from my body and examining it with such care that I almost stopped breathing. He leaned down and blew across the slices of marred skin.

"Come on." He pulled me into the adjoining bathroom and lifted me onto the counter like I wasn't diseased anymore. Maybe instinct had kicked in. Maybe he was going to snap later and he was just warming me up.

He was causing very severe trust issues in my heart.

Slade pulled out a first aid kit and some witch hazel wipes. He ran the wipes down my fingers then grabbed some antiseptic, gently rubbing it across the cuts.

I jerked in pain.

"Sorry." He said it like he meant it.

I stared at him like he'd lost his mind.

And he stared back like he wanted me to help him find it.

Too soon, the moment was gone as he wrapped my fingers in Band-Aids and then cleaned up the mess.

We locked eyes. His swirled with uncertainty, mistrust, so much pain I wanted to reach out and pull him in for a hug, but given his recent behavior he'd probably think I was trying to sleep with him. So I went for "Thank you" instead.

He nodded his head once. And then left me sitting there on the bathroom countertop wondering how to merge the two versions of him into one that made sense.

◆ ◆ ◆

"Hey, baby girl." My dad pulled me into his embrace while my mom took one look at me and handed me the glass from her hand. It was champagne. Because that was all she drank. Champagne. We had wineries everywhere, but she said champagne had always made her feel more mysterious. She was quirky and adorable, and the minute my dad had set his eyes on her he'd known they were meant to be. Maybe that's why I jumped head over heels for Slade. I thought it was possible for me too.

My first mom died when I was a baby, but Lilah had been my mom since I was a year old, the only mom I really remembered.

I kissed her on the cheek and downed her glass.

Her eyebrows shot up. "That bad?"

"Worse. Actually." I sighed and held my glass out.

She poured. "I hope you have a driver."

"I'll steal one of Dad's." I winked at my father, who was already digging into the calamari and piling it onto my plate.

We'd always had money.

But love was held to the highest standard, that and respect; money was there to change others.

Not us.

I smiled as my dad reached for my mom's hand and kissed it, all the while using his free hand to shove a plate of food in my face.

I gave him a look, then dove in.

"So, how's the job?" Dad asked in the casual tone that meant in about five minutes he was going to ask me to come back to work.

His bluish-silver eyes twinkled as he adjusted his bow tie then ran a massive hand through his dyed dark-brown hair.

With a sigh I leaned back in my chair. "It's work."

"A job should never be work," he countered.

I narrowed my eyes at him. "Trust me, with the way things are going, I'll probably be begging to get back on the payroll."

"We paid you?" he asked.

"Very funny. Actually, I think I need a raise."

He ignored me and poured a glass of Cab Franc. My eyes watered a bit as he held the glass to me and then swirled the liquid. "Look at the legs on this one."

"You say that to all the pretty reds." I winked and took the stem with two fingers, then held it to my nose, inhaling deeply. "Mmmm, raspberries? A hint of . . . is that chocolate?"

He shrugged.

"Jalapeño?"

"This woman"—he jutted his finger at me while talking to Mom—"has the best nose and palate in the world."

I beamed at the compliment, because for the past few days I'd been beaten down by the one and only man to ever fully see me naked and give me an orgasm.

"Baby girl?" Dad leaned in. "Everything okay?"

"Yeah." I choked out the word with every ounce of mental strength I had. "Just tired." I let the wine sit on my tongue as I savored the flavor. When I set my glass down, both Mom and Dad were waiting impatiently for my response.

"Full bodied, with a hint of tart, it would pair extremely well with a good Dubliner cheese or a sirloin."

"That's my girl." Dad clapped slowly and then poured a round for the entire table. "I love you." He leaned in and kissed my cheek.

And all was right in the world again.

Chapter Eighteen

As promised, I let one of Dad's drivers take me back to my apartment, and because I was a little buzzed and a lot emotional, I dug into my purse and pulled out two of the magazines, sat down on my couch, and started to read.

I read about his fiancée getting pregnant.

A light bulb went on when I realized he'd been flying to Puerto Vallarta a few weeks later.

Huh, so both of us were escaping our current situations.

Is that why he gave another name?

I did the same.

Were we both that mistrusting?

Or just in that much need to be different people?

I kept reading.

The details all seemed the same until I got to the part about his father's fatal heart attack and the mental toll it had taken on him. Drugs? Really? Rehab? Angry outbursts? I frowned.

Loss did bad things to good people.

I traced a finger over his beautiful smile. He was at the World Cup, hugging his dad while his dad wiped away a tear.

I knew that feeling.

Accomplishing something great and having your parents be proud of you. I'd had a crap day, and just being with my dad made the day end on a happy note.

As my eyes started to get heavy, I lay down on the couch and grabbed a blanket. Slade had lost his happy.

His support.

He'd lost one of his best friends.

I fell asleep with a frown, wondering how I was going to make sure the cranky bastard had a friend he could trust—who didn't want something from him.

How do you give someone a present they don't think they want or need?

He wasn't mine to save.

And I didn't even like him ninety percent of the time.

He'd hurt me.

He'd made me feel insecure.

Ugly.

He changed the way I saw myself.

He didn't deserve my help.

But I was going to give it anyway.

Because it was the right thing to do.

Chapter Nineteen

SLADE

I stared at the breakfast casserole like it was poison.

Not only had Mackenzie labeled it so I would know what it was, but she'd left a pink sticky note on the side: *Heat for forty minutes at 350.* I ripped the note off and crumpled it in my fist.

Did she think I was an idiot who didn't know how to cook?

Why the hell was she leaving me food?

It had been three days since I'd helped her with her bloodied hand. Extreme paranoia had followed that episode, making it almost impossible to sleep. Had I been too rough? What if she got blood poisoning? The cut went septic? Should I have sent her to the hospital? Even let her drive herself home?

It was stupid shit.

All of it.

But I couldn't stop the rerun of what-ifs that kept slamming into my brain. It got so bad that the minute she showed up the day after, I'd been so relieved that I'd stared at her a solid two minutes before grabbing my duffel and leaving. She probably thought I had a learning disability.

Thus the sticky notes.

Because ever since that morning.

Food.

All the food.

I had premade food for breakfast, lunch, dinner. She'd even gotten the secret recipe for my smoothies and had one waiting for me this morning, all before humming her way around my house feeding my dog.

I slammed the door to the stainless-steel refrigerator and leaned against it. My phone started buzzing. I picked it up from the counter immediately. I never missed calls.

I'd learned my lesson once.

"Yeah?" I barked into the phone.

"Slade?" Mom's voice was tired. "Are you feeling alright?"

I frowned. "Yeah, why?"

"You haven't been by this week . . ." Her voice was filled with so much sadness my chest hurt. My parents might not have been together anymore, but they'd still enjoyed a friendship that went beyond that of normal divorced couples.

Mackenzie chose that moment to walk by with Alfie attached to his leash and looking happier than I'd ever seen him. You'd think it was impossible since she walked him twice a day, but the little guy was packing on the pounds.

"We'll be back!" Mackenzie said in a clear voice that I knew my mom could hear.

"Who was that?" she said almost the second the door clicked shut. "Was that a woman?" She perked up so much my heart broke all over again. "You're dating!"

"Not—really." I scowled. "She's just—"

"Oh, I can't believe it! I've been so worried about you! Is that why you haven't been visiting? Because you've been with this girl? Oh, Slade." And that was when she burst into tears. I didn't have the heart to say no.

She was crying because she thought I was happy.

I could be happy.

I could fake it.

I did it once, right? After all, Hugo had been happy—not a care in the world.

Just channel Hugo.

"Yeah, I was going to tell you," I lied through my teeth. "But it's still . . ." I gulped as I stared out the kitchen window. Mackenzie's ponytail bounced with each step, and Alfie kept looking up at her as if he had a new favorite human. "New," I finished. "It's still new."

If *new* meant *nonexistent*, then sure, that's what it was!

"Oh, honey." She blew her nose. "Do you think you can bring her by at some point?"

Shit. "Yeah, Mom, I'm really busy with the team right now, but I'll do it soon, alright?"

"Oh! I can't wait! I'll get the albums out just in case it's sooner rather than later."

I cringed and squeezed my eyes shut. "Yeah, you do that. I gotta go, Mom."

"Oh. Okay! Love you!"

"Love you back." I hit end and stared at my phone for a few brief seconds before it registered that I was going to be five minutes late to practice. I ran out of the house and tried not to stare at Mackenzie as I drove by.

Tried.

Failed.

Same thing. Right?

Chapter Twenty

His car was gone by the time Alfie and I made it back. A small part of me had just begun to feel like maybe since the whole cutting-my-hand incident he'd been nicer, then he did something like just stare at me like I was a complete waste of human space, which hurt.

But I wasn't giving up.

And since I knew the way into a man's heart was through his stomach, I baked, I cooked, and I made sure that at least he wasn't hangry half the time.

"There you go, buddy." I unleashed Alfie and went to grab a bottle of water only to trip over Slade's duffel bag.

"Shoot! Alfie, I'll be right back!" I didn't know why I was talking to the dog like he could answer, but maybe my loneliness was manifesting as thinking that animals could understand me.

I dashed out the door with the duffel bag, got into my SUV, and probably broke at least two laws trying to get to the stadium in time. Traffic was horrible, like it always is downtown no matter what time of day, and his house wasn't exactly close. It took a good twenty minutes on a normal day, when people didn't drive five miles an hour and do their makeup in the rearview mirror.

I honked my horn.

Got flipped off.

Honked it again.

And nearly broke my slingback mules in an attempt to sprint into the stadium. I didn't exactly know my way around, but Alton had been friends with one of the players, close enough friends that he was one of the groomsmen at our wedding, which only made me sweat more when I thought about seeing him. Because seeing him would remind me of Alton.

Of freaking Joanna.

Of them moving on together while I was working for Slade.

What the hell kind of name was Joanna, anyway?

I speed-walked into the front office and held out the duffel bag. "Hey, Slade Rodriguez left his—"

"On the field." Security eyed me up and down then told me to put the bag on the conveyor belt while I went through a full TSA baton scan. I was surprised he didn't force me to take off my shoes.

When I was done, he grabbed a guest pass and handed it to me only after I gave him my license to copy and my social security number.

Really?

They played soccer!

It wasn't like I was trying to stalk Russell Wilson!

I didn't really watch sports.

I mean I knew sports were a big deal through Alton, and I knew players made good money, but soccer involved running.

I preferred a cycle bar, with a nice little instructor who yelled encouraging things like "You can do it!" versus running for an hour and imagining chasing a bottle of wine.

"May I go now?" I asked in a voice I hoped sounded sweet rather than strained and irritated.

"Yup." He winked.

I narrowed my eyes, grabbed the duffel, and picked up the pace until I made it into the stadium.

The first thing I noticed was the lights.

The second?

The giant banners hanging from the upper deck, one for each player, and the amazing amount of seating.

Huh, did they fill this thing up every game?

"Mack?" I'd recognize Jagger's voice anywhere. And then he was running toward me like we were long-lost friends. If he asked me about Alton, I was going to lose it. "What are you doing here?" He picked me up. He really did give the best hugs out of anyone on this planet. The perfect amount of tight and warm.

When he set me back on my feet, I actually felt better. "Hey, Jagger, how's practice been?"

He rolled his eyes. "Between you and me, I'd rather hang out with you and—" He stopped himself. "I'm sorry for what happened. I should have called."

I waved him off. "Water under the bridge. He has Joanna now."

"Fucking Joanna." Jagger winked and wrapped his arm around me just as Slade made it to my side.

"Forgot this." I handed over the duffel bag.

Jagger stiffened and then stared down at me. "Wait . . . tell me this wasn't your first choice after Alton?"

"Alton?" Slade's eyes narrowed. "Who the hell is Alton?"

"Her ex—"

"I need to get back to the, um . . . dog." I couldn't help the slight cringe under Jagger's intense gaze and Slade's confusion.

"Why do you have his duffel bag?" Jagger released me.

"Why wouldn't she?" Slade sneered.

I pressed my hands into my temples. "I'm his, er . . . housekeeper and dog walker extraordinaire." I shrugged. "You know, pays the bills." Confident wink, slight smile. I started to slowly back away as the rest of the guys walked over, including the coach.

"That you, Mackenzie?" One time. I'd met that stupid coach *one* time and sent him one case of wine! And this was how I was rewarded?

"Yeah, hi!" I gave a small wave. "I was just leaving."

"Stay." He grinned. "And thanks again for the wine last Christmas. The wife wouldn't shut up about it."

I shrugged. "It's the best."

"Housekeeper?" Jagger repeated. "Dog walker?"

Slade rolled his eyes. "I just moved. I needed help."

"So you hired a billionaire's daughter?"

And just like that.

Outed.

"Thanks, Jagger," I grumbled.

"What?" He looked genuinely confused. "Everyone knows who you are. You were on *Vogue* last year during Wedding—" He made a face. "Sorry, sore subject."

"Ya think?"

"Wedding?" Slade just had to ask.

"You know what would be great right now?" I spread my arms wide. "If I just went . . . away, and you guys did your thing, with the cleats and . . . running. Balls. Do your thing with your balls."

Jagger hid a grin behind his hand while Slade's lips twitched.

"Stay." Coach had me in a viselike side hug that immediately caused sweat under my arms. "I insist."

"Well," I said through clenched teeth. "If you insist."

"Let's go, men." He clapped his hands.

Slade's eyes narrowed at me before he shook his head. "Have you always been a compulsive liar, or is this new?"

"Oh, it's new." I flashed him a middle finger. "And this whole jackass routine you've got going on. That new too, or has it always been in your possessed, flesh-eating soul?"

"Flesh-eating." He nodded. "Nice. And honestly, it comes and goes, depending on the company."

"Lucky company." I glared.

We were at a standstill.

I wanted to lunge at him, poke those perfect eyeballs with my pointer finger, and kick him in the balls.

"Slade!" Coach called.

"Better go play with your tiny balls, Slade. And before you say something childish like 'You would know,' remember"—I lowered my eyes—"I really would."

His face broke out into a smile. That was all it took to transport me back to the guy I'd first met, not the one I was working for. His smile quickly faded, though. It slid into the abyss of whatever anger and sadness he was carrying around in a suitcase.

Forcing me to remember all the reasons I was trying to cheer him up.

Why fighting with him felt more helpful than good—just another one of life's great mysteries.

Chapter Twenty-One

SLADE

Drill.

Run.

Drill.

Run.

Repeat.

I had no time to look at her because she was sitting as far away from our practice as she physically could. It pissed me off that Jagger knew her.

And it pissed me off that I'd been such a tool. And she probably had more money than I'd ever seen in my entire life.

The things I said.

Even if they were true.

Still weren't right.

My neck felt hot and itchy as I peeled my shirt off and dribbled the ball between the cones, right left, right left, fake, strike.

Repeat.

More sweat fell from my forehead until I was almost blinded by it, and when we started to scrimmage and I was pegged against Jagger, I almost tripped over a shoelace when he blew a kiss over at Mackenzie and pulled his shirt off. I never knew it was humanly possible to take off a shirt that slow, but he accomplished it with finesse that would probably earn a triple take from the stands.

"Trying to seduce the help?" I asked in a bored tone.

He rolled his eyes. "I would give up my entire soccer career for that woman to look twice at me, so yeah, I guess I am, though I wouldn't be such a dick. Her dad owns most of Seattle and has a winery empire that would make an Italian weep."

"Winery empire," I repeated as Coach blew the whistle. "Then why is she working for me?"

"Why. Indeed." He said the words slowly as though savoring them, and then the second whistle went off and all thoughts of Mackenzie vanished.

Chapter Twenty-Two

What was that about not liking soccer? Not understanding all the running? The sport just earned a new fan. I watched the guys run back and forth as I tried to focus on their intricate footwork instead of the sweat dripping off multiple six-packs and pecs.

Slade had taken his shirt off first.

And I swore to myself that if I started staring at his body I was going to cut out all sugar for a month—including wine. It was a bet with myself, against myself, in order to protect myself.

I squinted at the opposite end of the field, then watched as Jagger tried to dribble the ball around Slade, only to get it stolen.

I would not clap.

I would not be impressed with Slade's feet.

Or his abs.

Or the fact that he was easily the best player out there.

Ignore, ignore, ignore. "Watch out!" a voice called. I blinked to the right and saw the ball sailing toward my face.

I ducked just in time and almost face-planted against the chair in front of me.

"Sorry." Slade jogged over. "My tiny ball must have slipped."

I glared. "Wouldn't be the first time, would it?"

"I bet you'd love to find out," he countered.

"Yes. I would love to find out and then somehow chain your body to a bed so I can force you into marriage . . . seriously, it's on my bucket list right next to tea with Satan."

He barked out a laugh. "Yeah, alright, catlike reflexes."

I scowled. "I was paying attention to the game."

"If you were paying attention you would have seen it coming."

I sobered. "Sometimes it's hard to call the shots when you don't realize you've been put in a game, Slade."

His face went from mocking to something else that I couldn't pinpoint until he started walking away with his head down.

Shame.

◆ ◆ ◆

I stayed until the end, then tried to sneak out, but my heels were like loud bombs going off against the concrete once I made it off my plastic seat.

"Mack!" Jagger called. "Wait up."

I forced a smile and crossed my arms. "Yeah?"

He was still shirtless.

Still shiny with sweat.

Still showing absolutely no body fat.

Jagger ran a towel down his chest in what could only be described as slow motion. His grin was the perfect mix of arrogance and beauty, and when he did an effortless I-just-look-this-way hair flip, my jaw nearly came unhinged from my face.

"I know things with Alton are probably still a bit . . . raw."

Oh good, my favorite topic of conversation. Being abandoned. My stomach clenched so tight I felt like I was going to hurl all over his cleats. It didn't work with Alton, and apparently I didn't even know how to do a one-night stand right without the guy assuming I wanted to marry him.

I clenched my hands into tiny fists and waited for the rest of whatever Jagger was going to say, forcing my eyebrows nearly into my hairline so I looked more surprised than sad.

"So . . ." He grinned wide. "I was thinking—it would be fun to go to dinner, just as friends. Like I said, I know things are still new even though it's been over six months, but maybe you could use someone to talk to other than Slade's fucking dog. Besides, the only reason you'd be working for that dick is because you can't stand to be in the same room as the one who left you at the altar."

You know when you expect one thing? And life throws you something completely different? Something so unexpected and just . . . kind, that you lose all logical control of your emotions?

It happened.

Rather than lie through my teeth like I had been for months.

I let a tear fall.

And then another.

And then I was in Jagger's arms while I cried softly against his chest. It wasn't just Alton; it was Slade too. It was the fact that I'd always seen my world with Alton, even though part of me knew it didn't quite fit, only to have the best hours of my life with a complete stranger who made me feel free—and then realize it was all a farce.

Jagger embraced me like we were best friends, his arms secured tightly around my body as I slowly got control of myself and then pulled away and wiped under my eyes. "Did I just lose my chance at a nice dinner by crying over your potential friendship?"

His clear blue eyes locked on mine. "No, you just made me wish I had been a better friend to begin with."

"You were Alton's friend."

"Ouch." He sighed. "I wanted to be yours more than his. You're prettier, and his name is Alton, so that's already a scratch against him."

I laughed, tears still in my eyes. "Dinner it is, then."

"What's your number?"

I fired it off and immediately heard a buzz in my purse.

He winked. "Just sent you a text."

"Great." I beamed, feeling lighter than I had in weeks, just as Slade walked by and purposely bumped into Jagger.

"He always like this?" I wondered out loud.

Jagger hesitated a bit, then said, "On the field . . . yes . . . off the field . . ." He didn't say anything more. "I've never seen someone look so . . ." It's like he couldn't find the word, like it didn't exist in the English language yet.

A word did not exist to describe Slade.

To describe the man he was.

And I couldn't figure out if that meant he was just that extraordinary or the exact opposite.

"Send me your schedule." Jagger pulled me into his arms again and kissed my forehead. "And let me know if you have any food allergies, can't have you dying in my arms."

"Hah." I rolled my eyes and started to walk off, then stopped and called after him. "Hey, Jagger . . ."

He paused and crossed his arms.

"Thank you."

Another wink.

I drove back to Slade's house feeling lighter than air—that is, until I made it into the actual house and saw that Alfie had had a little . . . problem.

"ALFIE!" I roared. "No, no, no, bad boy!"

He whined and then puked something up that looked a hell of a lot like a bird. There was dog poop all over the main hallway, in a trail that led into the huge kitchen. I followed it, covering my mouth. A giant puddle of God-knew-what was near the barstools.

I shuddered, grabbed an entire roll of paper towels, a trash bag, and floor cleaner just as I heard the sound of a sports car's engine turning off.

"No!" I stared wide-eyed at the door, then glared at Alfie, who was panting and smirking like it was the best day of his life. Probably because he finally got whatever the hell that was out of his system.

The door slowly opened.

I closed my eyes and waited for the yelling.

And then opened them when Slade said nothing.

He stared at Alfie, then at me, then back at Alfie. "Which one of you did this?"

I clenched my teeth. "Before you start yelling at me, remember that I brought you the duffel bag, and I cook for you. Remember that I'm a human and that you shouldn't throw things just because you're pissed off at the world, alright? Got it?"

He opened his mouth.

"Wait! Always count to ten so you don't do something you'll regret."

He sighed, then slowly held up one hand and started a fun little countdown. One, two, three fingers, he continued until he had both hands up, then dropped them and turned to Alfie. "Hey, buddy, are you sick?" He knelt down as Alfie waddled over to him and licked his thigh. "I'll get you into the vet."

"Not to interrupt, but I think he ate something . . . like a bird or rodent or whatever that object is down the hall, and you know . . ." I made a puking motion.

"That's one strike." Slade stood. "Two more and you're fired."

"How is this my fault?" I asked. At least he wasn't yelling. "I was bringing you your bag, the bag you need—"

"I have a spare." He shrugged. "I always keep a spare at the stadium, and even then, I can run circles around those guys barefoot and blind. But I do appreciate it. What I don't appreciate is people who are incompetent at their jobs."

I was going to kill him.

With my bare hands.

"Alright." I crossed my arms, apparently I was getting used to the smell of dog shit since I was actually standing there without puking. "How am I incompetent?"

"Easy." He stood to his full height. "Your main priority is to make sure Alfie gets exercise and is well taken care of—he clearly ate something he shouldn't have, on your watch." He moved closer to me until I could smell his aftershave. It sent memories sailing down my spine and, regrettably, my thighs as I tried not to look away in embarrassment. "Second, you left him alone in the house while you came to the stadium. You need to crate him if you're gone for a long time."

"Had I known I was going to be gone for longer than a half hour—"

He pressed a finger to my lips.

They parted on impact.

Like he was a freaking lip whisperer.

"Always prepare for the worst," he said in a hoarse voice before pulling his finger away.

"That's not a way to live, Slade."

It was one of the first times I'd said his name out loud, rather than using Hugo.

He tensed and then gave his head a shake. "Trust me, it's the only way." He grabbed the paper towels from my hands. "You're dismissed."

"Dismissed?" I said, trying not to screech. "Dismissed?"

He let out a sigh like I was the annoying, angry one. "You can go home, I'll clean up. And Mackenzie?" My body did not react with chills. It didn't. I rebuked said chills and decided it was just nippy in his house . . . with the heat on . . . "Stay away from Jagger, alright? He's not . . . fuck." He growled. "Just . . . you're my employee, alright? It looks . . . bad."

I gaped. "I'm so sorry. I had no idea having a friend would reflect badly on your already stellar image."

"Friend?" He barked out a laugh. "Yeah, no, Jagger doesn't have friends who are women. Trust me, he doesn't want your friendship, he wants your perfect tits and amazing ass, alright?" The minute the words fell out of his mouth he sobered and then looked away like he'd just been caught with both hands, legs, and his balls in the cookie jar.

"Perfect tits and amazing ass . . . huh?" I shrugged. "Better watch it, sexual harassment is no joke."

I handed him the spray. "Enjoy cleaning up shit. And Slade? I'm allowed one friend."

"You have friends." He said it so matter-of-factly that I almost choked up again.

"People like us don't get to have friends . . . at least not ones we trust." I grabbed my purse and reached for the doorknob.

His hand was on my shoulder. "Look, I'm sorry for—"

"See you tomorrow."

"Stay away from him."

"Have a lovely evening!"

"Mackenzie!"

"Food in the fridge!"

"Mackenzie, I'm—"

I was already getting in my SUV and starting the engine.

I promised myself I wouldn't look back.

And three seconds later.

Did exactly what I shouldn't have done, as the man with the orgasms and hateful words stood on the doorstep and watched me leave.

His eyes penetrating past the shield of my car and into my chest, and for two seconds I contemplated turning around.

Chapter Twenty-Three

"Jagger asked her out," I growled as I took another bite of pizza and wiped my face with a napkin.

Matt's confused expression wasn't helping. "Who's this 'she' you're bitching about?"

I let out a grunt. "Mackenzie."

"Okay . . ." he said slowly. "And she must have said yes?"

"Damn it, why am I the only person in the universe who actually sees through his constant bullshit? He's a fucking womanizer!"

Matt's eyebrows furrowed like he was in deep thought; he even stopped chewing.

"What!" I roared.

"Have I ever told you what a joy you've been recently? No? I wonder why . . ." He started chewing off another piece and then leaned back against the couch. "Something tells me Mackenzie's a big girl. She can take care of herself."

"Why didn't you tell me who she was?" The pizza tasted like cardboard in my mouth as I made eye contact with him and waited.

He stared me down, then finally said, "Does it matter?"

I laughed.

He started choking.

I pounded him on the back. "What the hell, man?"

"Sorry, it's just the last time you laughed was at least a year ago."

"I call bullshit." I sobered. "And it's more of an ironic laugh, not one full of humor."

"And you're laughing ironically now because?"

Guilt crept down my spine. "I, uh . . ."

"Damn." He tossed his napkin on the table. "Tell me you didn't seduce her already. Tell me we don't have a lawsuit on our hands. She works for you, man! She signed a contract! You signed a contract— well, actually, I acted on your behalf, but you can't touch the help! Especially if the help is worth more than two of you!"

"Seriously? That's . . ." I frowned. "If she doesn't need to work . . ."

"Maybe she just enjoys your cheerful demeanor," he said sarcastically.

I pulled at my long hair and stared into the glass of water. "I slept with her."

"Fuck." He grabbed his phone.

"About a month ago," I added.

He dropped the phone in his lap and narrowed his eyes at me. "I'm confused. You know her?"

"Long story short . . . she was the woman I was with the night . . ." I couldn't bring myself to say it. "That night."

"You went on vacation with her?" Yeah, he still wasn't getting it.

"We met on vacation," I clarified. "On the plane . . . and we kissed—the plane lost an engine and she thought she was going to die and one thing led to another and I just . . . I was drawn to her and she was so fucking happy and carefree and in need of an adventure while I just wanted an escape. It was . . . perfect, until . . ." I threw my hands up in the air.

"And she was fine with a one-night stand with soccer's biggest star? I hope you made her sign something for legal, hell, do you still have the paper? What do I tell you, always travel with the paper—"

"She didn't sign shit . . . ," I said quickly. "She thought my name was Hugo."

"What the hell kind of name is Hugo?"

"I panicked! I just wanted something normal, alright? And it's not like she was honest! She told me her name was Ashley!"

Matt pinched the bridge of his nose and closed his eyes, then grabbed his phone and pointed it at me like I was getting disciplined. "You realize this can blow up in our faces even more, right? Tell me you've turned on the charm with her, tell me that she's not going to go to the press, or worse, try to claim you got her pregnant."

"We used protection."

"Oh good, you used protection. Well, that solves everything!" Matt jumped to his feet. "What do you want me to do? Do you want me to back her into a corner? Force her signature on something? What's the play?"

I sighed. "I'll get her to sign something . . ."

He exhaled. "Good, we just need her to agree to not talk about it to the press. The last thing you need is more bad press, and a woman scorned is a scary thing. Reporters are fantastic at getting them even more pissed off, or convinced that you somehow owe them for psychological damage because the orgasm was too hard."

I winced.

I didn't tell him the rest.

I didn't tell him she'd been a virgin.

I didn't tell him that I'd taken something from her that she hadn't given anyone else.

I didn't tell him I was a dick to her.

I didn't tell him I left her alone in her bed.

I didn't tell him that I was petrified she would tell Jagger and make things worse for me. Out of everyone in the universe, he had a legitimate reason to hate me the most for what went down. For what I did. What I encouraged.

My thoughts spiraled out of control until I felt Matt touch my shoulder. "Hey, you okay?"

I flinched. "Yeah, just tired."

He patted my arm. "Get some sleep. And keep me updated, alright?"

"Yup." I stared at the pizza box long after the front door closed, and then with increasing bitterness and misplaced rage, I grabbed my cell and walked into the kitchen in search of the phone number she'd left attached to the fridge on yet another sticky note.

Woman loved her sticky notes.

Me: Hey, it's Slade, I'm going to need you to sign some legal stuff for me in the morning, if that's okay?

Mackenzie: Are you suing me?

Me: Why the hell would you think I was suing you?

Mackenzie: It just seems like something you would do, that's all.

Me: On what grounds could I even sue?

Mackenzie: Oh, I don't know . . . incompetence.

My stomach felt sick.

I had been such an ass, and this was me trying not to be. It's like the guy that smiled and laughed was trapped inside this angry body that refused to let go of anything.

And the more I refused to deal with it.

The more the anger took control.

And the more I needed someone to blame for it rather than myself.

What would my dad say?

Other than go dig a hole?

Me: I'm sorry.

That was all I had.
And even typing it had my hands shaking a bit as I waited for her to lash out.

Mackenzie: I'll pick up coffee for you in the morning.

Me: That's it?

Mackenzie: You're forgiven.

Mackenzie: For one instance of yelling . . .

Me: How many instances have you kept track of?

Mackenzie: All of them. Sleep well!

Chapter Twenty-Four

MACKENZIE

I braced myself for another stellar day with Slade and Alfie. At least Slade would be leaving for practice soon, and then I could unpack more boxes and take a nice long walk.

I juggled the coffee carrier in one hand, my purse in the other, and tried to type the code in without spilling. I finally managed to get it when the door suddenly opened and Alfie came barreling out with Slade.

I jerked back, catching my left foot on the stair, and saw my life flash before my eyes as the world tilted backward and I landed flat on my ass with searing coffee all over my white shirt.

"Shit!" Slade was at my side instantly, pulling me to a sitting position on the concrete. "Are you alright?"

"I'll make it." I gave him my best smile as he helped me to my feet. "Sorry about the coffee."

"Sorry about the concrete on your ass and the spilled coffee. Alfie was getting anxious, and I didn't want a repeat of last night, so I was going to take him out front."

"Gotcha." I tried wiping at my shirt, but it was completely ruined and starting to stick against my bra like a second skin.

"Why don't you find something to wear from my room?" he offered in a nice tone that reminded of the guy I'd met on vacation. "And I'll take Alfie out."

"Sure." I gulped, struggling a bit as I recalled the taste of his lips on mine. "Okay."

We walked past each other. He cleared his throat. I cleared mine. Like we both had the same frog, just different reasons for swallowing it.

I deposited my purse on the kitchen table, then slowly made my way up the stairs and into his massive bedroom. The same boxes were scattered around like he still wasn't sure he was going to stay in Seattle.

With a sigh I walked over to the dresser in search of a white T-shirt I could knot at my waist or tuck into my black skinny jeans.

The first drawer had socks.

The second held numerous tanks, and finally a cute band T-shirt that looked like it would be way too small on him.

I tossed it on the bed, then peeled my wet shirt over my head just in time to hear barking.

"Traitor," Slade said under his breath when Alfie came running into the room. I had nothing on but my bra. He looked his fill like he was actually allowed to after the way he'd treated me.

Shame washed over me. In a new way.

Shame that he could see me and not be affected.

Shame that I was that easily forgotten.

Left behind.

I quickly turned around, grabbed the shirt, and pulled it over my head, then pulled my hair out from underneath.

"Nice choice." He seemed amused.

I looked down, noting how it fit tight across my chest. "This can't be a guy's shirt."

"You would be accurate in your assessment. I was actually planning on burning all memories of the fiancée. I must have grabbed one of her

108

shirts without noticing it . . ." He shrugged. "Silver lining? That was never tight across her chest."

"Are you calling me fat?"

His eyes widened. "No . . . I know it's shocking, but I actually mean it as a compliment, you have nice . . ." He shook his head. "Never mind, let's go sign shit."

"I think this house has seen enough shit," I grumbled, glaring at Alfie. He whined and started licking my heel.

With a sigh I bent down and kissed him on his head. "No more mice or birds, and if you see a pet parakeet . . . self-control, buddy, self-control."

He licked my hand again and tried nuzzling my body.

Slade folded his arms as a pained expression crossed his features. "Let's go."

"Yeah." I stood and followed him back to the kitchen while Alfie trailed behind us, nearly falling head over paws down the last few stairs because he built up so much speed. The guy ran sideways, he was going to be big.

I smirked as his paws slammed against the kitchen floor in an effort to stop himself from running into the table.

Slade stepped over him and grabbed a stack of papers from a black portfolio.

I sat at the table and waited for him to say something

He didn't.

He just handed me a pen with a weird expression on his face.

I narrowed my eyes. "What exactly am I signing?"

"Another NDA, nothing fancy. I just need to cover every angle, every possible outcome . . ." He drummed his fingertips on the table. "Do you want a cup of coffee?"

"As long as you promise not to throw it at my chest," I teased lightly.

His eyes lowered. Damn, the man had the lazy, half-lidded gaze down like a champ. He didn't answer, just turned and went over to the Keurig.

I pulled the cap off the pen and skimmed the first page. Everything looked normal until I saw the words *Puerto Vallarta.*

"What?" I bit down on my tongue and read further. "Sexual relationship?"

A mug of coffee appeared in front of my face. "Here."

I took the coffee, set it on the table, and crossed my arms. "Is this what I think it is?"

His calm demeanor was really starting to piss me off. I'd rather have him angry than silent. "It's an NDA—one I would have given you in Mexico had—" He shrugged. "It's something I missed, alright? I need you to sign it."

Tears stung the back of my eyes as anger surged to the surface just a little bit faster than the sadness and embarrassment. "You're a piece of work, you know that?"

He sighed and then put both of his hands on my shoulders like I was the one that needed to be calm. "Mackenzie, it's to protect both of us, alright? What if a reporter asks you about me? If you sign something, you don't have to say shit." The asshole actually smiled like he'd just made it all better. And I wasn't stupid! I didn't have to say anything with or without the NDA.

"No." I dropped the pen.

"No?" He ran a hand through his overgrown gorgeous hair. "What do you mean no?"

"I mean no. I won't sign it. I wasn't . . . I don't need your money. I don't need your fame. Trust me, the last thing I want is to be in the spotlight. I'm taking care of your houseplants, for crying out loud!"

"Do I even have houseplants?"

"That's not the point!" My chest hurt. I jerked away from him and stood. "That's . . . you're making it . . . you're making what happened between us . . . like a business deal gone wrong. You're making it . . . so heartless."

Slade wiped his face and sat back in the chair. "I'm protecting you."

"No! You're protecting you. Because you're all you care about! This isn't about me! This is all you. And you know the worst part? I missed you. I missed you so much, and when I found out you were gone I felt so used. You were so—"

"Don't."

"Tender," I whispered. "You're not even that person. It wasn't even real, you know? It wasn't . . ." I wrapped my arms around my stomach. "I'm going to go take Alfie for another walk."

"Mackenzie." He stood and grabbed me by the elbow. "I'm trying, can't you see that? I'm doing the best I can!"

"Do. Better." I grabbed the leash.

"Fuck!" I could hear his loud, angry footsteps as he followed me into the entryway. "Would you just stop walking away and listen for one damn minute!"

"No!" I bent down and hooked the leash to Alfie's collar. Before I knew what was happening, Slade grabbed my hand and pulled me against his chest. I stumbled and braced myself against his biceps.

"Let me go," I said weakly.

His golden gaze darted to my lips and then back up to my eyes. "What's it going to take for you to sign this? To promise me you'll never go to the press about that night. To promise me you'll never come back and write a tell-all for some blog about your night with—" His eyes lit up and then he was kissing me, backing me up into the wall, his tongue deep in my mouth, his taste etching itself on my soul.

My heart thudded to life as he pressed his body against mine, trapping me, tasting my lips between his in slippery hot kisses that made my blood heat. The back of my head pressed against the wall while he cupped my chin with his hands, tried a different angle, then kissed the corner of my mouth again and again before pulling away breathless

"Sign it. Please."

I slapped him across the face.

Uh-oh. Not part of my plan.

In fact, I was so shocked I did it, I immediately covered my mouth with my hands. "Never . . . kiss me again to get me to do something. You've already taken enough, don't you think?"

I wouldn't let him see the tears escape my eyes in rapid succession.

I wouldn't let him hear the sound of my heart breaking for a second time since seeing him again.

I wouldn't let him think he'd won.

I would, however, call Jagger first thing after my walk with Alfie.

Chapter Twenty-Five

I shouldn't have fucking kissed her.

I saw her tears.

And it haunted me the entire ride to practice. When I passed her on the street, she didn't look up, didn't acknowledge me even though Alfie started barking.

Shit.

I dialed Matt's number. "Hey, I need you to send flowers to my house."

Matt sighed like I was the most irritating client in the world. "Sending flowers to yourself to make your lady friend jealous? Is that what we're doing here? Nothing better up your sleeve, huh?"

"Ass." I rolled my eyes. "They're for her, not me."

"Shit, what did you do? Again?"

"Nothing."

"Slade."

"I asked her to sign papers."

"How'd that work out for you?"

"She said no." I got on the freeway and clutched the steering wheel the way I still wanted to clutch her hips.

"End of story?"

"I may have"—I coughed—"tried to persuade her."

"Be honest. Are we talking lawsuit sort of persuasion?"

I gulped. "Well, I guess since I technically employ her—"

"Well done, Harvey Weinstein, let me know how they treat you in prison."

"I just reacted!" I said defensively. "I wasn't even thinking about using the kiss to persuade her, I just—"

"Damn, you need a keeper."

I stared straight ahead. "Just send the flowers, alright?"

He cursed. "And the note? What should that say? 'Please don't press charges, my dick knows not what it does'?"

"*Sorry.*" I croaked out the word. "Have it say *I'm sorry.*"

He let out a low whistle.

"Yeah." I took the next exit and sped toward the stadium. "Sometimes the simplest messages are the ones that mean the most."

"How poetic of you—did you just pull that out of your ass?"

I ignored him. "Gotta go, I'm at practice."

My mouth felt different, it kept reminding me that the reason for the difference was the fact that it had touched hers intimately and liked it. I pressed my lips together then licked, tasting her there.

I hadn't been thinking.

I'd just reacted! Poorly. Really. Poorly.

It seemed that was the only thing I was good at lately, making a mess of things.

"Why do your lips look swollen?" Jagger asked once I walked into the locker room.

I gave him a funny look. "Why the hell are you noticing my lips, Jagger?"

His eyes narrowed. "I would tell you to stay away from her, then again you'd take that as a challenge, so I'm just going to say this . . . she's too good for you."

"True," I admitted. "Which means she's really too good for you."

He shrugged. "I'm her friend."

I laughed. "Yeah, alright. You do know the definition of friendship, right?"

"This coming from the guy who only has one friend?"

I squeezed my hands tight, thinking back on when she'd admitted she couldn't trust people, that she didn't have friends.

More shame heaped on my already heavy shoulders.

"Isn't fucking your employee frowned upon?" Jagger asked out loud.

"I'm sure it is. Probably a good thing that she didn't work for me when we did!"

His eyes widened.

And I mentally punched myself in the face.

It just slipped!

"Tell me that was a sick joke." He looked pale—why the hell did he look pale?

"It's none of your fucking business," I growled, trying to sidestep him only to have him slam me against the nearest wall and ball the front of my shirt in his hands.

"Her ex did a number on her, you asshole. Tell me you weren't her rebound." He shook his head. "The guy never even slept with her, said he wanted to save it for marriage and then just . . ." He let me go. "You know what? This is bullshit. Stay away from her."

"Funny, I said the exact same thing to her last night, to stay away from you. What makes you think you're any better than me? Huh?"

"Easy." Jagger shrugged. "I'm not an idiot. Girls like her? They aren't fucking one-night stands, you dick."

I kept my face impassive.

When inside, my chest cracked a little.

It was never supposed to be a one-night stand with her.

But it had been.

And I'd left.

I didn't have a leg to stand on.

And for the first time in months, I was finding it hard to blame her for my father's death instead of myself.

Jagger walked out, slamming the door behind him.

And as I passed one of the mirrors and glanced up.

For the first time in my existence.

I hated what I saw.

Chapter Twenty-Six

The doorbell rang.

I prayed it was a misplaced pizza or some lost fries. I needed something to make me feel better about this morning, and I imagined it would just be another strike against me if I cracked open a bottle of wine during the workday.

Plus I was making amazing headway in his bedroom.

I cringed.

That sounded wrong.

It also made my mouth tingle.

And made me wish that the kiss this morning was more than a crap seduction to get me to sign a stupid piece of paper.

Every time I thought about it, I was insulted all over again.

When I finally reached the door, I was fuming.

Two dozen roses were held in the space between me and outside. "Are you Mackenzie?"

"Yeah."

"Here you go!"

"Who are they from?" I called to his disappearing form.

"It says on the card." He chuckled.

Why was that funny?

I put the roses on the kitchen table and searched for the card. It was nearly hidden behind the most beautiful yellow rose I'd ever seen.

Mackenzie.

I'm sorry—Love, Jackass

I burst out laughing as my eyes filled with tears. Huh. I tapped the card against my thigh, then grabbed my phone from my back pocket and typed out a text.

Me: I take it you're jackass.

Slade: If I die today, I imagine Matt would be more than happy to put it on my tombstone for you. Think of it as your final revenge.

I smiled and typed back.

Me: Thank you. For the roses. They're beautiful.

Slade: Thank you for not poisoning me in the near future?????

Me: See you soon!

Slade: Mack . . . .

I grinned, I liked being called Mack by him.

Me: Yes?

Slade: You're not really going to put arsenic in my Wheaties.

Me: Good talk!

Slade: Mack . . . I'll bring you wine.

My breath caught.
I didn't know what to say.

Slade: Remember, I know your weaknesses—all of them.

My thighs clenched as I tried to ignore what that made me think of.

Me: We'll see about that.

Slade: Don't challenge a player, it won't end well for you.

Me: Don't piss off the woman who makes your food—it won't end well for you ... either.

Slade: Stops off at nearest store to get the most expensive wine available ... happy?

Me: Cab Franc.

Slade: I'll take your word for it ...

Me: :)

I was grinning way too hard at my phone screen and easily forgetting all the shitty things he'd done, the way he'd treated me, because of stupid flowers and a few flirty texts.

I buried my feelings again, or at least tried, and then went back upstairs to dive into the last box.

It wasn't labeled.

I cut it open and paused.

Trophies.

So many trophies.

Awards.

From high school and college.

And in every single picture was a smiling father holding his son close and giving a thumbs-up to the camera.

There were at least three old photo albums underneath the heavy trophies. I picked up the heaviest one, sat on his bed, and cracked it open.

My eyes widened.

They were engagement photos.

A smiling Slade holding a soccer ball up to a beautiful girl who could pass as a supermodel, she was giggling and accepting the ball like it was a ring.

I vaguely remembered the picture from the news, but I hadn't paid much attention since I was dealing with my own stuff, and even then, I didn't really follow sports. The next few pictures were of teammates.

In one of them he had his arm wrapped around a guy on one side and his fiancée on the other.

Slade was looking at the camera.

They were looking at each other.

I sighed and kept flipping through his memories, through his personal life, like I had a right to.

Alfie got up from his spot in the middle of the room and started barking toward the door.

I quickly slammed the album shut and then put it back in the box. I didn't want to take any chances that he'd get pissed again. And I still had three weeks with him before I promised my dad I'd be back.

My stomach clenched.

I wasn't ready.

Clearly I wasn't ready if I preferred the company of a man who slept with me then treated me like shit over and over again.

Only to apologize with flowers.

At least he said sorry.

That was twice now.

I yawned and slowly made my way down the stairs, sniffing the air. What was that smell? Thai food? Chinese?

I rounded the corner and stopped in the kitchen.

Slade had grabbed two wineglasses and was pouring the exact bottle of wine I would have picked out from my family's winery.

"Hope you like fried pork," he said without looking up.

"Roses, wine, and now you're feeding me?" I made my way farther into the kitchen. "If this is another plan to wine and dine me until I'm so happy I sign that damn paper, I'm going to have to give you a hard pass."

He set the wine down and braced his body against the counter. "I'm not going to ask you to sign the paper again."

I exhaled.

"I'm hoping you'll come to your senses and do it on your own, with or without the wine, and if you don't . . . well, I guess that's a risk I'm going to have to take." He handed me a glass.

I swirled it around and sniffed it.

I was just about to take a sip when he said, "Why?"

"Why what?"

"Why are you working here? For me? It makes no sense. You don't even need to work. According to Matt you're worth more than two of my rotting corpse. It doesn't make sense."

My gut clenched further as I twisted the wine stem between my fingers. "Probably for the same reason you're in Seattle and not the UK."

He frowned. "Your fiancé cheated on you and got knocked up too? Huh, small world." He gulped the wine like a savage.

I glared. "Sip slower. And no, Alton didn't get knocked up. You have to have sex to get to the baby part, and he wanted to respect me and my father—his boss." I took a long sip, savoring the lingering flavor. "He did, however, leave me at the altar. In my wedding dress,

And now he has a Joanna. Oh, and did I mention I grew up with him? Was practically groomed for him? Yeah." I sipped some more. "So going back to my job, doing something I love—well, it takes the fun out of it when you have to stare at the guy who didn't have the balls to at least say something before I was forced to walk down the aisle in front of seven hundred people, not including the live media and *US Weekly*."

He cringed. "He's a fucker. You know that, right?"

"Cheers." I raised my glass. "You two have something in common."

"I deserved that," he muttered as his eyes flashed with guilt. "It's just . . ." His face twisted with pain. He drank more of his wine, then chugged the rest of it and exhaled. Monster. "That night, when you and I were together . . . my dad called. I'd been ignoring my messages, I was . . ." He swallowed slowly. "Busy." He looked away. "He called to apologize for being upset over my move to Seattle . . . he died three hours later. Heart attack." His voice lowered. "I never got to tell him I loved him. I never got to hear his laugh again. He was my best friend. My hero."

My throat clogged up as my legs took me around the island and into his arms. I pulled him in for a hug.

His body sagged against mine.

We hugged in his kitchen for a solid three minutes—at the very least.

When I pulled away, I whispered, "You're still a jackass."

He laughed.

It sounded beautiful.

His smile was there and then it vanished as quickly as it came.

I thought he was angry again, and then he was serious as he cupped my chin with his hands.

He was barely touching me, and my body hummed to life.

I stepped away.

I had to.

I didn't trust him.

I couldn't.

"So." I shrugged. "You have one box left—"

"Why did you pull away?"

"Because I don't know you," I said. "Not this version at least. And even if I did, I don't trust either version of you. Sorry."

He nodded slowly. "Friends, then?"

"Wow, two offers of friendship in such a short time. I must look desperate."

"Between the two of us, I don't think anyone would peg you as the desperate one." He grabbed the bag of takeout and jerked his head toward the living room. "Let's go eat while you make your decision."

"My decision?" I followed after him.

"Yeah, if I'm good enough to be in your inner circle."

"You're not."

"Yeah, the minute I said *good enough* I regretted it." He smirked.

It made me smile, and then we were both smiling at each other like idiots.

I reached for the napkins.

At the same time he did.

Insert awkward laughter.

I cleared my head and then held up my hands. "Look, we can be friends. On one condition . . ."

"Only one?"

"Try kissing me again, and I'm cutting your heart out and feeding it to Alfie. And . . ." Don't cry. Do. Not. Cry. "We don't talk about it."

"It?" He seemed confused.

This was hard.

"Mexico." I swallowed against the dryness in my throat and looked down at the coffee table.

The pain was almost too much.

It didn't matter that he had a backpack full of sorries.

He'd made me feel alive.

Then killed my soul in one fell swoop.

Because people like Slade, they were used to thinking about one thing and one thing only.

Themselves.

And there wasn't room for two people in the picture.

I was okay with it.

I just had to make sure he knew where the line was—at least it would make the next three weeks more pleasant.

He held out his hand. "Agreed."

I pressed my palm against his.

Why did it feel even worse that he agreed we shouldn't talk about it when I was the one who asked in the first place? My stomach dropped a bit as he held onto my hand and didn't let go. With a little jerk he had my body closer to his as he whispered, "Soy sauce?"

I inwardly groaned as my cheeks heated. His penetrating golden stare wasn't helping matters, and all my brain seemed to be able to focus on was the fact that those eyes had seen me naked, those lips had touched every part of my body, and those hands, the ones that had my body trembling—they were dangerous without him even touching me.

What was I thinking?

Three weeks of this guy?

I was probably better off with the jackass.

Chapter Twenty-Seven

I groaned as another camera flashed. I was in a pissy mood. Which wasn't rare for me lately—but for the first time, it wasn't images of my father that burned my brain.

It was an image of Mack shoving fried pork into her mouth.

Fried. Fucking. Pork.

It haunted me all night, and the next day when she walked into the house and handed me a black coffee and a gluten-free muffin and started unpacking groceries, I had tunnel vision.

Her. All I saw was her unpacking groceries.

And my brain did a little click.

She was talking.

I heard nothing.

She was moving around.

I stood still.

The world buzzed around me.

But she was in my house like she belonged there. She was in my life regardless of how horrible I'd been to her, how much I'd hurt her, how much I still had to keep myself from lashing out at her for reasons beyond my realm of understanding.

She was constant.

Beautiful.

And she was the only woman on the planet who didn't want something from me—who forced a friendship on me when all I'd wanted to do was kiss her for my own selfish reasons. But she'd hugged me, touched me, and didn't do it for herself.

It was for me.

In fact, everything she did was for me.

And I'd fucked it all up by not only putting the cockblock in place, but making her feel less than.

Less than.

When she'd only ever been more to me.

I gulped as guilt slammed down against my chest until it hurt to breathe.

"Earth to Slade." She waved in front of my face. "Did you hear anything I just said?"

Damn, her lips were pink today. I had a serious obsession with pink lips of all varieties.

I gave my head a shake. "Yeah, sorry, no. I was . . . thinking."

"You looked about a second away from thinking yourself into a stroke. Next time let the people you pay do the heavy hitting." She winked. "Matt wants you to meet with him tonight at some new restaurant. He said he'd text you the details. And you have that doctor appointment after practice."

I rolled my eyes. "You gonna remind me to brush my teeth too?"

"Yup." She popped the *p*. "And don't forget to floss, say your prayers, and look both ways before crossing the street." She snapped her fingers. "Should I get you a reflective vest like we have for Alfie?"

"Very funny." I grabbed my bag. "Do they come in a size big enough to wrap around my eight-pack?"

"I don't know. Why don't I call Walmart? If anything, I'm sure we can find something small enough for your dick." She beamed.

I narrowed my eyes. "That was low."

She just did a little curtsy and continued unpacking beef jerky and cheese sticks.

"What's with the groceries?" I jabbed my finger at the paper bags. "Do I not have enough food for you?"

"Pringles aren't a food." She opened up the pantry door and walked in. "Seriously, Slade, you're going to be late. Don't forget about your appointments, and try not to get struck by lightning on the way to practice."

"And why would I get struck by lightning?"

Thunder boomed outside.

I nodded. "Gotcha, let me just grab—"

"I put the umbrella in your bag." She poked her head out of the pantry. "Have a good day."

She smiled.

And again I was paralyzed. "Look, Mack—"

"Go!"

"I'm trying to—"

"Slade. When you're late you have to run more."

"Damn it!" I slammed my hands down on the granite. "Then I'll be fucking late, stop trying to manage me!"

Her pretty blue eyes went wide.

"Let a man apologize!"

"Do you always yell your apologies?" She crossed her arms.

"When the person is impossible to deal with, yes!" I roared and then stomped over to her, testosterone pumping through my system. "I'm fucking sorry. I know we've been over this. I know I promised I wouldn't—"

"Then don't," she whispered. "That can be your apology."

I licked my lips. We were at a standstill. I wanted to talk about the elephant; she wanted to pretend it wasn't standing between us.

"Fine." I hung my head. "Thank you for the food, thank you for the umbrella, thank you for reminding me of my schedule, and thank you for being . . . you."

She stilled.

Moisture gathered in her eyes.

And then I returned the favor.

I pulled her in for a hug.

Not for me.

For her.

Because I didn't know what else to do—and because she didn't trust words, at least not mine. If she needed actions . . .

I would give her actions.

I was struck by an intense feeling of longing at that moment in the middle of my kitchen.

And it only increased when I felt her heart beat through her chest. And as I left the house and drove to practice, I knew I would hate the day that she wasn't standing in my kitchen anymore.

I would hate that day.

And it was coming too soon.

Another camera flash went off as I made my way into the swanky restaurant that Matt demanded I meet him at because, according to him, they had the best calamari in the world.

The man had a weird fetish for calamari. If a restaurant didn't know how to make a good calamari, he believed that the rest of the menu must be shit.

I didn't even have to open my mouth once I approached the stand in the main lobby of the restaurant.

The host looked up at me and grinned. He had on a three-piece suit and wore black-rimmed glasses. He was bald but had a young face. "Right this way, Mr. Rodriguez."

I ducked into the dimly lit room. Sconces lined the walls, and each table had a line of blue fire and blue-black glass rocks in the center, making it possible to see people's faces pretty clearly in the dark.

Matt stood and shook my hand once I made it to our corner of the room. I exhaled, thankful that he let me sit against the wall so I could see every angle of the restaurant. I hated having my back to the crowd; it always made me feel like people were staring, and I couldn't see them, which made me even more anxious. People were brave when they couldn't see your eyes.

This way the staring would have to be blatant, and typically people got too embarrassed to continue, which I appreciated.

Sometimes a man just wants to eat a steak in peace.

"Let me guess." I sat. "You already ordered the calamari, ate all of it, and ordered more?"

He lifted his wineglass. "Cheers to best friends."

"Cheers." I lifted my empty wineglass.

"That's bad luck, and you've had enough of that," Matt said, lifting the bottle and pouring some into my glass before clinking it against his and handing it to me.

"Isn't that the truth?" I grumbled to myself.

And then because I was drinking wine . . .

I immediately thought of Mack.

Sure enough, the label was completely black and had her family's name etched across the top in white.

I ran my thumb along the label.

"Should I, uh, leave you alone with the bottle? Or can we talk business?"

I jerked my hand back and sighed. "Sorry, business, let's talk business."

Damn it, I could even smell her!

What the hell was wrong with me?

I took another long sip as Matt pulled out his phone and started talking about sponsors and Instagram promotions.

I got another whiff of perfume and sniffed the air.

"You're acting more manic than normal." Matt leaned forward. "Are you . . . are things—"

"What the fuck?" I growled, gripping the wine stem so hard I was afraid it was going to shatter between my fingers. "She's on a date with him!"

"She?" Matt turned around just as Jagger sat down three tables away from us.

Mack's back was to me.

It was bare.

Please, God, let her be dressed.

I tilted my head to the side. There was a black scrap of something on her legs and hopefully covering her breasts.

Jagger caught my eye and grinned.

All the middle fingers.

That's what I wanted to send him.

But I had to be mature.

Responsible.

There were cameras.

"I'm going to murder him." I started to stand.

Matt jerked me back to my chair and hissed, "Don't."

"He's clearly using her!" Did we really need him on the team? I knew people. I could destroy evidence.

A little strangulation.

Run him over with my car.

Or all of my cars.

I grinned.

"I know that smile, you aren't killing him."

"Why?" I gritted my teeth. "He's not as valuable as me. I'll make him a martyr, he'll thank me."

"Yes, his ghost will haunt you for life and write songs about how you plotted his death." He snapped his fingers. "Focus. We're here for business and good food. We're not here to talk about how to find a hit man because the guy is sharing a bread basket with Mackenzie DuPont."

I stared harder. "He broke her bread for her. She can break her own bread, you dumbass!"

Matt groaned into his hands. "Where are we with that NDA?"

"Never mind about that." I waved him off.

"Oh good, you slept with her again? Kissed her senseless again? Do I need to send a flower van this time?"

"Nothing like that." I couldn't take my eyes off her naked back. "I brought her takeout, we agreed to be friends . . . there was hugging."

He choked on his wine. "Cool, did you braid hair later and prank call all the guys in your class too?"

I kicked him under the table.

He grimaced and bit out a curse. "And that's why they pay you so well. I think I'm bleeding."

"She's . . . I mean we're . . ." I poured more wine. "It's complicated."

He snorted as Jackass Jagger scooted his chair closer to her.

"I'm killing him tonight."

Matt just sighed. "You can't tell me that if I'm supposed to be your alibi. At least be smart about it."

"I'll go Dexter on his ass. He won't know what hit him."

"One day, soccer's biggest star, the next, murderer. Yeah, just think of the headlines. I think you should do it. I'm in your will, right?"

"Don't make me kick you again," I growled. "Let's just fucking order and get out of here before I really do walk over there and slam his face into the nearest table. I'm not feeling calm . . ."

Another snort. "Yeah, the steam coming out of your ears and the alarming shade of purple on your face wasn't a dead giveaway."

I glanced back at Matt. "Why are we friends again?"

"Because I shaved off one of your eyebrows at soccer camp when you were sleeping."

"Right." I nodded. "That explains everything."

Chapter Twenty-Eight

I'd texted Jagger the minute Slade left the house. Well, first I had to stop my hands from shaking. And then I was tempted to throw some water on my face.

Slade hugged me.

He pulled me against his hard body.

And I was haunted with memories of that night, of being free, with him. And I couldn't go there. I couldn't. It was a slippery slope and I would end up eating Twinkies on my couch missing him and Alfie while putting on ten pounds of emotional eating weight.

And Slade?

He'd be just fine.

It would be a blip on his radar.

A fun time with the help.

And he'd probably refer to it like that too. All obtuse and arrogant.

"So . . ." Jagger had his long brown hair slicked back, making him look older than his twenty-seven years. It made his eyes pop and gave way to such a sharp profile that he could probably cut glass with either side of his face. No double chin for that guy, bastard. He'd probably age well too, like fine wine. He'd be . . . a spicy Merlot with hints of bing cherry and a robust aroma. "How are you doing?"

"Is this a date or therapy?" I said it in a teasing tone, but I was serious.

He handed me a piece of bread like I wasn't capable of reaching across the table myself. I wasn't sure if I liked it or if it annoyed me.

Once I had my bread buttered with enough calories and fat to make me sigh in bliss, he answered. "Can it be a little bit of both?"

I offered a smile. "Huh, that must be how friendship works?"

"It's one of life's great mysteries: communication, words, sentences that build into emotional paragraphs actually help you understand where a person is coming from." He winked. "Deep stuff."

Okay, I was warming to him, even if he handed me bread. But if he ordered for me . . . all bets were off.

And if he suggested a salad, I was going to throw a lot of words at him, none of them kind or cheerful.

"I'm doing . . . good. Thank you for asking. Actually"—I pointed at him—"I'm doing better than I was, still not back to normal thanks to an emotional terrorist that finally backed down and apologized, but . . ." I lifted a shoulder. "Yeah."

"Emotional terrorist, huh? I know one of those . . . has an ego the size of China and probably refers to himself in the third person when he's alone."

I choked on the bite I took and reached for my wine to wash down the bread that had lodged in my throat. "You know? I think I may sneak into the house late at night and see if he does exactly that."

He snorted. "I wouldn't, he'd probably assume it was an invitation."

The blood drained from my brain, leaving me light-headed.

Did everything come back to sex?

And why couldn't my brain exorcise all those moments in Slade's arms?

I cleared my throat and looked down. "Sorry, not one of my favorite subjects. Besides . . ." I pasted on my best smile. "Now that we're trying to be friends, things are better, and if for some reason he reverts back, I'll just clean Alfie's teeth with his toothbrush and then dip it in the toilet for good measure."

Jagger barked out a laugh. "Yeah, remind me to stay on your good side."

"Well, dinner's a good start."

"I'd say so." He returned my smile just as someone approached. "Oh, we aren't ready to or—Hey . . ." Jagger started coughing.

I stared at the menu, then felt a foot tap mine under the table. My eyes jerked up.

And there he was, in all his glory.

Alton.

I gasped.

Jagger's eyes widened a fraction before he smoothly said, "What's up?"

Yup. What's up.

I narrowed my eyes and stared across the table while Alton shrugged. "Nothing, just trying to sell more of our wine to the restaurant, decided to check it out for myself." He turned to me. "Your father was impressed with their calamari."

I just stared at him, unable to form words.

This was the second time I was forced to see him. To speak to him. When I didn't want to do any of the above.

Jagger spoke for me. "We haven't ordered yet."

"Are you guys . . ." Alton made a motion with his hand between us. "On a date?"

"I'm wearing a dress," I said in a pinched voice. "What do you think?"

Alton lowered his voice. "Isn't that kind of an unspoken rule between friends, Jag?" He shoved his hands in his trouser pockets and rocked back on his heels. He really was thin compared to Jagger, and Slade had at least thirty pounds of muscle over him.

"Seriously?" I didn't mean to shriek. "We're adults sharing a meal. It's not a crime."

134

"I didn't say it was," Alton said in the sort of voice typically used to calm people down, the kind of voice that only makes a person want to lash out more. "All I'm saying is it's . . . frowned upon."

"Frowned upon?" came another voice.

One I dreamed about at night.

One that belonged to a name I screamed out more times than I'd care to admit. Hugo . . . my Hugo.

Welcome to hell.

"Slade." Jagger inclined his head. "We were just talking about you . . . Question, do you think this place is big enough to fit your ego? I'd say it's a close call."

"Alton, meet Slade Rodriguez. Slade, Alton Davis."

"If this dick," he said, pointing at Alton, "can fit nothing but hot air into that giant head, then I guess it makes sense that my ego can fit here, right?"

I tried not to smile.

I failed.

Jagger even seemed relieved.

"Mack." Slade ignored Alton's sputtering. "Can you stop by the house after dinner . . . ?"

"House?" Alton repeated, voice shrill and posture rigid.

"Hell no!" Jagger laughed. "She's with me right now, you get that, right? God, you're such an asshole!"

I let out a long sigh. "I don't know if that's a good idea."

"Just to talk," Slade added.

"What the hell? Why would she talk to you? Wait a second . . ." Alton's eyes widened. "Are you—"

"One sec." Slade held up a hand in front of Alton's face. "Please, Mack."

It was the eyes.

It was always his stupid golden eyes.

They made me want to say yes to everything and tell my heart to shut up.

"I, uh—"

Jagger cleared his throat. "Slade, admit defeat, man. You had your chance, and your true colors showed, big shock. Go sit down before you embarrass yourself."

"Chance?" Alton piped up. His teeth ground together as his eyes narrowed.

I groaned into my hands.

"Damn right I had my chance." Slade clenched his teeth. "And I'm still haunted by her tight thighs and breathy moans—you're fooling no one, I know what you want. But she's mine."

I gasped. Again.

Alton gave me such a look of disappointment that I was ready to drown him in my water glass. "You slept with him?"

In retrospect, I should have just owned up to it rather than sitting in silence while my ex started throwing insults, but I was in shock.

"What? Our marriage doesn't work out so you just spread your legs for some soccer playboy with an accent!" He turned red.

Jagger threw down his napkin and stood.

At about the same time, Slade grabbed Alton by the shirt and punched him across the jaw.

"Son of a bitch!" Alton said from the floor.

"You're a piece of shit," Slade growled.

"Better shit than slut!" Alton said, blood trickling down his chin as he tried to get up.

Before Slade could throw another punch, Jagger beat him to it.

Alton went down for a second time.

And that was when I heard the sirens.

I grabbed the bottle of wine from the table and started drinking straight from it once a cop walked in, followed by another.

And put all three men in cuffs.

"He started it!" Alton roared.

I almost kicked him in the ribs.

"Shut the hell up, you pussy," Slade sneered. "I can see your man tits from here."

Jagger choked out a laugh and then added, "He has one testicle. Literally."

Alton's face flushed while wine almost spewed out of my mouth. Matt made his way over to talk to the cops.

People were clearly enjoying the show.

And I was so frozen in shock that I didn't know how to react or what to do.

But when Jagger was talking to the cop with Matt and Alton, Slade turned around and whispered, "Sorry . . . again."

My answer? "I like chocolate too."

He grinned. "So you're saying I have to send chocolate with the flowers next time?"

I nodded.

"Done."

"And Slade?"

"Yeah." His eyes locked on mine.

"You're my hero."

"Funny, that's always something I've wanted to be to someone . . ."

My eyes filled with tears.

We stared at one another and the world faded around me. His golden eyes didn't leave mine for a few seconds before the cop escorted them out of the restaurant.

"Do you think you can talk your father into persuading Alton not to press charges?" Matt asked once they were in the cop car.

My chest ached a bit. "I'll try."

"Thanks." He patted my shoulder. "Head on home, get some sleep . . . they're not going to jail, but I see some community service in Slade's near future, and to think he'd been doing so well . . ."

Instantly, I felt guilty. "It was my fault."

"Nah, he threw the punch, but something tells me Alton deserved it."

I gave him a silent nod.

"Then I'm sorry the fucker didn't pass out cold."

I laughed. "Thanks, Matt."

"Yeah, yeah, it's really fun, my job . . . keeping their asses out of jail, losing sleep, balding—"

A smile tugged my lips upward. "You aren't balding."

"Don't make me show you the spot. It's embarrassing."

I stood and gave him my hand. "Should I grab the tab for the wine?"

"Already taken care of when I saw Slade make his way over. I know the guy. When he sees something he wants, he gets tunnel vision and doesn't think, he just . . . executes. It makes him a hell of a striker, and sometimes a hell of a human."

Chapter Twenty-Nine

I reacted.

Poorly.

Again.

But the bastard was just sitting there insulting the world by breathing, let alone speaking about her in a way that was so disrespectful—if I see him on the street I'm taking all hateful vengeance toward Jagger and Dextering it on Alton.

Simple.

"One testicle, though?" I wondered out loud as the cop took off the cuffs and gave me a look that said I really needed to stop talking if I wanted to make it back to my house and not a jail cell next to a guy named Billy who has some things in his trunk he wants to show me.

"Think about it." Jagger massaged his wrists while Matt discussed terms with the cops. "Is there any chance in hell you'd want that woman"—he pointed at Mack's disappearing form as she got into an Uber Black SUV—"to know that you have one of something that you should have two of?"

"Huh." I rubbed my chin. "You'd think he'd be so sexually repressed that he would have just taken the chance, plus when you love someone . . ."

Jagger stared at me like I'd grown three heads.

So I stopped talking.

"No, continue." He crossed his arms. "I think we were having the closest thing to a moment I've ever seen."

I rolled my eyes. "I'm just saying, it shouldn't matter. Things like that don't matter, not when you're with someone."

It wasn't a topic I liked to discuss.

Loving someone.

Loving anyone.

And losing them.

Loving them with your soul—only to discover you never even had their heart, like with my ex-fiancée.

It's the worst. It feels like a death—maybe not as bad as my father dying, but it sure as hell didn't make me feel like I wanted to go ahead and do it again.

The risk? Was too high.

The reward? Well, I never had the reward, because she took it from me the minute she decided to sleep with someone else.

"Hey, you still with us?" Jagger walked over and touched my shoulder.

I frowned at his hand. "You're touching me."

"You looked ready to cry."

"Bullshit. I was just . . . thinking."

"Also disconcerting." He moved his hand just as Matt walked over to us with a wide, encouraging smile.

"Fixed," he announced.

Jagger and I both stared at him.

"What is?" I was the first to ask.

Matt wrapped an arm around each of us. "Walk with me, boys."

"You're using the voice," I pointed out. "The one where you deliver the bad news but try to convince me that it's good news by your wide smile and high-pitched voice."

Jagger coughed on a laugh.

Matt just ignored me and released us, then turned, pressed his steepled hands to his mouth like he was praying, and took a deep breath. "Mackenzie's going to work on Alton not pressing charges. He says he's not going to, but he still could, and we don't want that hanging over us."

If that bastard touches her or tries to get her back . . . I gave my head a shake. No. I wouldn't let that happen. He was the asshole of all assholes, and I was well aware of my own behavior the past week.

"You both are going to do community service!"

Jagger kicked the curb while I just groaned and looked away from him.

"What?" Matt actually sounded surprised by our disdain.

"Community service," Jagger repeated, "usually entails work after all the work we're already putting in with practice, PR, the press, nonprofits—"

"First, you're lucky both your asses aren't in jail." Matt changed his tone. "And second, you're going to teach a soccer camp for one of the elementary schools. One full week of working as a team." He pointed between me and Jagger with a giant grin. "And the best part? The arresting officer was willing to do anything to get volunteers—the fact that it's you guys? Well, let's just say he's going to win Dad of the Year, and since no charges are being pressed—yet—you're free to go!"

"Fantastic," I said in a dry tone. "We'll get to teach elementary kids which direction to run in. Sounds like a blast."

"Speak for yourself," Jagger snorted. "You still don't know what direction to run in. Besides, do you really think you're the best role model?"

I turned and stepped forward until we were chest to chest. "This coming from the guy who did a burger commercial holding a ball in front of his dick with one hand while rubbing fries over a girl's stomach with the other?"

He flinched. "It was . . . art."

I burst out laughing while Matt pressed his lips together and let out a snort. "You ran ketchup down her thigh—and they had to pull it because people complained about the controversy."

"Sold a hell of a lot of burgers, though," Jagger said smugly.

I turned to Matt and sighed. "Didn't this prick sleep with the model too?"

"Careful," Jagger growled.

"Want to know what I think?" Matt asked.

"No!" we said in unison.

Of course he just took that as an invitation to keep talking. "You're both shit role models, and you both need to get your heads out of your own asses before you ruin what should be the best year of your careers, on the same fucking team together." He shrugged. "Make it work. You report Monday morning to Kamiakin Elementary. Oh, and bring some signed shit, because even though I know how worthless you two can be when you're in the same orbit, the kids don't, and they deserve better than your sad side-by-side-my-dick-is-better-than-yours game. Honestly? It's getting old."

And then Matt.

Our manager.

Friend.

Abandoned us in the middle of the street.

"That was . . . out of character," I finally said after a few minutes of silence.

"You think his blood sugar's low?" Jagger asked as he pulled out his phone.

"Maybe he's on a diet. He's like an angry soccer mom when he's on a diet. Remember when he tried that Whole 30 thing a year ago and almost burned down his house trying to find a Snickers?"

Jagger grinned wide and then looked up from his screen. "I have a confession to make."

"What?"

"I ate the Snickers the day before."

I laughed. "Does he know?"

"Hell no!" Jagger joined in the laughter. "He'd have my ass! He searched for three hours and flipped over his couch into that massive fireplace with nothing but hunger and brute strength. No. I told him it was probably in the living room."

"Ah, so the cause of the fire, all . . ." I pointed at him.

"Take it to your grave, Slade."

I chuckled. "Let's at least try not to let the kids see blood, alright?"

"Or us comparing dicks, because not only is that shit weird but people go to prison for it."

"Yeah, smart-ass, I'll . . . attempt to not kill you. You're lucky my anger is more directed at Alton right now. Fucking Alton. I hate him."

"I think he knows," Jagger said. "And if he forgets, he can just look in the mirror and remember who gave him the bruise."

"You helped."

"Because of Mackenzie."

Not because of you. I knew where the rest of that was going.

"He never deserved her in the first place. I could never quite figure out why they were together, and when things went . . . badly, it made sense."

"So you and Mack . . ." I cleared my throat.

"It's getting late." He shrugged. "We have practice." He turned around and started walking down the street toward his car.

"Is that your answer? Ignore the question?"

"You need to ask!" he called back.

"Are you dating her?" I hated the way that sentence tasted. Full of bitterness and longing.

"That was a question." He laughed and just got into his car. While I stood on the street and watched him take off. While I wondered if I'd lost her the minute I accused her of stalking me and forcing me into marriage.

I cringed.

A fucking van full of flowers.

Ten vans.

Shit, at this rate I was going to need to plant an entire garden for her and buy a flower shop just to stay on her good side or at least, possibly, get another chance to taste her mouth.

I sighed and made the slow trek back to my car, feeling more depressed with each step.

How was I supposed to win her if I wasn't even allowed to play the game?

Chapter Thirty

MACKENZIE

"Hey, Dad." I kissed his soft cheek and made my way past him into the enormous home he and my mom shared on Lake Washington. The marble floor seemed to swirl and come alive beneath my feet as I flipped on a light in the hall and walked into the kitchen to grab my favorite wine and my favorite wineglass to go with it.

Dad followed me, as was tradition when I stopped by late at night.

Wordlessly, he grabbed his glass and sat on the barstool opposite where I was standing. "What's going on?"

I took a deep breath, then took a drink of the dry red before speaking. It tingled against my lips and breathed life into my parched soul. "Alton was at the restaurant with you tonight."

"Are you asking me?"

"No, I know he was."

"Potential buyer, but I left early to make it home for Mom's and my show . . ." My parents were obsessed with *The Voice*, as in, they refused to be distracted and would save it until they could watch it together, full volume, one bottle of wine, a cheese board. It was basically a weekly holiday and excuse to drink. "Why? What happened? Did he talk to you?"

"Yeah." I cringed. "One sec." Two more small sips. "He sort of insulted me, in a very inappropriate way in front of my . . . er . . . date? And in front of the man I currently work for."

Dad sucked in a breath. "What did he say?"

I felt my face flush. "Let's just agree it was horrible and I almost cried."

"Honey . . ." He reached out. I took his hand and squeezed.

"So," I continued, using him for support, "my employer punched him in the face, and when he wouldn't stop saying cruel things, my date punched him in the side of the head. The police came . . ."

Dad released my hand. "What sort of punks handle things with a fistfight?"

"Ones trying to defend my honor and stand up for me. Something Alton wouldn't do in a million years."

Dad's face softened. "He's just not the fighting type, honey. He uses his words—"

"Oh, trust me." I scowled. "I know he uses his words, he needs someone to staple his mouth shut. The point is, he deserved it, and I don't want him to press charges." I licked my dry lips. "Dad, you didn't fire him after the wedding even though I begged you to. I don't want to work with him, I don't even want to see his face." My chest felt heavy with each confession. "Since you're his boss, you have pull. Can you please just tell him not to press charges?"

Dad frowned. "Do you know if he did?"

"No. But I do know he was angry."

"Honey, he was punched in the face by two men. Of course he was angry—your date was a man, right?"

I narrowed my eyes. "As opposed to a turtle?"

"No." He laughed awkwardly. "I just meant, after Alton, if it were a . . . woman." His face turned serious. "That would be okay."

"Thanks? I think?" I gave my head a shake. "But it was a man, an attractive man—we're getting off topic. I just need you to talk with

Alton, let him know it would reflect badly, or could reflect badly, on us." It wouldn't, but I was hoping that would at least help sway him.

Dad stood. "Honey, I understand your concern, but if Alton wants to press charges, I'm not going to stop him just because you want to protect some punks who don't know how to fight like men."

"But—"

"Topic closed." He smiled like it wasn't a big deal that he was basically choosing Alton over my needs or wants—again. Playing favorites . . . or at least that's what it felt like. Why was I suddenly remembering all the times I had to compete with Alton for my dad's attention? For the accolades that made me think I needed to do whatever it took to be part of the boys' club.

I'd begged my dad to fire him or at the very least put him in a different department after Alton left me at the altar, but my dad said keeping Alton was business, not personal. I was making it personal.

Of course it was personal! He. Left. Me.

And while I appreciated my dad's strong business sense, sometimes a girl just needs a hug, she needs to be told it's okay to make it personal! I loved my dad but he wasn't acting like my father, he was acting like a shrewd business owner, which was a side of him I rarely saw or maybe just refused to acknowledge.

"Dad." My eyes filled with tears.

He pulled me into his arms. "Trust me, things will look better once you get some sleep. Are you staying the night?"

"No." I jerked out of his embrace, possibly for the first time in my life. His look was a mixture of confusion and hurt. "I'll just take another Uber home."

I walked past him. I held my tears in.

And two minutes later when my car pulled up.

I felt those tears slide down my cheeks and drip off my chin.

Fight for me.

I closed my eyes.

I wanted someone—someone to fight for me. Not try to do what was best for me.

A vision of Slade slammed into my consciousness.

He might be a lot of things.

But when I'd needed him most.

He threw a punch.

Even if he said things he shouldn't.

I appreciated that punch more than he'd ever know.

"Hey!" I snapped out of my sadness. "Can we stop somewhere really quick, I'll tip?"

"Where to?" the driver called back.

I fired off Slade's address and prayed he'd still be up.

I didn't really have a plan.

Other than a thank-you hug.

And . . . something?

I told my driver I'd be five minutes.

I knocked on the door twice.

Nothing.

And then two barks.

Cursing.

I smiled just as the door opened, revealing a shirtless Slade and low-slung sweats on what could only be described as the V straight from heaven.

I should have taken that bottle of wine from my parents'.

"Hi, hey, hi." I said hi twice, didn't I?

He frowned. "Are you drunk?"

"What?" I gave my head a shake. "No, do I look drunk?"

"You said hi twice."

"I was hoping you wouldn't catch that."

"Too obvious not to catch but cute that you're holding onto hope like that . . ." His lips twitched into a small grin while I narrowed my eyes.

"You're making this harder than it should be." I crossed my arms.

"And you make me harder than I should be. And yet, here I am." He crossed his arms.

Don't look down. Do not. Look. Down.

I gulped.

His smile broke out into a huge grin. "You were saying?"

I bit down on my bottom lip and then took a step toward him, then two, until I could smell his spicy body wash and minty breath. "Thank you. Just . . . thank you for standing up for me—even though you also confessed to the whole restaurant that I slept with you."

"Weak moment," he admitted. "And you're welcome . . . if that guy ever speaks to you again, just tell him I'm coming for his other testicle."

I burst out laughing. "Yeah, but maybe I won't word it that way?"

Slade stared at my mouth, then his eyes flickered back up to mine. "Great idea."

"So," I croaked and then wrapped my arms around his middle.

He stood still for a few seconds, making me feel slightly stupid, and then he was hugging me back.

He hugged just as good as he kissed.

With his whole body.

I closed my eyes.

And then, I stood on my tiptoes and kissed his cheek.

"My other cheek feels left out," he whispered in a dark voice that sent chills down my spine. I could have sworn his golden eyes were glowing at me as an electrical current of awareness shot through my body.

I rolled my eyes, trying to play it off, then moved to his right cheek, only to have him capture my lips right before I was able to make contact with his skin.

He kissed me softly, never even using his tongue as his lips slid against mine, and then he pulled away.

"You promised." I wasn't angry. Who would be angry? I was more . . . drugged.

"I slipped," he said in an innocent voice. "Plus it's really dark and it looked like you were going for my ear. You've been embarrassed enough tonight, can't imagine what would happen if you fell face-first against the doorbell."

"How . . . chivalrous of you." I shook my head in disbelief.

He put his hand on his chest. "Thank you, that was my aim."

We stared at one another for way too long without speaking.

It was becoming a nasty habit on my part.

So I cleared my throat, another nasty habit, and stepped away from the temptation, away from the cliff I wanted to jump off. The only thing that kept me grounded was the knowledge that last time I jumped . . .

The only one to break my fall was me.

And that was a very depressing and lonely thought.

"Night, Slade."

"You should stay." He leaned against the doorframe. "We can watch a movie."

"It's late."

"Dessert, then?"

"Slade." I eyed him suspiciously.

He hung his head. "You could sleep over?"

"I'll see you tomorrow."

He just grinned. "Had to try."

"I'd be disappointed if you didn't give it a little effort—friends, though, remember?"

"Only because you keep reminding me," he said softly. "Be safe."

"I live five minutes away. I'll be fine." I gave him a little wave and got back in the SUV before I did something stupid like say yes to a movie, which we both knew wouldn't have just been a movie.

It was late. I'd had wine.

He was being nice.

And he'd given me a sample of his flavor again, the way he tasted.

Of course it wouldn't be a movie.
It would be dessert in his bed.
And I'd hate myself for it in the morning.
I squeezed my eyes shut and leaned back against the soft leather.
Why did things have to be so complicated?

Chapter Thirty-One

SLADE

"Let's just get this over with," I mumbled to myself as I pulled up to the Kamiakin Elementary School.

Jagger was leaning against his car like he'd been waiting for me since the ass crack of dawn. I rolled my eyes and purposely took my time cutting the engine, opening my door, staring him down, slamming said door, and crossing my arms in response.

"You look radiant this morning, sunshine. Something crawl up your ass and decide to stay there, or do you always look like that and I've just now noticed it?" I grinned from ear to ear.

"You're probably just now noticing on account of your head being stuck in your tiny prick for God knows how long," he countered with a grin of his own.

"Touché," I grumbled as we fell into step next to each other and walked onto the field.

It was Monday morning—our conditioning practice started in two hours, and yet there we were. Getting a week pass so we could coach some kids who probably wouldn't know what a goal was if it hit them in the ass.

The younger ones were fun, don't get me wrong, some may even call them adorable—even with the runny noses and constant farting.

I just wasn't feeling it.

That meant I wasn't feeling inspiring because I wasn't inspired. Because I was feeling jealous about Mack's date with Jagger—and because she had barely answered my texts.

And maybe because every time Jagger pulled out his phone I wondered if he was texting her—I wondered if he was winning.

And then I felt like an ass for even thinking it.

She'd done nothing except be an easy target when it came to my grief. I wasn't sure why it was finally clicking for me, just how much I blamed her for my father's death.

Maybe it was a hard look at jealousy, staring its ugly face down and realizing that if I didn't do something, I was going to end up alone, without the only girl in my entire life who'd ever made me feel truly alive.

How's that for honesty?

"Who you texting?" I just had to ask as I leaned over Jagger's arm.

He shoved me away with his elbow. "Do you mind?"

I spread my arms wide. "Just a question."

"Dipshits." Matt made his way over to us with two Starbucks cups. He was wearing sweats.

I frowned. "Are you depressed, man?"

"Huh?"

"Yeah." Jagger took one coffee. I took the other. "What's with the sweats? Get dumped?"

Matt just glared between us. "You know what I need? A pet."

"Because you're depressed?" I added knowingly.

Jagger elbowed me. "He doesn't even have gel in his hair."

"A nice pet," Matt continued, "that almost lacks the will to live—I need that level of lazy so I feel like I'm actually adequate at taking care of things." He sighed. "No, I'm not depressed, I'm just here to help because I'm a good manager and a good friend. Seriously, if you looked up *saint* in the dictionary, my face would be smack dab next to Mother Teresa."

I took a few steps back and looked up. "Huh, I could have sworn I felt lightning."

"I heard thunder," Jagger added.

"God forbid you two ever become friends. I'd need a sedative," Matt grumbled. "The kids should be here any minute. Be nice, be inspirational, and try not to curse."

I laughed. "Yeah, okay, we won't curse." I made air quotes. "Matt, we know how to do our shit."

"Yeah, fuck, let us handle our damn community service like professionals!"

"Hell!" I said while Matt groaned into his hands. "Those little bastards won't know what hit them, huh, Jagger?"

"You know it, bitch."

Matt narrowed his eyes. "I think I found the common ground."

I snorted in disbelief. "Oh yeah, what's that?"

He pointed between us. "You both live to piss me off."

Jagger was silent, like the idea of us being friends again made him uncomfortable.

I frowned at him and then shrugged. "Doesn't mean I still don't want to kill him on a daily basis."

"Still upset over my date, I see," he announced just as one of the volunteers walked up with cones and a bag of soccer balls.

"She says you're just friends. I call bullshit." I shrugged.

Matt bit back a curse. "Stop with the language."

I turned and grinned. "And bullshit's what? A dirty word?"

"Fucking hate my job most days." Matt kicked the dirt.

Jagger burst out laughing. "Poor Matty."

Matt's eyes widened.

I burst out laughing. "I forgot about that nickname."

"Oh, it's a gem," Jagger added. "Remember? I'm Jaguar Jagger, you're Slade the Striker, and then we have . . . Little Matty." Nostalgia hit me hard and fast as a memory of us playing in our early twenties reared its ugly head. Game after game, bars filled with friends and food. We'd been poor as hell but happy.

Matt gritted his teeth and then flipped us both off, though he was cracking a smile as he turned around and jogged toward the volunteer.

I took a sip of coffee. "How do you want to do this? Start with some drills?"

"Sure." Jagger was looking at the grassy field. "Camp goes until eleven every morning—which means we can still get in our afternoon practice with the team . . . I say we go through a few drills, and you can teach them all about balls, that is, if you still have them after Saturday night."

"Good one," I said in a dry tone. "And that shitface deserved every punch I slung his way, plus I didn't see you jumping to your feet until my balls and I stepped in."

"Yeah, well . . ." He swallowed and looked down. "We used to be friends, remember? My first instinct isn't to hit my friends. You wouldn't know what that's like, since you don't really have any."

"I have Matt," I said defensively.

"You pay Matt," he pointed out. "When was the last time you even hung out with the guys?"

I started getting hot and itchy as I stared him down. "I hung out with my old team all the time. Look how that turned out for me."

Jagger's eyebrows shot up. "Funny, I heard a bit of a different story from a few people . . . especially about your ex."

"I know the truth," I said through clenched teeth.

Kids started shuffling onto the field.

You could tell the minute it registered that we were on the field. There was no way to brace for the onslaught of elementary school kids running at us full speed with no plan of stopping.

Jagger's eyes widened.

I closed mine briefly.

And then felt stickiness against my legs, arms. There was lots of jumping up and down, so I just went with it.

I started jumping up and down.

Jagger burst out laughing and joined me.

Soon we had all fifty kids jumping with us, and the adults watching in disbelief, before I blew a whistle and kicked things off with a game of freeze tag.

It was an easy way to get them warm. And it helped them loosen up around us instead of being starstruck.

Jagger blew his whistle after about twenty minutes of running around and basically getting bulldozed by all the tiny humans.

"Alright, everyone, I'm going to count you off in ones and twos. Ones go to Slade, since he's the number-one striker in the world." Cheers sounded around us. I actually laughed out loud when some of them started practicing their own kicks.

My ones were more than pumped to be on my team. The twos didn't seem to mind being on his, so all in all, it was a good start.

"Alright, ones," I called out. There was no way I was going to remember everyone's names at this point, but I could try. "We're going to run a quick feet drill. I'm going to line up the cones, and I need you to weave the ball through the cones like this." I demonstrated what I meant with ease while they all stared at me slack-jawed as though I'd just performed brain surgery.

"Alright, one by one, I want you guys to follow each other. When your friend gets to the end, you start. I'm setting up ten lines."

Once I was done, I blew my whistle and they started.

Everyone seemed to be having fun except one little boy who stood with the ball in his hands.

I tapped one of the kids on the shoulder. "Hey, who's that?"

"Oh, Danny?" He said his name under his breath like he was afraid someone would hear. "He, uh, his papaw died yesterday. His parents made him come still, they thought it would cheer him up."

My heart sank past my knees and onto the ground.

"And what's your name?"

"Mitchell." He puffed out his chest.

"Cool." I pulled off my whistle and handed it to him. "You think you can handle the team while I go talk to Danny?"

Mitchell's eyes widened. "For real?"

"For real." I grinned. "Once everyone finishes, blow the whistle, have them line up again, and run lines between the cones."

"But, Mr. Slade, what if they don't listen?"

"You have the magic whistle, they will," I said encouragingly, ruffling his hair. "Plus I'll be right over here watching."

"'Kay." He pulled the whistle cord over his head and crossed his arms, somehow managing to look very adult. I cracked another smile, then jogged over to Danny. He was still holding the ball close to his chest, like it was a teddy bear or security blanket.

"Hey." I gave him a head nod and then sat on the grass and patted the spot next to me. "Have a seat."

He lowered to the ground and crossed his legs, still holding the ball, still not saying a word. His sadness was palpable; I could feel it winding its way through me. Choking me.

Had anyone walked up to me and asked me how I was doing after my father died, I was embarrassed to admit I'd probably have burst into gut-wrenching tears at the time.

"It's Danny, right?"

He didn't say anything.

"I heard you're having a rough time . . ."

He scowled. "No offense, stranger that I don't know," he said sarcastically. Kid was probably eleven tops. "But I don't need to hear it. Any of it. It doesn't make it better."

"It doesn't," I agreed. "It sucks."

He looked at me out of the corner of his eye.

"I'm not going to tell you it's okay, I'm not going to tell you that you should be happy or that you'll see him again—I'm not going to tell you that sometimes life happens and we can't control things . . ."

He gulped as a wave of fresh tears ran down his cheeks. "Good."

"Yeah. Good." I nodded. "Screw 'em, right?"

His eyes widened.

"All the people still here that love you, that are in pain too, that want you to feel better—screw 'em."

He gulped. "Yeah."

"Yeah." I nodded, suddenly feeling like I had more in common with an eleven-year-old than anyone else in my life. Ironic. "My dad died . . ." My voice shook a bit. I couldn't stop the tiny tremors or the goose bumps that broke out on my arms. "He died of a heart attack a few weeks ago." Danny didn't say anything, so I kept talking even though it hurt my throat to get the words out. "He was at every practice, every game, he was supposed to be at all my new games. We were supposed to go on a trip." I choked over the word. "He was upset that I decided to come to Seattle, and when he called, I didn't answer the phone, Danny. I just . . ." Tears stung the back of my throat, but I couldn't stop talking. "I blamed everyone, including the person I was with when he died." I toyed with the grass in front of me. "I blamed everyone but myself because it hurt too much. Because it hurts, Danny. Because sometimes I don't think it will ever stop hurting, and sometimes we hurt a little bit less on the inside when we're mean and sad on the outside."

I felt something sweaty touch my hand.

I looked down.

Danny had his hand on mine.

I turned it over and squeezed it.

He stared down at my hand and then looked up at me. "You were Papaw's favorite player."

Shit, this kid was going to make me bawl in front of Jagger and elementary school kids.

"Oh yeah?" I rasped.

"He said you were the most inspirational . . ." He frowned. "Inspirational person, that if you could play for a league, someday I could too." He blinked back another tear. "Was he right?"

Typically, I didn't give kids false hope.

I liked to inspire but not make it so they thought they could wrangle the moon if they wanted to.

But with this kid?

I'd tell him he could be Captain America if that's what it took for him to believe that it could get better.

"Danny, he's right. It sounds like he was a good man, and I know he'd want you to be here playing your heart out—he wouldn't want you sad."

Danny put his head on my shoulder and whispered, "I don't think your dad would want you sad either, Mr. Slade."

I squeezed my eyes shut to keep the tears in. "I think you're right."

"I don't hear that a lot."

I laughed and then released his hand. "Danny, thanks for listening."

"I'm a good listener." He squared his shoulders to sit a bit taller and then grinned. "Do you think I can go play now?"

"I think you absolutely should." I stood and offered him my hand. He took it, dusted off the grass, and went flying.

He left the soccer ball.

I picked it up and flipped it over and nearly dropped it. In black marker etched across the white was the name Pablo.

My father's name.

I shook my head as fresh tears stung my eyes. I gave myself a few seconds to gather my emotions then trotted over to Mitchell. "How's it going?"

"I think I'm going to be a coach someday, I like bossing people around," he announced.

I burst out laughing, tears replaced with humor. "Yeah, yeah, give the whistle back, little boss."

He pouted but gave it back and joined the ranks.

And when Danny made his way through the next drill with a smile on his face, I had to ask myself if that talk was for him . . . or for me.

Chapter Thirty-Two

MACKENZIE

Something was different.

First of all he was whistling when he came home. Alfie even tilted his head in disbelief. I almost asked him if he was on drugs.

Especially when he swept into the kitchen, saw dinner on, and pulled me in for a hug, then kissed my cheek. "I was going to sell my soul for a nugget on the way home, then got your text that you made dinner." His eyes bored into mine. "Thank you, Mack, you're the best."

My heart did a little flip as I waited for the other shoe to drop, like *You're the best but there's too much salt*, or *You're super great, but this isn't working out.*

Instead he just grabbed a plate and then called over his shoulder, "Did you want any?"

"Uh . . ." I almost scratched my head and turned around in a circle. "Must have been a good day? Did you get a bonus or something?"

He stopped piling food onto his plate and turned, bracing himself against the counter. "Bonus?"

"Money," I clarified. "You know, green stuff. You buy things with it, in your case probably prostitutes."

He grinned and snorted out a laugh. "No. I spent the first half of my morning teaching elementary school kids which goal to run toward, and fought with your friend"—he made air quotes—"Jagger for the first fifteen minutes of camp."

"Ah." There he was. Air quotes and all. "It's a shame your community service includes teaching this generation's future." I grinned.

"Hah-hah." He wagged his finger at me. "I'd like to think we put our differences behind us when the kiddos are watching. Case in point, I didn't even swear."

"Wow! Turning over a new leaf, huh?" I teased.

He dug the fork into his chili, then dipped his corn bread in right after. "You know you're spoiling me, right?"

"That's my plan . . . you know, next to the shrine I keep by my bedside and the candles I light around your picture. Fingers crossed one of them works." I grabbed my purse and coat.

"Hey, I had a stalker email me a picture of her shrine—I doubt yours has a light show." He shrugged. "And she had at least twenty candles to your few, so you may need to up your game."

"She sent you a picture?"

"Over Instagram. You know how it blocks pictures? Her name was an old teammate's, clearly on purpose. I clicked and haven't gotten the image out of my mind for a solid three years." He took another bite and then nodded to the table. "Stay, hang out."

"You don't pay me to hang out." Keep it professional, keep it friends. He was being nice because . . . because he doesn't like Jagger. Focus!

Slade frowned. "What am I? The worst company in the world? The worst friend?" He pulled out a chair for me. "Sit down and tell me . . ." His eyes roamed over my body a bit. "Tell me . . . about your day."

"Curious, it seems like you're trying to have a conversation with me without sliding in the term *NDA*, kissing me, insulting me, or forcing your friendship on me . . . are we . . . adulting today, Slade?"

He grinned wide. "You're a smart-ass, you know this, right?"

I nodded. "I come by it honestly." With a huff I got up, grabbed a bowl, and made my way over to the stove. I put in two heaping spoonfuls and was already taking a bite out of the corn bread when I sat down.

"That was possibly the biggest bite I've ever seen another human take out of corn bread up close," he observed, making me almost choke.

I reached for his water.

Drank.

And then put it back.

"Get any corn bread floaties in there?" He jerked his head toward it.

"If I did, it will be a special sort of surprise," I fired back.

He laughed. "I like this."

"What?" I blew across my chili. "The risk of backwash?"

He set his spoon down and stared at me so hard I started getting uncomfortable. Those golden eyes were like laser beams, and they saw more than I wanted him to.

They saw past my humor.

Past my sarcasm.

Sometimes I thought they saw through to the hurt girl who just wanted someone to see her and say, "You, I want you. Nobody else."

"You," he said like he could read my mind. "Me." I deflated a bit. "Us." He shrugged. "I like us getting along . . . I, um . . ."

"Don't." I shook my head. "Don't ruin things by getting serious."

"This is serious." He half growled. "I'm trying—no, scratch that, I want to try . . . with you. I want to be better, I don't want to be the guy who lets one tragic thing in his life turn him into a man he doesn't recognize . . . I guess I just wanted you to know I'm trying."

I gulped. "I know."

"And I'm glad we're friends."

My heart crashed against my rib cage, then sailed to the ground. Why was I stupid enough to become friends with the guy whose kisses were seared into my soul? Why?

"Me too." I forced a smile.

He returned it with a wink. "Hey, Mack?"

"What, Slade?" I reached for my spoon.

"You're a bad liar."

I glared. "I'm not lying."

"That would be lie number two."

"I'm not . . ." I huffed. "Of course I'm happy we're friends."

"Is that why you're gripping your spoon the way you gripped my—"

I shoved a piece of corn bread into his mouth. "Sorry, you looked hungry still."

It fell onto his chili.

He shook his head and chewed the part still in his mouth, then whispered so low that chills erupted down my arms. "I'll wear you down, Mack . . . and look at the bright side. If you don't want my friendship . . . and you don't want me as an enemy, there's only one logical choice."

"I refuse to be your mother." I smirked.

"Got one of those."

I shifted in my seat a bit as he pointed his spoon in my direction and said, "Game on."

"Good luck finding someone to play with," I said in a sweet voice.

"Looks like I already did. And she's days away from throwing in the towel, and I can't wait for the minute that happens—when you realize that he isn't what you want . . . that he won't make you scream the way I did—that he never could."

I ignored him for five straight days after that conversation.

And for five straight days.

He asked me to stay for dinner.

For five straight days I wondered if his kiss still tasted the same.

Five days of avoiding the media firestorm of the fight that broke out at the restaurant and the questions regarding Slade's interest in me, as well as Jagger's. Five days of wondering if he was right about Jagger. I knew in my soul, there was really only one way to find out.

Chapter Thirty-Three

I woke up extra early to make sure I didn't make an ass out of myself and ruin her surprise.

She seemed so focused on making sure I was fed that I figured food must be important in her life—like wine. It was at least worth a shot.

I mentally braced myself and then physically grabbed the countertop and repeated out loud, "Don't be a dick."

I'd spent five days trying like hell, and every time I saw Danny I tried a little bit harder. If he could make it through, I could make it through. But I still had my moments, hell, I had a lot of moments. It helped that she stayed for dinner but I think that was only because she didn't trust me to clean up after myself, considering the way she found the house on that first day. It also helped that I had no choice but to play nice with Jagger every day this last week.

I'd like to think we created a cease-fire.

And then I'd see him texting and lose my shit all over again.

I was ready to throw his phone into the trash.

Pathetic, but every time I thought about them I defaulted back into jackass territory, and while I still had chest pain when I thought of my father's death, a small part of me understood that she wasn't the reason his heart stopped.

I just needed to get over the fact that instead of talking with him, I was balls deep inside her—but it had been different.

It wasn't meant to be a one-night stand.

It wasn't.

No matter how many times I tried to convince myself it was.

And the simple fact was that it wasn't fair to want her so badly that I was willing to commit murder just so Jagger wouldn't know how good she actually tasted.

I ran my hands through my hair and checked the baked French toast one last time. In a moment of weakness I'd actually called my mom for the recipe, only to have her burst into tears because it had been Dad's favorite.

So emotionally, I was already spent—meaning I needed to try extra hard not to stick my foot in my mouth. This week had been a mixture of heaven and hell. Heaven because I finally felt like I was dealing with my shit—I had an elementary school kid to thank for that. And hell because I was still dealing with my shit while trying to not beat the shit out of anyone who looked at Mack wrong, and prove to her that friendship wasn't all that was on the table.

The front door opened. I leaned against the counter. Stood. Leaned again. Hell, at this rate I was going to be waiting with a red rose clenched between my teeth.

"What smells so good?" Mack's footsteps sounded down the hall, and then she was facing me. Her hair was in a high ponytail, her simple white T-shirt and boyfriend jeans looked so adorable with her gray Converse that I almost forgot about breakfast and just picked her up into my arms so I could feel her.

"Slade?" She waved a hand in front of my face.

"I like you in Converse best, I think," I finally answered. "And white. You should wear white all the time."

She smiled. "Thank you?"

"Welcome." I beamed. "Now, sit and I'll share a secret family recipe with you, but"—I grabbed a fork and pointed it at her—"you can't share the recipe, alright? Or I have to kill you so Grandma Rodriguez's ghost doesn't haunt you like it does Uncle Jose—he still screams at night."

"Seriously?" she said with heavy sarcasm. "What did he do?"

"Posted it on a cooking blog." I shrugged. "Went to bed and woke up screaming an hour later. Every night, same time, same scream, just ask my aunt. One night we found a rolling pin in his sheets."

"So? Anyone could have grabbed one from the kitchen."

"Theirs had just broken—they needed to buy a new one."

"Oh, so your grandma's ghost is like Santa, that's sweet." She took the coffee I handed her and sipped slowly while I stared at her in disbelief. "What?"

"Sweet?" I started pulling out the French toast. "There's nothing sweet about a ghost that gives a grown man night terrors."

"But at least now he has a rolling pin." She nodded triumphantly. "Right?"

I shook my head. "A ghost is a ghost. Just don't share it, and you'll never have to worry about smelling Bengay when you're trying to fall asleep."

She spewed coffee back into her cup. "Do I want to know?"

I shuddered. "No." The French toast had caramelized perfectly. I set a piece onto a plate and dished out more for myself, then handed her a fork. "Eat up."

"You . . ." She stared at the French toast. "You made me food?"

I shrugged. "You seem hell-bent on getting me to eat. Don't seem so shocked. I'm just trying to see how many times I can get your mouth to water when you see me—and what better way to do that than with food? Hell, it would make my life if your mouth started . . ." My eyes lowered to her gorgeous pout. "Watering . . . whenever you heard my name."

She shifted in her seat.

I grinned knowingly.

And then grinned harder when she sent me a seething glare.

She took a bite.

Closed her eyes and let out the most erotic groan I'd ever heard in my entire life.

I clutched the edge of the table with my free hand so I wouldn't reach for her.

"And that too." I dug in to my own food with my free hand.

"What?" Her eyes popped open.

"The moan . . . I didn't get to hear it the way I want to, but I still got to hear it."

Another bite disappeared into her mouth, and then she licked the caramel off the fork. "You're manipulative."

"I know what I want. Big difference."

She pointed her fork at me. "You're lucky this is the best thing I've ever tasted."

"Does that mean you're going to moan again?"

"Stop, you're ruining my moment with this glaze." She tossed a napkin at my face.

"Should I leave you alone with the entire dish?"

"I don't trust myself not to go all the way," she whispered like the dish could hear her. "And nobody wants to see me unbutton my too-tight jeans to make room."

I smiled. "I don't know, I think I'd fucking love to see that."

"Because I'd be partially undressed?"

"No." I leaned in and licked my lips. "Because nothing looks better than a woman satisfied."

Her lips parted.

I reached across and swiped my thumb near the corner of her mouth, then sucked the glaze from it. "Don't you agree?"

"I . . . uh. Yes."

"I have to go to camp and then practice." I turned and grabbed my duffel from the floor, then put it in front of my constantly hard dick—her fault. "Enjoy my family's secrets."

"Wait." Her hand jutted out. "Thanks again, it was really . . . sweet. You know, the opposite of what you typically are to other humans."

"Yeah, deserved that." I sighed. "Are you ever going to forgive me?"

"Maybe when you grovel."

I leaned down and whispered in her ear. "Baby, if you want me on my hands and knees, all you gotta do is ask."

I left her with that parting thought.

And me with a raging hard-on.

Which I needed to get rid of immediately so I didn't get arrested on my last day of soccer camp.

I grinned as I made my way to the car.

All in all, not the worst Saturday I'd ever had.

Chapter Thirty-Four

Worst. Saturday. Ever.

Jagger wouldn't stop staring at his phone with a shit-eating grin on his face, and I couldn't stop trying to peer over his shoulder to see what put it there.

"Slade," he said without looking up. "Look over my shoulder one more time and I'm punching you in the dick."

I jerked back. "Can't a guy be curious?"

He put his phone away and crossed his arms. "Curious is asking if I have a cold. Creepy is when you keep trying to read my texts and breathe down my neck in the process."

I scowled. "I was just . . . bored."

"Bored." His eyebrows shot up. "Have to admit, that's a new one."

Idiot. Table for one.

I was waiting for a smart retort to pop up in my brain. Instead, I stared at him slack-jawed like I'd just been hit by a ball.

Our kids started arriving then.

Danny was finally smiling.

All was right with the world.

Except it wasn't.

Because my world, however cash filled it was, didn't include the one thing that Jagger apparently had.

Her.

Fuck, I'd been an idiot for blaming her.

For letting her go.

For thinking I could last without tasting her again.

I would do things differently.

But that was the shit part about life—you didn't get do-overs. You got one chance, and then maybe if you were lucky and you screwed up—you got another.

I was out of chances.

"You look sad," Danny said, coming to stand next to me. The kid had his arms crossed and was wearing one of my jerseys. "Mom says low blood sugar makes me moody. Here." He handed me a warm, half-melted protein bar. "This should do the trick."

"Sure will." I laughed. "Are you sure you weren't supposed to eat that, though?"

"Gross, like I would ever eat the cookies-and-cream flavor. I already tossed a peanut butter one in my bag. That one was in my pocket!"

Sure. Was.

"Thanks, man." I opened it and took a bite to show my appreciation while he beamed to the rest of the kids running up.

I choked it down.

No choice since he kept looking at me to make sure I was chewing.

"Alright, Team Striker, gather around."

It was Jags against Strikers for our final day. If we won, Jagger had to shave his head. If Jagger won, well, my famous locks were on the chopping block.

I took a deep breath. "Men, we have one goal today. Keep me from being the laughingstock of my team. I gotta be honest, guys, I don't have a round head. It's shaped like an ugly football, and I'll probably never get a girlfriend if I have to shave my hair." They started snickering. "Lads, I could not be more serious if my life depended on it. Do you want me to die alone?"

"No!" they cheered.

"Guys! We're a team! Leave no man behind. I'm counting on you! My future self is counting on you! Now, go out there and have fun! Team Striker on three. One, two, three, Striker!"

They ran out screaming.

Jagger sent his out in similar fashion.

We stood side by side watching our handiwork as they warmed up.

"They grow up so damn fast." I shook my head. "I swear Mitchell grew a hair on his chin this week."

"Brady told me he found a hair on his balls, I guess they both win."

We both burst into laughter as the guys ran around us emitting their own happy noises.

"If you ever lose the love of the game . . . just watch it through their eyes, huh?"

"Yeah." He nodded and, without looking at me, coughed out, "You did good."

I cupped my ear. "I'm sorry, lots of horns honking and people yelling, what was that?"

He gave me a shove. "You did good, jackass."

"No cursing!" came Matt's admonishment from behind us.

We turned, and Jagger shot Matt a death glare.

"You killed our moment, man!" I roared at him.

Matt held up his hands, eyes wide.

"Here we are ready to hug it out." Jagger shook his head in disappointment.

"Start fresh," I offered.

"And you"—Jagger spat the word *you*—"just had to lecture us about our language."

Matt pinched the bridge of his nose. "I quit."

I burst out laughing. "You like the smell of money too much. Besides, where would we be without our glue?"

"Oh, you two?" He pointed between us. "Probably dead on the street somewhere. But me? I'd be in the Bahamas. Thanks for the reminder. Not painful at all."

I just rolled my eyes. "Thanks for coming to the game, now watch me kick Jagger's ass."

"Your golden-brown locks are mine, Rodriguez!" Jagger grumbled.

I narrowed my eyes and tilted my head. "That come out the way you planned, or are you really regretting—"

"Shut it."

Matt laughed just as the ref blew the whistle.

My guys ran over to me. I gave them high fives, grabbed my clipboard, and knelt down. "Remember what I said, guys, my future wife needs you to win, nobody wants to marry a football. Amen?"

"Amen!" they shouted.

I sent them off with a giant smile and prayed they wouldn't make me a hairless cat after Mack's own heart when I knew in mine—she really preferred bulldogs.

I gave Jagger major side-eye.

Yeah, I wouldn't stand a chance with no hair.

Chapter Thirty-Five

MACKENZIE

Alton: Your father spoke to me.

I stared at the text while the French toast turned to a rock in my stomach. The last thing I wanted to do after having such a great start to my Saturday was see a text from the guy who accused me of being a whore in front of the guy who rejected me and the one who was . . . what was Jagger doing? It seemed genuine, and I hated that my trust issues were filtering into the way I saw him.

My phone pinged again.

Jagger: We need a redo.

I smiled at the phone and responded. He'd been texting me throughout the week, nothing serious, just asking about my day, telling me about his. Complaining about Slade—the usual.

Me: What were you thinking?

I could tell he was typing since the dots were dancing.

And while he was typing out whatever he was typing out, my eyes fell to the French toast that Slade had made for me—as if he wasn't busy enough with camp and practice, he woke up and made me something that instantly kicked my day off right. I smiled just as Jagger replied.

Jagger: My place tonight.

I gulped, feeling instantly guilty.

And chewed on my bottom lip. Why did that seem more personal than dinner?

And why did I suddenly feel like I was cheating on Slade when all he'd done was make me breakfast and apologize for his crappy personality? You know, after being sweet all week long, teasing me, forcing me to stay for dinner. I stared down at my phone.

I didn't overanalyze.

I just responded.

Me: I'll bring wine.

Jagger: You better . . .

I was about to put my phone away when Alton texted again.

Alton: Look, I don't know what kind of influence those guys have over you. The fact that you even slept with one or hell who knows? Both of them? Reflects badly on you. Not on me. I just reacted. Like any concerned friend would. I'm worried about you, and it's wrong of you to take out your own guilt by tattling to your father and trying yet again to get me fired. It's business, it's not personal.

I imagined reaching through the screen and squeezing both hands around his neck.

I almost married this guy?

The one who didn't stand up for the girl?

Alton would never be a hero.

And honestly he didn't have the brains to pull off the villain.

He was too focused on himself and his own career than anything. Heck, Alton was the kind of guy who would be more worried about his stocks than the fact that the building was burning. I'd just chosen to focus on everything else. I'd ignored the truth right in front of me. I was business to him. Nothing more.

Me: You called me a whore. And yes. I slept with Slade Rodriguez. Not because I was desperate. Not because I was sad. Not because I wanted to see what it was like. And . . .

I felt a tear slide down my cheek and continued.

. . . not because I was trying to trap him into marriage. I had no ulterior motives other than finding adventure in someone's arms, finding something I'd been searching for my whole life and capturing it in that moment because I could. Because I can . . .

I sent the text.

And then I stared back at Jagger's name and frowned.

I refused to think about the texts the rest of the day and grabbed the leash for Alfie. It wasn't long before I got lost in cleaning out the final box. It was nearing the time when Slade was supposed to be home. And finishing that box meant my days with him and Alfie were getting fewer and fewer, until they disappeared altogether.

My phone went off several times.

And each time I saw Alton's name across the screen, more bitterness took hold. He had no right to be angry. I stashed my phone back in my car where it belonged and gritted my teeth.

My body. My choice.

And every time I ignored him, my heart tried to remind me of how good it was with Slade, how tender he was, how loving . . . I squeezed my eyes shut and forced the thoughts away.

I had to convince myself that the man in Puerto Vallarta didn't exist.

Because if he did?

I wouldn't let him go.

Alfie came and rested by my feet as I pulled out a few pictures and dusted them off. The ones that seemed the most important—Slade with his father—were the ones I put around his room. A photo of him and his father after winning the World Cup was on his nightstand. And another at what looked like a birthday dinner, I put in the bathroom. It just seemed right to have them out and not stashed away, especially since he was such a huge part of Slade's life. I stored the trophies in his office, and when I came back to the final picture of him, his old teammates, and his ex-fiancée?

Well, that one I put in storage.

If he wanted to burn it later he could.

When I was done, I took a look around the room.

"You sure spend an awful lot of time in my bedroom," a freshly showered Slade teased as he leaned against the door and crossed his arms. "Just don't look in any of the drawers, don't want to embarrass you."

I rolled my eyes. "Oh, I already saw the blow-up doll."

He laughed. "Riiiight . . ."

"I stored her in the closet fully inflated, just in case," I added, making my way closer. "Oh, and I added another box of extra-small condoms, you're welcome."

His smile just widened. "It's not an insult when we both know you're lying, you know this, right?"

I just shrugged as his eyes fell to the nightstand.

He was quiet.

Too quiet.

I braced myself for a fight. I hated that I had to.

He clenched his teeth and then picked up the picture and stared at it. "I could hear him screaming when I was on the field."

I sucked in a breath.

"Hundreds of thousands of people, and yet I could pick his voice out . . ."

"What was he saying?" I asked quietly.

Slade stared at the picture so hard he didn't blink. "'Don't give up.'"

"Did you listen?"

He put the picture down and looked over at me. "We won, didn't we?"

"I don't really follow soccer," I said to lighten the mood.

He actually cracked a smile. "Trust me, I'm well aware you don't follow soccer. Had you known who I was, you would have been peeling your shirt over your head the minute you saw me on the plane."

I shook my head. "You do realize that's not everyone's reaction to you, right? Mr. I-have-such-a-high-opinion-of-myself?"

He took a step toward me. "*People* magazine says my sweat smells like an orgasm, so . . . maybe it's others that have too high an opinion of me."

"Bingo." I spread my arms wide and laughed. "So, I should get going. I'm glad you aren't upset about the pictures. I just figured they needed to be seen."

"Wait." He held up his hand. "Where are you running off to? I mean isn't there dinner?" Okay, now his smile was wide, happy. Oh no. He pressed his hands down on my shoulders. "It's like you've got a hot date to get ready for."

He meant it as a joke.

We'd been joking with each other all week.

This wasn't any different.

Except I didn't find any humor in it.

I didn't laugh.

His smile fell as his eyes laced with panic. "Right?"

"Not a date," I said quickly. "But Jagger said he wanted to reschedule our dinner."

"Jagger." His nostrils flared and then he seemed to calm himself before he exhaled in obvious frustration. "He wants one thing from you, and it's not friendship."

"Are you telling me you're better company?" I countered.

He opened his mouth and closed it, then whispered, "I've been trying."

I sidestepped him as his hands fell to his sides. "I'll be sure to bring a sticker in on Monday."

"Wait!" He grabbed my elbow. "Monday? But today's Saturday!"

I nodded slowly. "And tomorrow's Sunday . . . what's your point?"

"Alfie still needs a walk."

Was it my imagination or was he sulking?

I was not falling for the puppy-dog look in those golden eyes or the soft pout of his mouth when he pressed his lips together in frustration over me not being at his house.

"You're a kicker." I shrugged. "Use those muscular legs and take him out for a walk."

He grinned, still pressing his fingers into my skin. "Striker, and what's that about my muscular legs? Were you . . . staring?"

"No!" I said quickly. "I mean I just assumed, because of the running, and the—balls."

He pressed his lips together harder, like he was trying not to laugh.

"Soccer balls," I corrected.

"Oh, good, because you lost me there for a minute, thought you were talking about my balls." He winked. "Besides, the team I was coaching won the championship camp game, meaning Jagger had to shave his head, and I didn't even make the bastard shave all of it, so when you see a high-and-tight-looking fool—that's him, just in case you're confused about your . . . date."

I felt my cheeks heat. I was still thinking about the balls. His balls. I cleared my throat. "Thanks for the heads-up. And congrats on the win." I pulled away. "So I'll just see you later! You have my number if you need anything."

His eyes lit up. "You're right, thanks for the reminder! Have fun with Jagger." Before I could stop him, he was pulling me into his arms for what I thought was a kiss, but ended up being a really tight hug. His lips brushed my ear. "I'll miss you."

It was my undoing.

Being missed.

Wanted.

I reacted more strongly to that sentence than I would have had he kissed me.

And I could have sworn he knew it as he watched me walk away from him toward another man.

He'd miss me.

And the sick part.

I wasn't even out of his house.

And I missed him too.

Chapter Thirty-Six

Jagger lived closer to downtown Seattle than I would have thought. His penthouse apartment was exactly how I would imagine a bachelor pad, all dark colors with lots of reds, and enough expensive electronics and gadgets to make any guy salivate.

He'd texted me the address the minute I was in my car trying to decide if I should cancel and go back in to Slade.

His text sealed my fate.

Well, that and an adorable picture of him and his new haircut and a ton of littles standing around him with huge smiles on their faces.

That was how I found myself on his couch a few hours later with his arm wrapped around me, and a bottle of wine sitting between us. I blamed the children.

He had a gourmet cheese board I'd seen at a high-end grocer last week—he didn't make it, not like Slade. And it didn't even matter. I bought cheese all the time like that! Ugh, I was going crazy second-guessing myself and unfairly comparing him to Slade. I stared at the plate.

Why did I care that he didn't make food?

It wasn't like he was a lazy guy.

He was just a guy.

Not all guys cook, Mackenzie!

I shook my head.

"Something wrong?" he whispered in my ear. I shivered. I forgot how close we were sitting—his body was so warm I was almost overheated, and the few times I turned to look at him, his eyes had darted to my mouth like he was trying to decide how I would taste— and if I'd let him in the first place. "Hey, Mackenzie, where are you?"

"Right here." I finally looked at him.

His blue eyes lit up a bit as he cupped my chin with his hand, rubbing his thumb across my lower lip. His head descended. I froze.

And then my phone went off on the coffee table.

I jumped back and grabbed it.

Slade: Where's my detergent?

Jagger read over my shoulder and let out a snort of disbelief. "Really? He can't find his own detergent?"

"I do his laundry," I admitted, then typed out, Did you try the laundry room, genius?

Jagger barked out a laugh.

Slade: It's not in here.

Me: It's there.

Slade: Would you bet your life on it?

Me: No, I'd bet yours, though!

Slade: That's hurtful . . . oh, I found it!

Me: Great! Good night!

I put my phone back on my lap just as Jagger shook his head. "The guy's clueless, isn't he?"

"I don't mind it . . ."

And I didn't.

I didn't mind taking care of him, and part of me felt like maybe he was playing dumb about the laundry detergent. I'd seen him do his own ironing plenty of times.

"Why are you growling?" Jagger asked.

"Nothing, I just—"

My phone buzzed again.

Jagger groaned.

Slade: Did you leave any French toast?

Me: I put the leftovers in the fridge.

Slade: You almost ate the whole pan.

Jagger glanced down. "You ate that much French toast?"

"Stop looking over my shoulder." I elbowed him while he held up his hands in surrender. "And it was . . . good. He's a good cook, alright?"

"Wait, ass pants made you . . . French toast?"

"It was baked," I said, reliving the texture in my mouth. "It had this syrupy brown-sugar glaze and I think he even put brandy in it."

"Damn. I may have underestimated him. I mean I had my suspicions when he didn't make me shave all the hair off my head plus my eyebrows, but still."

"Eyebrows too?" I smiled to myself and typed back.

Me: I didn't eat the whole pan. Anything else?

Slade: Do we have wine?

I took a deep breath.

Me: Look in the cellar.

"He has a wine cellar?" Jagger asked out loud.

"I said stop!" I laughed. "Okay, movie, we were watching a movie, right?"

"Uh . . ." A crestfallen expression crossed his face before he nodded toward the flat-screen. "Yeah, that's exactly what I had in mind for the night."

I settled back against the comfortable couch. Jagger held me tighter. Five minutes went by and then there were six consecutive buzzes of my phone.

"Are you serious? If that's Slade I'm going to block his number on your phone, the guy's such a fucking cockblock." He laughed. "I mean he gives me so much shit during practice, the camp, I hate that I actually respect him now and—"

I pulled away. Shook my head for good measure, not even hearing the rest of what he said, and gave him a sharp look followed by "Excuse me?"

His expression went from frustrated to panicked before he shrugged. "Look, it's a common phrase, don't read into it too much."

"But why would you use it on your friend?"

"Mackenzie." He wiped his face with his hands. "Can we not do this? Don't be the girl that reads into things and ruins what should be a really good time."

I didn't think he meant it as a put-down.

In fact, I knew he probably wasn't thinking anything, but I was jumping to conclusions.

But after all those texts from Alton.

It was enough for me to feel emotionally awkward and more than ready to go home.

I stood.

"Mackenzie." He gripped my hand and tried tugging me back down. "Seriously, I'll stop talking. The guy just drives me crazy. On purpose. We'll just watch the movie."

I glanced at the texts on my phone.

Slade: Come back.

Slade: I know he's with you.

Slade: Tell him I'm plotting his death.

Slade: I'm not joking.

Slade: Hurry home so I don't go to prison.

Slade: I miss you . . .

"No . . . ," I said in a harsh whisper. "I think we should just call it a night." I smiled down at him. "Thanks for the wine and food, but I should be going."

"Shit." He said it so quietly that I almost didn't hear it. When he stood, he had a defeated look in his eyes.

And when I grabbed my things and walked to the door, he reached for my hand and squeezed. "Mackenzie?"

"Yeah?" I squeezed back.

"I never stood a chance, did I?"

"Next time, don't lead with being a friend if what you want is something more," I said truthfully.

"Would it have even mattered?" His eyes shifted like he was trying to read my emotions to see if there had ever really been a chance.

The question hung between us like dirty laundry that needed to be acknowledged, taken care of.

I exhaled and shook my head no. "He and I—"

"He's a dick at least ninety percent of the time," he finished. "Promise me that when you get him out of your system you'll give me a chance."

"Get him out of my system." Why did all the men around me, except the one I wanted, try to control me? Put me down? Make me feel bad about myself because of my own feelings? Why? "What makes you think that's what's happening next?"

He stared me down. "Because I've seen that look before . . . the day his fiancée told him she was pregnant and was willing to do anything to keep him. Even though she betrayed him she couldn't bear the thought of letting him go. His grip on her was too deep, she made a mistake and would have sold her soul to keep him."

"I don't want to hear about it."

"You think you even know what the truth is?" He shook his head. "He doesn't care about anyone but himself."

"Bye, Jagger." I threw my purse over my shoulder and power walked to the elevator as the door shut quietly behind me.

Was it too much to ask for one man not to assume the worst of me? To support me?

I wanted a partner.

Not someone who knew better and ruled over me.

I wanted the danger of jumping off the cliff while my partner not only encouraged me to do so but said he'd jump next to me—regardless of whether we both landed in shark-infested waters.

Together.

Forever partners.

Maybe it didn't exist in real life.

But for a few brief moments in Mexico.

It had.

Chapter Thirty-Seven

SLADE

I was slightly buzzed from the wine.

And drunk from the taste of the French toast, or maybe just drunk with the knowledge that she'd eaten so much of it, enjoyed it, that I'd satisfied her.

I flipped through more channels.

I'd texted her forty minutes ago.

And still nothing.

I tried not to think about her being with Jagger—because thinking about that made me think about taking his head off, and he was my teammate, we'd be playing in games together soon—I would need to trust him, not murder him.

Shit.

I groaned into my hands and wiped my face.

I should just go to bed.

Instead, I checked my phone again.

I'd done nothing right when it came to Mack, except make French toast. I didn't even send the flowers myself.

I typed out a text to Matt.

Me: I told her I missed her.

Matt: You don't drink during the season, why are you drunk texting me?

Me: Not drunk. She's with him.

Hell, he was right. I was drinking. Why was I drinking her away? It wasn't working worth shit!

Matt: Then maybe you should have been the cheerful sexier option, idiot.

Me: I am sexier.

Matt: People magazine did a poll, you won by two percent.

Me: Two percent is still winning and I'm damn cheerful!

Matt: Yes, so cheerful that you yell out your cheer loud and clear and then save your smiles for your dog.

Me: That doesn't even make any sense.

Matt: Go to bed. Nothing good happens after midnight and you need the sleep.

Me: I fucked up.

Matt: I'm sighing really loud right now. What do you want to hear? That there's a chance?

Me: Finally! Yes!

Matt: Alright then! Go get 'em, tiger, she's totally going to forgive you. In fact, if you send enough money in her direction, you can even marry her, screw the whole NDA. Just put a ring on it and be done!

Me: Very funny. You know I'm not ever getting married. I just . . .

Matt: Use her for sex and I'll help Jagger bury your body.

Me: I would never do that.

Matt: Don't lead her on if you don't plan on following through.

Me: I won't. I swear. I'll make sure she knows it's not a one-time thing.

Matt: You can't hear me, but I'm groaning really loud into my hands.

Me: Do that shit privately, man. I don't want to know about shower time.

Matt: You. Are. A. Dick.

I ignored him. He called me a dick at least eighty percent of the time I was around him. It was nothing new, and it wouldn't be the last time. I set my phone on the coffee table and willed a text from her to come through.

Only to hear a knock on the door.

I jammed my knee against the coffee table in an effort to sprint toward the door, and nearly tripped over an equally excited Alfie as we made our way down the hall.

I stopped, took a deep breath, then opened the door and tried not to look tired. "Hey, Mack."

Her eyes narrowed. "You're fooling no one. I heard you running to the door, and poor Alfie looks ready to have a heart attack. You know he can't do long distance!"

I stared at my bulldog in disbelief. "It was forty feet, tops. If that's long distance, we need to cut back on snacks."

"But he's such a good boy!" she said in a high-pitched voice as she got down to eye level and started loving his face.

Irrational jealousy pounded through me. I cleared my throat to get her attention.

She just kept ignoring me. "Aren't you, buddy? Aw, Alfie, I missed you." Bastard licked her face and whined, then looked up at me as if to say, *I win.*

Damn it, I should have been more worried about the dog all along! I cleared my throat again.

"You want a bath on Monday? Yeah!" He wagged his nonexistent tail and started to dance around in circles when seconds ago he'd looked ready to pass out.

I rolled my eyes. Leave it to my dog to be more dramatic than me.

Mack caught the movement. "What?"

"Nothing." I knelt down and rubbed his belly. "Can't a guy be jealous about bath time?"

"It's typically a bad thing when humans get bathed by another human," she pointed out.

"Not true." I inched closer. "Bathing can be very—" Her eyes flickered to my lips.

I sniffed.

Her eyes widened. "ALFIE!"

"Why!" I waved in front of my face. "Alfie, no, man, you gotta stop with the gas, you're going to chase her away! Oh, it's full of protein." I gagged. "Like eggs or something."

She held her nose and turned away to take a breath. "It's his superpower."

"I need to ask the vet what to do, because that's not natural. It's not."

She burst out laughing as tears of mirth filled her eyes. "You *would* have a dog with a toxic ass."

"Hey! He just . . . has an extremely sensitive stomach."

She stood while Alfie seemed to be grinning between the two of us as if to say, *Look, I didn't ruin the moment, she's still here!*

"So." I held the door open wider. "How did it go with Jagger?"

She stepped into the house.

I shut the door.

Locked it.

Briefly wrestled with the idea of putting a chair and armoire in front of it. Then I followed her into the living room.

The bottle of wine was out.

Over half of it was gone.

My glass was empty.

She picked up the bottle and drank straight from it.

I whistled as my eyebrows shot up in surprise. "Must have gone well, then?"

"He called you a cockblocker."

I couldn't stop grinning.

"That funny to you?"

"It's funny that he said it out loud when he was trying to play the friend card . . . not that I think he's incapable of being a friend, but when it comes to you? No man would be able to do that . . ."

It was out before I could stop myself.

And just like Jagger the shithead—I'd outed myself.

I rubbed the back of my head and stared at the floor. "All guys are . . . idiots."

She was silent.

Though I did hear the sound of the wine bottle tipping back again.

"Did you really lose the detergent?" she asked in a soft voice.

"No," I admitted.

"And the French toast?"

"Where else would it be? The dishwasher?"

"And killing him?"

"Oh, that's still on the calendar, thanks for asking." I beamed.

She set the wine bottle down on the coffee table and slowly made her way over to me.

I sucked in a breath, waiting for her to announce that she was going home since she already checked in on my sanity.

Instead, she set her purse down on the chair next to my legs and then pulled her coat off, draping it beside her purse.

I could hear my own heartbeat as my eyes zeroed in on her pink lips. "Does this mean you're staying?"

"Do you want me to?"

I reached for her.

Only to have her dodge me and lift her shoulder into the air. "Movie?"

"Movie." I tested the word with my mouth and decided that I didn't like it, not at all. "Sure."

A movie?

Really?

"What do you want to watch?" I grabbed the remote and tried not to inhale as she breezed past me—God, she always smelled so good.

She grabbed a blanket from the couch and wrapped it around herself, then yawned.

I made her yawn.

YAWN.

"Something with some action," she decided out loud.

"What kind of action?" I hinted a bit.

And it went directly over her head. "You know, like Bruce Willis."

Damn it.

"Yeah, I can find something . . ." I skimmed the channels. A *Die Hard* marathon was on cable. I clicked on it and sat.

My body rock hard.

My resolve rock solid.

My brain mush as she moved her head to my chest and wrapped an arm around my middle, like I was the best fucking friend she'd ever had.

I squeezed my eyes shut and tried to think of anything but the way that arm felt brushed up against my skin.

Sweet hell.

And when she tried to get closer, I wrapped my arms around her and just held her there.

"Was I too easy?" she asked about ten minutes into the movie.

"Are you fucking kidding me right now?" I growled. "If he called you easy I'm going to—"

"Not him." She shook her head. "Alton."

"Alton wouldn't know his ass from his penis if someone drew him a diagram. No, you're not easy. He's just a pompous prick with too high of an opinion of himself."

"You're not just saying that?"

"He left you. At the altar, Mack. You went on vacation. You wanted an adventure . . ." I squeezed her tighter. "Never apologize for wanting to live."

I meant it.

"Thanks."

"Mack, any girl that saves herself for the man she's going to marry and then gives it away the way you did is so blindly trusting of other humans. It says so much about you, about your character. And the guy who took it without looking back? Well, let's just say that guy is just as much of an asshole as the one who let you get away."

"Oh yeah?" she whispered. "Why's that?"

"Because for a few brief moments of his life he had it all—and threw it away because he couldn't see past his own mistakes."

We were quiet the rest of the movie.

She fell asleep in my arms.

So I picked her up, refusing to let her go even if she did wake up for a second, and placed her in my bed.

Where she should have been since the day I walked away without a second glance.

Next to me.

In my arms.

In my life.

Where she was always supposed to be.

When my eyes flickered to the portrait on the nightstand, I smiled. A real smile. Because with the way the picture was facing her—it almost looked like my dad was laughing in approval.

And the best part?

It kinda felt like he was.

Chapter Thirty-Eight

MACKENZIE

I woke up with the picture of Slade's dad staring me down. Sunlight crept through the windows of his massive bedroom. And I had a hundred and ninety pounds of muscle wrapped around me.

Shirtless.

Tears pricked my eyes.

This was how I was supposed to have woken up in Mexico.

It wasn't fair.

I tried to slowly pull away.

But he kept me pinned at his side, his nose nuzzling my hair, his voice deep and raspy, and for the first time since working for him, his accent wrapped around me with warmth. My entire body melted.

"Sunday." He sighed into my neck. "Remember?"

"I know, I just, I have family dinner and—"

"Perfect." He pulled away, leaving me confused.

"Perfect?" I repeated, voice filled with sleep. "Why is it perfect?"

"I'll go with you."

"I don't know if that's a good idea." I shook my head. "My dad and I are fighting, and I may not be his favorite person right now."

"Mack, I would do anything to fight with my father again . . . don't let something come between you, even if it seems too large to ignore. Work it out."

I sat up and faced him. "You're right."

His eyes lit up. "Damn, it sounds even better than I imagined it."

I threw a pillow at his head.

He blocked it with his hands and then tackled me against the mattress. "I'm inviting myself."

"I see that."

"I'm also taking you out on a date today."

"And I'm saying yes?"

His eyes narrowed. "Of course, you do know who I am, right?" I could tell he was teasing, though.

"Careful before I suffocate you with that same pillow."

He smiled and then sobered immediately. "Let me spoil you today."

I tried to swallow past the knot in my throat and finally got out, "No yelling? Or accusing me of trapping you into marriage?"

He scowled. "If anyone's trying to trap anyone, it's me . . . trapping you. And fair warning, Mack, I always play to win." He lowered his eyes to my chest.

I looked down.

And I was in nothing but my bra and underwear.

I let out a little gasp. "You, you!" I jabbed my finger at him. "You took my clothes off!"

"I asked your permission." He winked and then got out of bed wearing only a pair of Nike joggers and a smile. "I took your grunt and snore as your stamp of approval."

I buried my face in my hands and groaned.

"Hey, at least Alfie knows he's not the only one who makes noises in his sleep."

I grabbed the sheet and followed him into the massive bathroom just as he dropped his pants and turned on the shower.

I turned away. And nearly passed out when I felt his body behind me, his hands on my shoulders. "Join me."

"I shouldn't."

"You really"—he ran his fingers down my arms—"really should."

"I'd be naked."

"Most showers take place that way, yes, unless you'd rather wear this sheet?" He pulled it down my body until it pooled at my feet.

Next he was unhooking my bra.

I shivered as it fell to the floor, then swayed as heat pulsed between my thighs the minute those same fingertips tugged down my underwear. I felt both longing and loss when he moved his hands.

"Come on," he urged. "The water's hot."

So it really was a shower?

No seduction?

Why did I feel disappointed when that's what was necessary so I didn't get hurt again?

Why was I standing there naked in his bathroom?

I hurried into the walk-in rain shower and nearly moaned when the hot water hit my face.

"See?" He chuckled. "I have all the good ideas."

"The best ideas . . ." I let the water pour over my face and then opened my eyes.

He was staring at my mouth.

Not my naked skin.

But the thing that he saw every day.

As if he was so obsessed nothing else mattered.

"Slade!" Matt's voice boomed through the large bathroom. "Seriously, answer your phone, you got the Gucci deal."

My eyes widened in panic as Slade shoved me against the nearest wall and pressed a finger to my lips.

"I'm naked, don't come in," he shouted over his shoulder. I took that opportunity to stare at his dazzling cheekbones, plump lips, and perfect hair even under all the water . . . and gulped.

"You realize I've seen you naked more than your own mom, right?"

"Don't make shit weird, Matt!" he yelled back while I gave him a *Really?* look.

His eyes narrowed as he ran that same finger down my chin and then tugged my lower lip with his teeth, bringing just enough pain with all the pleasure.

I reached for him, only to have my hands slide down his slick, hard stomach.

"Do you . . . are you? There's wom—do you have company of the female variety? God, you're such a jackass. You text me last night lamenting the fact that Jagger and Mackenzie were in the same room together alone—almost fucking crying into a bottle of wine—and now you're with another woman? See! This is why I told you to stay away! Guys like you don't deserve pretty trust-fund daughters with more brains than you have in your tiny head!"

With every word my smile grew wider until it felt like I was going to bust up laughing.

Slade chuckled under his breath, then whispered to me, "I wasn't crying . . . my eyes were dry, I used eyedrops, not real tears."

"Sure?" I said.

"But I did text him like a bitch."

"Huh, Slade Rodriguez, insecure? I wouldn't have guessed." I nuzzled his neck just as he slammed a hand against the wall like he wanted Matt to be anywhere but a few feet away from us.

"Who are you talking to?" Matt roared. "Did she sign an NDA?"

"Fuck the NDA!" Slade yelled back at about the same time I said, "Hey, Matt!"

"Mackenzie!" Matt shouted. "Slade, what did you do!"

"He made me take a shower!" I yelled.

Slade grinned. "Nothing happened!" And then he lowered his voice. "Yet."

I gasped.

"I should have just gotten a cat," Matt muttered.

"What was that?" Slade yelled.

"A cat! I should have gotten a cat! And now I have you and Jagger and another pissy athlete that yelled at me when you beat him out for Gucci. You need to be there next week for the photo shoot, they want to use body oils to bring out your muscles in the pictures. Good luck with that one."

Slade scrunched up his nose.

"And keep it in your pants!" Matt yelled. "You too, Mackenzie! I'll be watching, well, not watching because that crosses a very professional line, and we both know that sexual harassment is—"

"Matt!" Slade laughed. "Go. Away."

"Right. Doing just that." I thought he left and then his voice was back. "Seriously, Slade, don't . . . just . . . please don't do anything stupid."

"Do I often do something stupid?"

Matt was silent.

I wrapped my arms around Slade's neck and pulled him close until the tips of my breasts were sliding across his chest.

He let out a groan.

"Seriously," Matt added.

Slade looked down at my lips, captured them with such ferocity that my head slid back against the tile, and then pulled back just long enough to whisper, "Too late."

Chapter Thirty-Nine

It had been years since I'd just made out with someone for the sake of making out and not to prime them for more.

I'd forgotten how erotic kissing was.

I'd also forgotten how hard it was when a beautiful naked woman was rubbing against me not to slam her against the wall and pin her there.

I dug my hands into her wet hair as she opened her mouth to me, and hot water fell between our bodies as we kissed. I tasted water against her mouth, with each part of her lips I drank. Her hands dug into me, clung to me like I was going to let her go, and it broke my fucking heart that she might actually think I would do that because of our history.

I wasn't letting this go.

Her go.

I pressed my palms against hers, interlocking our fingers as I tried to put space between our bodies, but she fought me every way. I laughed against her mouth. "Professional athlete, Mack, nice try, but you'll lose."

"We'll see," she panted, and then she started sucking on my tongue. I dropped my hands, she walked right into my arms and crushed her mouth aggressively against mine. I was so hard I couldn't see straight, and her soft body rubbing against me was not making the situation any easier.

"Bad." I licked a droplet of water off her bottom lip. "Idea."

"Good idea."

A frisson of tension spread down my body as I drove my hips against her in search of release.

Her eyes hooded, the slight part of her lips drove me fucking mad as I stepped completely out of her embrace, chest heaving. "I can't."

"Nature says otherwise." She reached for me. I let her because I was weak for her and had been getting progressively weaker where she was concerned.

"Mack." I bit out her name with a harsh whisper that had my brain telling me how easy it would be to bury myself inside her and take what I'd been wanting since seeing her again.

She dropped her hand, looking crestfallen, from her swollen mouth to her primed, wet body.

I tugged at my hair, then wiped the excess water from my face and took a deep breath, and another, then finally just looked away. "Shower, it was supposed to be a shower."

"It is a shower." Her confident, sexy voice was killing me inch by inch. My body was confused as to why it wasn't already pressed into hers, and my blood throbbed so hard I couldn't think straight.

"I want . . ." I licked my lips. "No, I need to do this right . . . not in the shower . . ."

Her face lit up. "Does that mean you want me to stop getting wet?" She reached for the knob.

I hung my head and groaned. "You're going to be the death of me. Stay wet, always stay wet." I grumbled the last part. "Let's just . . . wash . . . the Jagger off of you, and then we can go meet your parents."

She frowned. "How did shower sex go from Jagger to my parents?"

"Easy." I grabbed some body wash and lathered it up in my hands, then ran it down her shoulders. "I want you smelling like me, not him. And I want to meet the people who gave me you."

She gulped, and her wide-eyed gaze left mine as if she was afraid to stare too long, afraid to look too hopeful. "Do you really think you should say things like that to me? Might give me the wrong idea."

"Oh yeah? And what's that?"

She lifted a shoulder as I ran the soap down her belly. "That you want to keep me."

I knelt in front of her and pressed my face between her thighs, whispering against her slick, heated skin. "Consider yourself kept."

When I looked up, her breath was coming out in harsh gasps like she was already that out of control just from the buzz of my mouth.

I gripped the sides of her thighs, dug my fingers into her flesh, and tugged her legs apart.

Her hands fell to my shoulders for balance. "Slade?"

"Mack?" I winked up at her. "Hold on tight."

"Afraid I'm going to come apart all over your head or something?"

"Afraid?" I repeated. "No, I'm counting on it, in three, two—"

She tasted like she was already mine.

Don't ask me how I knew it.

But a man doesn't forget his first taste.

A man doesn't forget the way a woman responds to his lips, his tongue, the way her body heavily rested against my mouth with each lick. The way she moaned without even realizing she was moaning. The way she braced one hand against my shoulder, the other in my hair, pulling, directing, loving the ride I was taking her on as her thighs quivered.

Steam billowed around us as I cupped her rounded ass and jerked her against my mouth, opening to receive her, ready to drink her dry and stay there forever.

"Yes, that, just like that," she panted, her body giving out. And I took it all, every ounce she had, and realized I wouldn't survive leaving her a second time without losing my mind—my soul—my heart.

And for the first time since my father's death.

I looked forward to the idea of being lost in something other than my own grief.

Being lost in her.

Chapter Forty

She couldn't walk.

I thought she was just trying to make me puff out my chest and pound it a bit while we walked into the country club.

No.

Not the case.

She was walking funny, and I hadn't even been inside her again.

I smirked and then squeezed her hand. "My mouth made you stumble—I can't wait to feel your thighs clench around my—"

"Dad!" she blurted loudly, cheeks flushed. "You look . . ." Another gulp and stumble. "Great."

He frowned. "Have you been sleeping?"

"She's sleeping just fine," I interrupted and held out my hand. "Slade Rodriguez."

His eyes narrowed. "Ah, the aggressive one." He didn't seem impressed as he looked me up and down, taking my measure as though I were an unfamiliar insect invading one of his vineyards. "Alton told me all about you."

Mack paled. "You guys talk more than—" She stopped herself but I could tell she was angry, hurting.

With a sigh, I forced a smile I wasn't feeling, and only because I knew that Mack needed support and would hate herself if she didn't fix whatever had gone wrong between her and her dad. "Should we sit down?"

Everyone was seated around a circular table, a few bottles of wine were in the middle, and the plates were already set out in front of each chair.

Her mother stood and shook my hand, then pulled Mack into her arms and whispered something in her ear.

Mack quieted. "No, I don't understand."

"Not here." Her mother's smile was bright as she turned her attention to me. "So, I hear you play soccer."

"Yes, ma'am." I put on my best commercial smile and helped Mack into her seat, then took mine. "I just moved here from across the pond."

"You don't have much of an accent," her father said. I loved it when people like him pointed out the obvious: you're not wearing shoes, you don't look like a soccer star, shouldn't you be taller?

I gritted my teeth. So far things were not going how I'd planned. I could usually charm the silver off a coin. "Yes, well, my mother's American. I spent a lot of time in the States."

They both nodded as if that explained everything.

I turned to Mack, who'd suddenly gone motionless. "Alton."

Seriously? This guy again? He needed a warning alarm! I watched as he moved to sit down next to us.

His hair was slicked back, his pants were fucking ironed and starched to death, and his button-up went all the way up to the top button—he looked like a tool. I'd never wanted to punch someone so bad in my entire life.

One-testicled piece of shit probably didn't even know what a G-spot was.

I made a mental note to show Mack later—without the watchful eyes of her parents scrutinizing us—and glared at Alton as harshly as I could.

204

"Mack, don't make a scene. You're obviously still upset over what Alton said. I brought him here to apologize to you."

Good thing I'd invited myself.

I cleared my throat. "Did he actually tell you what he said?"

Alton sat straight, hands in his lap. His eyes roamed over the table before he answered. "I don't believe it's appropriate for polite company."

"Because it wasn't fucking polite," I snapped.

Her mother let out a little gasp behind her hand like I'd just announced I kill puppies for fun, while Mack scooted her chair closer to me.

"Is he your bodyguard now?" Alton asked, looking between us. "Or should you come clean about your behavior?"

"My . . . behavior?" Mack looked genuinely confused. I was with her on that one. What the hell was this prick getting at? "I'm sorry, you must have mistaken me for some other upstanding citizen. My behavior is none of your damn business."

"Mack—" Her father sighed. "Alton is here to fix what's been broken. You should be happy to put everything behind you!"

"I would put it behind me if you gave me time and didn't force him to speak to me, and didn't defend him when he called me a whore!"

Her mom's eyes widened as Alton's jaw dropped. "It wasn't—"

Her father craned his neck toward Alton. "You said it was a simple insult taken the wrong way."

"It was." Alton narrowed his eyes.

"This is bullshit." I held my hands in the air. "Sir, no disrespect, because clearly you've built an empire by reading people and being business savvy, but this guy is a fucking idiot. He's playing you. I'm going to just go out on a limb and assume he wants you in his pocket because he wants deep pockets and power. But he announced to an entire restaurant, and with media present, that your daughter spread her legs for me, then accused her of sleeping with another player—which was completely untrue. It may not seem like a big deal to you. People say horrible things—but when it's said about someone like Mack, someone so pure and beautiful, and clever, and . . ." Mack's eyes filled with tears. "So fucking strong . . . well, that's not right. The fact that you didn't fire his ass the day he walked out on her isn't just alarming— it's abhorrent. And the fact that you didn't stand by your daughter the minute she came to you for support—that's inconceivable."

Her mother's jaw dropped.

And then her father stood, turned, and looked at Alton, really looked at him as Alton opened his mouth to speak.

"Don't." He held up his hand and then looked back at me for a crazy minute like he was deciding if he liked me or not. Without looking back at Alton he said, "Pack your bags."

"You can't be serious!" Alton roared. He glared at Mack. "You bitch!"

I was out of my seat before Mack could stop me.

Thankfully, her father grabbed me before I could launch myself against Alton's face.

"It's not worth it, son."

His strong hands held me back, calming me.

And mentally crumpled like the sad human I was.

Son.

Son.

Son.

Memories flashed.

I squeezed my eyes shut against them.

And then shook my head as Alton kept hurling insults at me, her family, Mack . . .

" . . . wrongful termination!" he roared. "I'll sue you. I'll sue all of you!"

Her father made a motion with his hands and two security guards came over to our table and grabbed Alton by the arms.

"Don't fucking touch me!" he snarled. "You think I stayed with her because I loved her? It was the easiest way to the top!" An evil smile crossed his face. "So innocent and stupid." He jerked away from one of the security guys. "I wasn't saving shit for you—I was just too busy fucking someone else."

Her father threw the punch this time.

While Mack covered her mouth with her hands.

Her mother started chugging her champagne with wide eyes.

Alton arched backward and went sailing to the floor.

"It's really been such a rough week for that guy." I grabbed the bottle of wine in the middle of the table and handed it to Mack. "Just an idea, but if you thrash this over his head, nobody's going to judge you." I nodded encouragingly.

She took the bottle with tear-filled eyes and then gave me a watery smile. "I was thinking more along the lines of ripping out his only remaining testicle."

Alton was carried out.

Ice was brought for Mack's dad's hand.

Not the strangest dinner I'd ever been a part of, but a close second.

"So, son." Her dad looked at me earnestly. "I owe you an apology."

"Let me take your daughter on a date and we're even."

He cracked a smile. "Like I could stop you."

I just shrugged.

"Alright, Mack . . . stay out of the tabloids this time."

I winced. "We'll try . . ."

"You?" He pointed at me.

I nodded. "Yeah, unfortunately."

"Just how famous of a soccer player are you?"

The table fell silent and then Mack squeezed my hand and kissed the back of it. "Dad, he's the best in the world."

Chapter Forty-One

"So that wasn't awkward or weird at all. Sorry about all the hugging, my dad's a hugger." She sighed as we walked into the stadium.

I'd told her I had dessert planned for us.

Her eyes had lit up like the dessert was going to be of a physical variety, so when we came to the stadium I knew she was curious about what I had planned.

"I didn't mind," I said honestly, and I didn't. Hugging was intimate—my dad had been a hugger, it reminded me of him. "I can't believe he asked me to go golfing with him." I hoped to God Alton somehow crashed our bonding time and I could beat him with my wood.

Mack grinned up at me. "Do you even know how to golf?"

"Please." I snorted. "I can handle all balls, even my own, big shock. I know, let it sink in for a minute."

She slapped me playfully on the chest. I caught her hand and kissed her fingers.

"I'm sorry for being a dick to you. And I'm sorry that I may unintentionally snap back into dickish behavior because I'm me and I have no filter and I just . . . well, Matt calls me a bull for a reason."

"You have no peripheral vision." She sighed. "It's okay, I'll just make sure that all you see is me in front of you so you never have to worry about what's next to you."

"Not gonna work, Mack, not when I want you by my side."

She sucked in a breath as we walked into the dimly lit stadium. "So where's dessert?"

"Dessert one is out there." I pointed to the field. "Dessert two? Right next to me. I'll make sure we're primed and ready for it, though, none of that quick vacation sex . . ."

She ducked her head against my chest as we walked in the dark. I stopped us, checked my phone. "In three, two, one."

A spotlight hit the field.

And a giant piece of chocolate cake sat in the middle with two spoons, two chairs, and a lit candle on the table.

Mack laughed and took off running.

And I just watched her.

I watched her joy.

I watched her live.

The girl who was so worried about dying on the plane. The girl who didn't want the life she had—who needed to spread her wings and fly out on her own.

I wanted that girl. That woman.

I didn't want the one her parents wanted her to be.

I wanted the one who would jump off a cliff because it was scary.

And I was going to make sure that everything we did was for the woman she wanted to be.

Not the one she had become.

I jogged after her. "Initial thoughts? Cute or trying too hard?"

"Cute." She pulled up a chair and reached for the fork. "This feels like we're both breaking in and having a cheat day, I love it."

"Hah, I told Coach ahead of time, but you're right about the cheat day."

She didn't even wait for me, just dug into the cake and took a huge bite that ended up spreading chocolate across her lips. She licked the excess off, and my body jolted at the motion. "This . . . I think I like this better than your mouth."

"Well, cake time is over," I growled, then reached for the plate.

"I'm kidding!" She licked her lips again. "Tell me you baked this and I'm never letting you go."

"Hah, I didn't." I lowered my voice. "My, um, my mom did."

Her fork clattered to the table before she picked it up again and stared through me. "Your mom?"

"Yeah, I kind of texted her and asked for a favor and then blurted out that there was this beautiful girl I wanted to win over after being the jack of all asses, not that I needed to since she'd already guessed weeks ago that I had someone in my life I wanted."

"I see what you did there." She pointed the fork at me. "Keep talking . . ."

"Her next text was a simple 'Chocolate, and when do you need it?'" I laughed.

"Your mom's a genius, can I . . ." Her eyes darted away from mine. "Can I maybe meet her someday?"

I grinned. Loving the way she asked if she could meet my mom, like I didn't want that more than anything. "You can meet her any day you want. She doesn't live far from me." I cleared my throat. "It's, uh . . . it's been hard since my father's . . . death."

Mack reached her hand toward mine and gripped. "I'm so sorry."

"I need to say something. You asked if you were easy and it got me thinking. I know we both swore we wouldn't talk about that night, but I also promised not to kiss you and I broke that rule several times already. I just"—I exhaled—"need to get this off my chest."

Her nostrils flared, her breathing deepened.

"It wasn't a one-night stand for me," I confessed. "I know I said that in the beginning . . . accused you of . . ." I sighed. "I can still smell your skin."

She tilted her head. "Because I'm sitting across from you?"

"No, not like that." I searched for the right words, probably making a complete mess out of everything. "I mean, I could still smell your skin, I could still taste you . . . weeks later. You'd been a part of me, and I felt so guilty that I still thought about you instead of my father. I blamed you for his death even though you didn't do anything. I blamed you for me not getting to hear his voice again." I held her gaze even though I was terrified of what I might see in her eyes. "I didn't want to blame myself, it hurt too much, and then the guilt just ate away at me, the guilt that I should be mourning him—not still dreaming of you."

"Slade." She took a deep breath, and her tongue flicked her upper lip. "It's okay to live your life while you mourn, and it's okay to feel guilty. It's okay to miss him, to give yourself permission to grieve. And I don't blame you for blaming me. I'll take it." A tender smile lit her face. "If it makes it easier to deal with—I'll take the blame, I'll take it all."

I stood. Walked over to her chair. Pulled her to her feet and kissed her hard. Imprinted my mouth on hers.

"No," I said between heated kisses. "You don't need to take the blame, but the fact that you'd be willing is enough for me to want to show you how much I care about you, how much I want to see where this can go if we let it—if we trust each other."

She wrapped her arms around my neck. "Trust, huh?"

"Yeah, trust." I held her close. "Think you can trust me?"

"You'll have to prove yourself there, Mr. Rodriguez."

I reached down and swiped the chocolate frosting off her plate, then leaned in and whispered, "Count on it."

I pressed the chocolate to her cheek and patted it there.

"Slade!"

I ran like hell.

She chased me.

And when she wasn't even close to catching me I stopped, turned, and held my arms open wide.

She hopped into them and I licked the chocolate from her cheek and slid my tongue across her jawbone and lips. "You taste so good I'm tempted to take a bite." I nibbled her lower lip, sucking more chocolate from her mouth. Her sugared tongue was so sweet I wanted more. I cupped her cheeks gently with both hands, diving past her lips again for taste after taste, and when the chocolate was gone—I didn't stop.

She melted against me.

The smell of fresh grass and the stadium mixed with the taste of her—it was something that I would never forget, something that would haunt me until I was a cranky old bastard talking about the good ol' days.

And one very specific day.

The day I kissed Mack on the field in the middle of the stadium—the night I promised I wouldn't let go again, the night I realized that if that smell of fresh grass, the feel of being in front of crowds of people, went away.

But I still had Mack.

It would be more than enough.

She swayed against me, her mouth still open, her lips parted like she couldn't get enough as she returned my kiss. The faint scent of chocolate hung between us.

A sizzle of awareness crackled.

"Mack," I rasped, pulling away. "Thank you for not giving up on me."

She sighed.

It sounded like a good sigh.

But I braced myself for rejection—God knew I deserved it.

"I just have one question."

"Alright . . ."

She leaned in, face completely serious, eyes locked on mine. "Have you had sex on this soccer field yet?"

It took me a few seconds to respond, and then my brain was going a million miles a minute. "First off, I would never have sex with one

woman while the taste of the one who got away was still on my tongue."
Her breath hitched. "Second, Matt said not to do anything stupid."
She nodded. "And third . . ." My eyes fell to her chest as she slowly
pulled the straps of her dress over her shoulders. "Third," I repeated
like an idiot.

"Third." She nodded. The dress was past her shoulders, then her
hips, a wiggle here, a wiggle there. I was hypnotized by the sway of
those hips, the faint scent of her arousal.

"Yeah, my third . . ." The dress hit the grass. I would never get that
vision out of my head: white sundress on green grass, gorgeous woman
in nothing but a nude thong in front of me. "Point." I finally got it
out. "My third point was that . . ." She tilted her head, then arched her
back, giving me an incredible view of her breasts. "Um, third, and um,
fourth points?"

"Yeah?"

"Fuck it, I have no idea why I'm still talking, get over here." I
reached for her elbow and pulled her close, then pulled my shirt over
my head, my movements by no means seductive or slow.

Everything was jerky—fast. Because my body wasn't going to last
without hers—in fact, I was sure any minute I would just combust all over
the field. They'd dedicate that small patch of grass to my sad, lust-filled
body and joke about it for years.

I kicked off a shoe.

It narrowly missed the table.

"No wonder you like kicking balls," she teased between soul-wrecking
kisses. I was torn between wanting to kiss her and wanting to get naked.
It was a problem.

"I'm good at . . . kicking," I said dumbly as my trousers finally
made it to the ground.

She laughed. "I like you this way . . ."

"Stupid?" I offered, gathering her up in my arms.

She laughed. "Not stupid, just . . . eager."

"So. Eager." I ducked my head, pressing a kiss below her ear, trying to slow my body down even though it was a losing battle. Blood pumped south. All it took was kissing her and my dick was ready to pound nails.

"There's no cameras or anything in here, right? Filming us?" She looked around the darkness.

"Wait here." I pressed a finger to her lips, then walked back to the table, put my hand in the spotlight, and pulled out the tablecloth with one fluid motion.

Everything stayed in place.

And I had something to cover her up with.

"Wow, and a magician." She hugged her arms to her chest.

"Party tricks. We all have them. You should see me open a champagne bottle."

She just laughed.

It was a nervous laugh.

Maybe I'd waited too long.

Or maybe she was just worried that I was going to turn into a giant prick once I got what I wanted—but that's why it was necessary. I wanted her to see that it could be different.

That the ending was going to be completely and totally different from last time.

"Here." I draped the tablecloth around her shoulders and then grabbed her hand and tugged her toward the stairs leading up to the seats.

I sat on the first step and held open my arms. "Sit on me."

With a small nod, she slowly hung one leg around me and then the other. She didn't lower right away, just locked eyes with me. Straddled me.

She was in suspension over me.

Her back to the rest of the world.

The tablecloth covering everything.

"Why the hesitation?" I teased as my cock strained toward her in an almost painful way. The cold of the metal stairs stung my skin.

"I just like making you wait—think of it as a training exercise in not always getting everything you want when you want it." She winked.

"Fine." I put my hands behind my head and shrugged. "Wait all you want, but we both know you're suffering too. You can be patient and I'll be here, I'll wait." I lowered my voice. "But your body doesn't lie." My eyes drank in her erect nipples and the rise and fall of her chest as I looked my fill of her narrow hips and strong legs. "I know your legs and thighs are starting to tremble, I know you're thinking about what it would be like to be filled so completely that you see heaven. I know that your core's getting hotter and hotter, ready to weep for me." I reached between her legs, spreading her apart with my fingers. "So . . ." Her body swayed. "The question is, how long do you think you can take it? Because I'm a patient man when it comes to everything in my life—except you. Not because I can't be—but because why the hell would I want to wait to devour every inch of you and make you mine?"

She leaned down, her lips brushed against mine as she gripped me in her hand and led me where she wanted me. Those few brief seconds, being touched by her, being guided—the most erotic in my entire life.

Because it was Mack.

And Mack—was all I wanted.

All I needed.

My tip brushed against her heat.

I gritted my teeth to keep from slamming into her.

I focused on our kiss instead.

On the way my mouth moved in sync with hers—I inhaled her scent, dug my fingers into her skin.

And when she sank all the way onto me with a gasp . . . and wrapped her arms around my neck, fisting her hands into my hair, gripping it so hard that I felt a sharp sting from her nails—I waited.

I memorized that moment.

That feeling.

I etched it on my heart.

"Why do you feel so good?" she whispered as she started to move. I gripped her hips and guided her pace. "Why? And if you say it's because you're Slade Rodriguez—" She clenched her teeth.

I moved my hands to cup her face as she increased her tempo, allowing me deeper inside her.

"Mack, I was going to say . . ." I clamped my jaw and rode out a wave of pleasure that stole my breath. "I feel good because I'm yours."

Our mouths collided in a crescendo of tongues and teeth. I braced my arms around her, pulling her closer, pumping my hips with each kiss. She met each thrust.

"Right there . . . right . . ." She shook her head like I was making her dizzy. "Deeper!"

Was tame little Mack yelling at me?

I chuckled and pulled almost completely out only to thrust back in deep, so deep I was seeing stars. "Only with you."

"With me?"

"Only with you has it ever felt like I can't get enough." I parted her lips with my tongue and deepened the kiss as her walls clenched around me, pulling me deeper, making me never want to leave her body.

Her nails dug into my shoulder as she held on, her body twisting in mine. I felt her release, felt every ounce of her drain, saw the look on her face when her eyes closed like her expression—her truth was too much for me to see. Her grip released on my shoulder just as another tremor ran through her.

I rested my head between her breasts and held on tight, running my hands down her back, feeling her muscles, her skin, memorizing the way everything seemed to buzz beneath my fingertips.

"I'm just going to stay like this forever," I whispered.

"I was just going to invite you to," she purred.

I smiled against her skin, trapped in the protection of her body, and closed my eyes. "Come home with me."

She didn't say anything.

I held her tighter. Afraid to let go. "Stay. Please. Stay."

When I opened my eyes and pulled away from her, she had tears in her eyes. No words were said as she nodded her head slowly and then wrapped her arms around me and whispered, "That's all I've ever wanted."

"To stay at my house?" I said, trying to lighten the mood.

"To be asked to stay," she said on her next breath, like she was afraid to speak it too loud.

Chapter Forty-Two

MACKENZIE

Don't be the weird girl who cries after sex.

That was the only thing I could think of as we drove in silence back to his house.

I had one more week before my dad expected me back at the main winery. One more week where I could both work and play with Slade.

I swore to myself to take advantage of that.

But first steps first, don't cry because he said everything that I've been wanting another human to say to me for the last few years.

Alton included.

It was too heavy of a thing to tell him, and though I wanted to trust him—needed to—I was still scared.

Petrified, actually.

It wasn't helping that Jagger's words haunted me, as if I didn't know the real Slade.

It gave me a headache thinking about it.

Was this the real Slade?

This sexy combination of the Slade from vacation and the confident albeit cocky celeb?

By the time we pulled up to the house and got out of the car, my nerves were a wreck, I was overthinking everything.

And it wasn't fair to him.

But he didn't push me.

He didn't even ask me what I was thinking about.

And when Alfie barreled toward the front door, I intercepted him so he wouldn't run into the driveway. "Buddy, you miss us?"

"Of course he does." Slade lowered himself to the ground. "You miss Mom and Dad, buddy?"

I froze.

Slade froze.

Alfie froze—tongue hanging out.

Slade cleared his throat. "You know what . . . I meant . . . in . . . joking. It was . . . a joke."

"It was funny?" I offered, scrunching up my nose.

He actually looked like he was blushing as he stared down at Alfie, as though the dog was the reason for his slipup, and then back over at me. "So, I'll just get the guest bedroom ready for you?"

I frowned. "Wait, what?"

He grinned. "See, that was funny, that reaction right there. You have this very Botox-free line that appears when you get pissed, divides your face right in half, sexy as hell."

I narrowed my eyes.

He whistled. "And paired with that *I'm going to spank you later* look—it's every guy's dream."

"You're a . . ." I gritted my teeth. "Huh, maybe I will take the guest room, Alfie would probably love to share a bed."

"That backfired in ways I didn't predict," he grumbled, getting to his feet and holding out his hand. "Also, if you sleep anywhere but my bed, you're going to have company and not just that of the farting variety." He jerked his head to Alfie. "I mean you, buddy."

Alfie whined and turned in a little circle. I laughed while Slade locked the doors and then wrapped his arms around me from behind, drawing lazy kisses with his tongue down my neck.

I shivered.

"See, that's the response I love . . ." He tugged my ear with his teeth. "You're so damn responsive for me—how the hell am I supposed to keep my hands off you?"

"You're not." I turned in his arms.

He devoured my next words, walking us backward toward the stairway. "I want more of you . . . I want all of you."

"You have all of me."

"I want it all the time. I want all of you every second. I want to hear you scream my name so loud your voice goes fucking hoarse. I want every step you take to be a reminder that I've been inside you, that I'm between your thighs." He oozed sexuality, his powerful body bracing me against the stairs, his golden eyes wild as he flattened his palm against my ass and jerked me forward. A tremor of want rippled down my spine as he lowered his head and coaxed my mouth open with his velvet tongue. "I'm not done yet. We're not done."

I exhaled against his lips. "Good."

Growling, he pulled me into his arms, our mouths knocked together in frenzied heated kisses that had me rubbing myself shamelessly against him. I grabbed two fistfuls of his hair, deepening the kiss as he braced himself against the wall.

"Keep doing that and Alfie's going to see you naked." He swallowed another scorching kiss as we stumbled into the bedroom.

Slowly, he set me on my feet.

I'd never seen a man's eyes so eager, so full of temptation and power. He was a perfect box named Sin—and I was about to fall.

Again.

My blood buzzed in my ears as he dipped his head. His mouth didn't touch mine, but the inches between our lips were so electric that I swayed toward him.

And then I was hit with cold air as he lifted my dress over my head and tossed it to the floor.

Before I could utter a word, he gripped my thong in a fist and ripped it from my body. "You won't be needing this tonight."

"What about tomorrow?" I licked my suddenly dry lips.

He just grinned. "Don't get ahead of yourself, wildcat, I'd hate for you to bite off more than you can chew."

My heart fluttered in my chest.

I pressed a hand against my skin to feel its beats—the beats were for him, in anticipation of his touch. Ready for anything he would give me.

His tugged his shirt over his head. My eyes greedily roamed his golden-tanned body and the bulging lean muscles that rippled beneath the surface of the most perfect skin I'd ever seen. He was more. More dangerous, more beautiful. I couldn't look away.

Abs like his shouldn't exist on real humans.

I kept thinking it was a trick of the light.

And then I touched them.

My knees knocked as I swayed and muttered, "Unbelievable."

"You're shaking." He grabbed my hand and brought it to his mouth, kissing each fingertip until he reached my pinkie, and then he linked it with his and tugged me toward the bedpost. "One foot on the bed, one on the floor, try to hold on tight."

I did. Because I wasn't thinking straight, and had he told me to lie facedown in the bathtub and oink, I probably would have done it without question.

I was facing away from him as the air crackled with electric heat between us. I could hear the faint murmur of the TV downstairs, Alfie scratching at the door. The patter of rain lightly falling on the roof. The smell of his aftershave as he moved the air behind me stirred my senses, and I waited for whatever was coming next.

And when I felt his rock-hard body behind me.

When I felt his length press against my skin, the heat burning every inch it touched, I squeezed the bedpost harder. Used it to keep me from collapsing to the floor.

He ran a hand around my ass, rubbing in circles before his brazen lips started nibbling from my shoulder to my neck. He slid his right hand from my hip to my belly button, and pressed down while his fingertips came into contact with my core. I rocked against him.

"Don't close your legs," he whispered, his breath hot in my ear.

"But it's hard not to."

"Trust me, this will feel good."

"Oh, I'm not worried about not feeling good, you always feel good." I closed my eyes tight as he toyed with me. I gripped the bedpost, my nails probably digging into it in an effort not to collapse against him or pull my legs together.

"Are you ready for more?" I felt myself on his fingertips as he dragged them back across my stomach and thigh, bracing my hips with both hands. And then before I could utter another word, he slid into me.

Filled me completely.

"This is . . ." I let out a moan when he started to move. He turned my chin back toward him and swallowed my next sentence as we moved in sync. I surrendered in a wave of pleasure. With the rain pounding overhead.

With the one man who'd hurt me more than anyone ever could.

I surrendered.

And I knew he could feel the minute I did.

The minute the very last piece of the puzzle righted itself.

The minute I told myself I was his and he was mine.

With our bodies joined and waves of pleasure rocking between us like a torrential storm. He urged me on with each thrust, with each wild touch, sending me into fits of arousal until it was overwhelming.

"Let go, Mack," he said between kisses. "It's time to jump."

With tears in my eyes I kissed him back and surrendered my body, my heart.

Everything I had. "Yours."

A smile graced his lips as he kissed me and then kissed me harder, and then with each punishing thrust he whispered my name like it was the only word he knew.

"Mack." He clenched his teeth. "My Mack."

And for the first time in my life—it felt like I wasn't going to jump and have to catch myself.

I had someone by my side. Just as eager to take the leap.

Just as willing.

To catch me after the fall.

Chapter Forty-Three

SLADE

I was afraid to fall asleep.

It was the stupidest thought that I could have in my head. But just because something was stupid didn't mean the thought magically went away or that you didn't obsess over it until you've convinced yourself all hell is breaking loose, and suddenly that one errant thought turns into complete insanity.

That was why I slept like shit.

Why every time I closed my eyes, I'd jerk awake.

Just to make sure she wasn't gone.

To make sure it wasn't a joke.

A way to get back at me.

When I finally did fall asleep, it was fitful.

And when I woke up.

It was in an empty bed.

My chest tightened as I put on a pair of sweats and searched the bathroom . . . no trace of her.

Maybe she went home to change?

I checked my phone.

Nothing.

My door was open. She'd probably fed Alfie before she abandoned me. I clenched my teeth as I slowly made my way down the stairs.

To the smell of bacon.

I sprinted into the kitchen.

And came upon the most beautiful scene—one that would be seared into my brain for life.

Gorgeous woman.

Cooking bacon.

Long, golden-brown hair hung halfway down her back, kissing my black shirt from the other night; it barely covered her naked ass. Ripping that thong was one of the best choices I'd ever made.

I smiled and leaned against the wall, crossing my arms as she did a little dance in front of the stove and twirled.

Alfie stared up at her with complete adoration and obsession, then stared me down like I was actual competition.

When I took a step toward them.

He let out a growl and rubbed his fur against her bare legs like he was trying to remind her how soft he was.

"Don't be territorial, Alfie, she still loves you," I said in a sleep-filled voice as I wrapped my arms around her from behind. "You look sexy in my shirt."

"I'll be even sexier once it smells like bacon."

"My exact thoughts." I chuckled against her neck. Her skin smelled like a mixture of my Opium cologne and soap. I grinned as I placed another kiss below her ear, then reached toward the skillet.

She smacked my hand with the spatula. "Not yet."

"Ouch!" I jerked away. "But it's done."

"It barely has any crispy!" she argued, eyes wide.

I held up my hands. "Did you just say it barely has any crispy? What the hell is crispy?"

"You know." She turned to the other skillet with eggs and stirred. "The crispy parts, the crunchy ones that snap in half and almost taste burnt."

"Woman, if you burn this bacon—"

"Call me *woman* and I'm burning more than the bacon." She allowed her gaze to drift below my waist, and I suppressed a cringe.

"Mack . . ." I braced her with both hands. "Please don't burn the bacon—or my penis."

She tilted her head. "What made you think it was your penis?"

"You looked down, you pointed, you smelled like rage and testosterone."

She burst out laughing. I decided that was how I wanted to wake up from here on out, with the sound of her laugh and the smell of bacon. "Yeah, okay, go sit down."

"Mack, you don't have to serve me, let me—"

"I like taking care of you," she said softly, and then her cheeks flushed as she looked away.

I sighed. God, I'd been such a dick. "I like it when you take care of me too . . . because I'm well aware I don't deserve it, not one bit."

Mack cupped my cheeks between her palms and pressed a hot, open-mouth kiss against my lips. "Bacon will solve everything, including the fact that you have that look in your eyes."

"What look?" I shrugged. "I'm just tired because I was in bed with an insatiable woman who takes direction too well and screams until her voice goes hoarse. Thought poor Alfie was going to break down the door at one point. You sounded like you were either getting murdered or having the best night of your life."

Mack threw a napkin at me. "Very funny. And the look that says you're thinking about skipping practice. You only have a few minutes before you need to show up, and you guys have your first game soon."

"Memorized my practice schedule?" I grinned.

She scowled. "I see that sex doesn't change your winning personality or inability to tamp down that ego."

"If anything, it makes it worse," I teased, smiling more in those few brief minutes than I had in weeks. "Are you going to paint your face and wear my jersey? Because I have to admit, I'd love that—would love it even more if you flashed me."

She grabbed a plate, piled it high, and shoved it into my hands. "No face painting because I'll stand out, and I hate . . ." She frowned. "I don't really like attention after the whole . . ."

With a curse I was pulling her into my arms. "Women like you should never have to hide—don't let that dick take your strength. Don't let him win."

Tears filled her eyes. "I'll . . . try, it's just . . . hard."

"He's a dumb jackass with one testicle—you really think he should have the upper hand in any situation? I doubt he can even walk in a straight line without stumbling on account of his uneven balls, bet the guy even wears special shoes so he looks taller."

"You finished?" She grinned.

"For now." I let out the breath I'd been holding. "He deserves to get punched in the face every day for leaving you at the altar." I shrugged, thankful the bastard had no brain cells and didn't go through with it, his loss, my gain. "Now I'm done."

"You volunteering as tribute?"

"I'd probably do it at a different time every day so he could never mentally prepare for the punch—I imagine he would eventually just go insane and die alone." I nodded encouragingly.

She patted me on the shoulder. "Eat your bacon and go to practice."

"Come with me."

"I have Alfie."

"Bring Alfie."

She rolled her eyes. "I need to finish dishes, and I noticed that the laundry needed—"

"Excuses." I grabbed her hand. "Come with me to practice. You can watch with Alfie—then during break we can grab lunch. Please."

She made a face and then slumped. "Lunch, no practice, and somewhere nobody would expect us to be, the last thing I need is to be on every magazine in the world . . ." She made a face. "Again."

"If the worst happens, we'll just run Jagger over with your car, problem solved. He'll be all over the news, and we'll be old news, and really, I don't mind driving . . ." I winked.

"Shocked." She grabbed a piece of bacon and tugged it between her teeth. Waves of jealousy mentally attacked that bacon as she let out a moan. One that wasn't for me, but for a dead pig.

Lucky pig.

Even Alfie sighed.

"Come," I tried again.

She let out a sigh that said she was giving in and then straddled my lap as she sat down, wrapped her arms around me, and whispered in my ear, "I like waking up with you."

"Does that mean yes?" I braced her hips with my hands.

Our foreheads touched. "That depends."

"On?"

She pulled back, uncertainty in her eyes. "Just tell me now, so I know."

"I'm completely lost."

"Was it . . . am I . . ." She bit down on her bottom lip. "I'm a grown woman, I can handle the truth, but I need you to tell me now."

"What am I telling you?" I whispered. "That you're beautiful? That I can't get enough of you? That I'm going to be dreaming about your thighs wrapped around me during practice?"

Her lips parted briefly. "No. That. I mean." She smiled. "I was just hinting that if this was a one-time thing—it's okay to tell me."

"I want you more than once. I took you more than twice." I pressed a kiss to her cheek. "It wasn't a one-night stand in Mexico, it's not a one-night stand now. I'm not doing this to get you out of my system— if anything, I'm obsessed with keeping you in my system, in my soul, in my blood. How's that for a confession?"

She pressed her lips together and then full-on smiled. "Pretty good, could use some work, but you still have jackass-like tendencies, so I'm forgiving."

I smacked her on the ass, then squeezed. "You'll pay for that later."

"Counting on it," she teased, crawling off me and grabbing another piece of bacon, nipping it with her teeth while she started humming and moving around the kitchen.

Unease rippled through my body.

Because the last time things felt this good—this . . . perfect. Was when I walked in on my best friend and fiancée doing reverse cowboy.

"You should hurry up." Mack poured herself another cup of coffee.

I jumped to my feet. "Don't forget lunch."

She was mid-sip so just waved while I ran back to the room to get changed.

And the feeling?

The dread.

Followed me all the way to the stadium.

Chapter Forty-Four

I gave Jagger a wide berth.

I was afraid if he opened his mouth I would force it shut with my fist and then end up getting pulled into Coach's office.

I didn't hate him.

Hate meant you wanted to kill someone.

And I'd like to think all the sex tamed me a bit, or at least my thoughts. Though I wouldn't exactly be upset if his dick just fell off and got run over by a semi.

"There a reason you're staring at that soccer ball like you want to hump it?" Matt took off his sunglasses and shoved them in his suit jacket. "Because I can leave you two alone if it's necessary—and I signed an NDA, so I can't say shit to the press about your kinky fantasies."

I sighed. "I was thinking, not about humping, just—" I gave my head a shake. "It's nothing, I know it's nothing. I just have a bad feeling."

"A feeling?" Matt repeated, his tone sharp, his expression concerned. "And when did this feeling start?"

"Post-sex. Breakfast. There was bacon, she was half naked and straddling me—"

"I really don't need that sort of detail." Matt held up his hand. "And I've known you for years, you're just gun-shy. Who wouldn't be, after last year?"

I shrugged. "Maybe."

Matt put his hands on my shoulders and pressed down. "Trust me. You're the kind of guy that gets worried when things are going right because he's so damn sure that they're about to go wrong . . . but that's not how the universe works, alright?" He dropped his hands. "So snap out of it and go kick some balls around so I can take your stupid Instagram photos."

I grinned at that. "Hey, that's how I get followers."

"You have twenty million. Do you really need more?" he wondered out loud. "I know it strokes your ego to get marriage proposals and compliments." He changed to a falsetto. "'He's so cute, so hot, I'd let him touch my balls.'"

I made a face. "The hell?"

"Oh, that was last night's message. He was fifty, I'm sure his balls are very hairy and in need of attention—if you want me to reach out I can—"

"Matt."

He laughed. "Fine, go do your thing, I'll snap ten and post one of them in a few hours, alright?"

"I want to look sexy as fuck, Matt!" I joked, turning and running right into Jagger.

He stumbled back.

I stared him down.

He shook his head and sidestepped me.

"What? No hug?" I called after him.

He flipped me off with his right hand and kept walking.

I grinned. "That's what happens when you get the girl."

Matt gave me a look that was more concerned than anything. "You realize it's not just about getting her—it's about keeping her."

"Not gonna be a problem," I said confidently—even though something still felt wrong.

And as I continued running off, doing drills, sprints, I wondered what it would take for the damn feeling to go away.

"Watch it," Jagger growled when I was so lost in thought I nearly ran into him.

"Sorry." I gave my head a shake. "I'm a bit out of it today."

"Sex does that to a guy." His nostrils flared, and he stood there. Like he was waiting for me to deny it.

"Guess it does," I said through clenched teeth. "Not that it's any of your business."

He scowled. "You're going to break her, like you break everything. Why can't you just leave it alone? Leave her alone?"

"What do you mean break her?" I stood with my hands on my hips. "She holds all the cards, not me. I genuinely like her, which is more than I can say about you."

"Funny." He hung his head. "I don't want to be that guy, Slade."

"The asshole?"

"Nah." He shook his head. "The guy the girl comes running to because the one that she really wants breaks her heart. Don't make me that guy. I suck at being that guy."

He turned on his heel and jogged off.

Leaving me wondering what he could possibly know that I didn't.

About Mack.

About my past.

I didn't break things.

If anything, I was the one who still felt broken.

Chapter Forty-Five

"Hey!" Mack walked into the stadium with a bright smile, her brown hair was pulled into a high ponytail, and her eyes actually sparkled. I'd never been the type of guy to get focused on all the tiny little details, but with her, I couldn't help but notice everything.

Even the three freckles near her nose.

The slight dimple on the left side of her face when she laughed really hard.

She had a scar just below her chin like she'd taken a fall when she was little. I could imagine that, a small Mack sprinting through the house and tripping over something.

I watched her make her way slowly across the turf.

She was dressed casually in black Converse, skinny jeans, and a long-sleeve shirt. It looked good on her.

"Hey," I finally called back, waiting for her to step into my arms, which she did, even though I was sweaty. "You made it."

"You're . . ." Her breathing picked up. "Sweaty."

"I hope this doesn't mean we have to break up," I teased, placing a kiss on her nose.

Her eyes flashed to mine. "Break up . . ."

"Wow." I reached for her hand and interlaced our fingers. "Mack, that cuts deep!"

She laughed and leaned her head on my shoulder, despite my sweat. It was like she didn't care. And I loved every bit of it.

"So not only am I not a one-night stand but . . . did you just basically call me your girlfriend? Moving a bit fast for a player, Slade."

"Hilarious." I stopped walking and pulled her into my arms then pressed my mouth against hers, tasting the mixture of coffee and spearmint gum on her tongue. "Be mine?"

"I'm already yours. You know that," her voice whispered softly between our bodies.

"Maybe I just like hearing you say it."

"That's more like it . . . it scares me when your arrogance isn't showing."

"I'm not sure if I'm offended or if that actually makes sense."

She looped her arm in mine. "Trust me, it makes total sense."

"Hah." We walked down the tunnel that led to the locker rooms and parking lot. I didn't miss the stares I got from teammates, with expressions ranging from knowing smirks to complete devastation.

Jagger.

Mack's breath hitched.

I wanted to stand in front of her, guard her from his leering eyes. I wanted to wrap her up in my arms and yell, "Nothing to see here!"

Instead, I chose the opposite of being my typical dick self and kissed her on the forehead. "I need to go shower really quick. Why don't you guys . . . talk."

"Did that hurt to say out loud?" She smiled up at me.

I groaned. "You have no idea. My throat actually hurts, but not as much as my chest . . . stop giving me anxiety, it's not good for my game."

She patted me on the chest. "I think you'll make it."

I sighed. "Just . . . don't let him touch you. Or breathe too much air around your space, and if he says—"

"I'm a grown-ass woman. Go take your shower so you can feed me. Oh, and Slade, you're paying."

I burst out laughing. "A gentleman always pays."

She winked.

It didn't alleviate the panic when she turned to Jagger.

When he got up and made his way toward her, a mixture of anger and sadness filled his features.

I exhaled and turned around.

With every step I fought the need to protect her.

To protect what we had.

To keep him from telling her what she already knew.

I wasn't good enough for her.

Would never be.

Chapter Forty-Six

"Hey." I shoved my hands in my back pockets and rocked awkwardly on my heels. Jagger was shirtless just like Slade had been, his muscles glistened. He was clenching his teeth. I could tell because his jaw looked ready to pop off his face.

Jagger would always be beautiful to look at.

But it wasn't Jagger that I wanted.

"Hey, Mack." He swallowed like he was trying to keep from saying something else, and then he reached out and pulled me in for a hug. "I'm sorry for what I said."

I sighed against his chest, wrapping my arms around his thick middle. "It's not your fault that Slade's jackass tendencies tend to rub off on people closest to him, and you did spend one full week coaching together."

I pulled away grinning.

His smirk was back. "Well, at least he let me keep my hair."

"Your hair?"

"I lost, the bet was to shave our heads, but he somehow convinced the players to make me shave my legs and arms instead. So now I have a high-and-tight haircut too."

"Tell me the truth . . ." He ran his hands over his newly cropped hair. "Did I chase you into his arms? Was it my fault?"

I let out a sigh. "Jagger, you offered friendship—I wasn't ready for more, not after everything that happened between me and Slade, and then . . ." He didn't need the gory details. "Never mind, the point is, no you didn't push me into his arms, but I probably wouldn't have sprinted toward them as fast as I did had you not made me feel stupid, like there was something I wasn't seeing with him. Trust me, when I walked into that house, I knew exactly what he was capable of—but the risk was worth the reward. You can't live in fear, you know?"

His face broke out into a soft smile. "Your maturity's good for him."

"I'll tell him you said so."

"Hopefully, we can still be friends—maybe you'll even tame the beast, crazier things have happened, right?"

"Right."

He nodded and was getting ready to walk past me when I grabbed his hand and whispered low, "One thing that's been bothering me."

"Oh yeah? What's that?"

"You said I didn't have the full story on his ex . . . were you alluding to something I should be concerned about?"

Jagger sighed. "His ex is a piece of work . . . just know . . ." He swore. "Shit, if he ever finds out I told you this he's going to kill me, alright?"

My stomach dropped and then filled with dread only to drop further. "What?"

He looked over my head like he was making sure that Slade wasn't coming out of the locker room. "Look, when you're as famous as he is . . . especially with how big soccer is overseas, they worship you . . . you're not just a celebrity, you're some sort of god. The things he gets offered on a daily basis, the women that throw themselves at him. It's normal to him, it's not normal to someone who isn't in the limelight or in the sport. His ex was the sweetest girl at first. I loved her. Everyone loved her. It made it easy for him to love her. But this life can turn even the best women dark—it ate away at her, the constant attention from other women, the flirting. The emotional cheating. Did he ever touch anyone? No. Did it matter when he was answering texts and Instagram messages? Did it matter when he had photo shoots with women all over him asking to do happy hour after? He didn't see her anymore. He didn't see . . ." He took a deep breath. "Cheating will always be wrong, but she didn't cheat because she ever fell out of love with him—she cheated to make him as jealous as he was making her. And when he didn't notice, she just kept doing it. It was a cry for help. And then it was too late and he just left her. He promised her forever, he gave her a ring. They both messed up, and the media made her the monster. That's all I'm saying. He's poison you don't even know you're drinking until you stop breathing. I wish I was wrong . . ."

"Why is this so personal?" I asked with a shaky voice.

"Fuck." Jagger just shook his head. "Because I dated her first."

"Excuse me?"

"Because," Jagger said through clenched teeth, "before she ever knew Slade—she was with me. Five. Years. She was mine. Engaged. And he ruined her forever."

"But—"

"Everything okay?" Slade walked up behind us and wrapped an arm around me.

"Yup!" I said way too fast while Jagger locked eyes with me one last time and then nodded his head at Slade and walked off.

I tried to stop the shaking.

The overanalyzing.

The stupid worries. Fears. The thoughts.

I didn't talk the entire way to the restaurant.

And when we walked in.

I saw Slade in a different light.

Fame was easy for him.

People asked for autographs.

He gave them.

They wanted pictures?

He gave them.

They wanted to talk soccer?

He handed over his time.

Two hours later, we were finally ordering and he had to be back at the stadium in twenty minutes.

I didn't realize it until I was back in my car, after a kiss goodbye.

His life was soccer. His life was full.

His life . . . didn't allow room for two loves.

Because he didn't let it.

Chapter Forty-Seven

"Right there, Slade, yeah, just like that, and smile!" The photographer, who introduced himself as J, fired off a few more shots. The model next to me wore a bikini bottom and a men's button-down shirt and was holding a motorcycle helmet. I was shirtless, in leather pants that were too tight, and I was sweating.

It wasn't a good sweat.

More like a get-me-the-hell-out-of-here sweat.

Matt gave me a thumbs-up from behind the camera.

And Mack stood next to him, her expression indifferent.

She'd been acting oddly ever since talking to Jagger—and when I approached Jagger about it, the jackass actually looked guilty, like he'd said or done something.

But every time I thought about asking Mack, she'd snap out of it. And it's not like our sex life slowed down.

If anything, it was crazier. I was hardly getting any sleep, and this morning I woke up with her mouth wrapped around me.

I told her it was one of the best mornings of my life.

And I meant it.

So why the face?

"Over here, Slade." J snapped his fingers. "Alright, now lean down and kiss her neck."

I hesitated.

Matt gave me a *What the hell, just do it* look.

And Mack looked down.

Fuck.

This was my job.

They were paying me to do this.

I started sweating even more, my legs dying a slow death in the leather pants and my dick reminding me that it needed blood flow or it was going to fall off in the next picture.

J sighed in irritation. "Slade, her neck, I need a slow kiss, then hesitate and look up."

Screw it.

I kissed her neck and paused.

J snapped a few more photos and cursed. "You look bored. Can you at least pretend you find one of the world's hottest supermodels attractive?"

Hell, I didn't even know her name.

It wasn't important.

She wasn't Mack.

"That your girlfriend?" she asked, peering up at me under long lashes, with bright-blue eyes and lips that had to be cosmetically enlarged.

"Yes." I offered a polite smile.

"So . . ." The model shrugged. "Pretend I'm her."

"I don't think that's—"

"Slade! Are we talking or are we working?" J yelled, then turned to Matt and started firing off words that made Matt's face turn red.

"Sorry!" I called. "I'll do better, I'm just . . . hot."

"Yeah, you are," the model murmured.

My heart cracked a bit in my chest. That had to be the reason it hurt to breathe, the reason I felt like I wanted to cut and run and turn down a ten-million-dollar Gucci campaign.

"Hey, the sooner you do a few good shots, the sooner you can take your girl out for drinks, alright?" The model winked. "Showtime."

She wrapped her legs around my waist and leaned back against the motorcycle.

"Yes!" J snapped more pictures and got closer. "Slade, I want you to straddle the motorcycle and then lean over her, take her bottom lip between your teeth and tug. Be sure to keep your chin thrust so you don't create a double chin."

I prayed Mack wouldn't be like my ex.

I prayed she'd understand that this was part of the job.

And if she didn't understand?

If she hated it?

I'd tell Matt no more campaigns.

It wasn't worth the stress pumping through my body as I leaned over and took the model's plump bottom lip between my teeth and pulled.

I felt nothing.

Nothing except sweat running down the back of my thighs.

Nothing but irritation when she moved her mouth closer and then slid her tongue past my lips, taking advantage of the situation in a way that had me feeling manipulated and guilty all at once.

"Yes, yes!" J shouted. "Damn, that's hot, the angle's perfect, you guys are going to love these." He took a few more snaps over what felt like a lifetime. "Keep kissing, part your lips, Slade, just a bit."

I parted my lips at about the same time the model grabbed my ass and squeezed. At least she wasn't moaning.

"Perfect!" J announced.

I jerked away from her and wiped my mouth with the back of my hand. "Are we good?"

"I think—" He looked through the shots on his camera and then nodded to the team of people behind the set. They gave him an okay. "Fantastic, thanks, Slade, I think the intimacy is what really helped get the passion across."

"Yeah." I felt sick.

Sick to my stomach.

I made my way over to Mack.

Her smile was fake.

I hated it.

Her body language was stiff.

I wanted to run myself over with the set motorcycle.

"Mack," I croaked.

Her smile didn't make it to her eyes as she reached for my hand. I squeezed it tight and didn't let her pull away.

"So, you must be the girlfriend?" Did that model ever quit? What the hell was her name again? Jana? Dana? Did it matter?

"Yup." I wrapped an arm around Mack and pulled her close, sweaty chest and legs be damned. "This is my girlfriend."

"Lucky girl." The model winked, then turned toward me and shrugged. "It was great working with you—let me know if you ever want to go get drinks."

I laughed.

She laughed.

Mack did not laugh.

"That's not going to happen." It came off ruder than I intended.

Matt's eyes widened when I glanced over at him. One message was clear: abort, abort!

"Excuse me?" She put her hands on her hips. "Look, I was just trying to be nice—"

"Nice is saying *good job* and walking away. Nice would be inviting both of us out. You're not trying to be nice." I narrowed my eyes at her. "I have a girlfriend. I love her more than I'll ever love whatever the hell you think you have that's special. I wish I could say it was nice meeting you. I'm disappointed that you're just as vain as every tabloid says you are."

"And you're a fucking dick!" she yelled.

"Hey!" Mack shoved me behind her. "He's my dick, you bitch, walk it off." Then she turned to me. "You ready?"

I burst out laughing. "I don't think anyone's ever claimed me as their dick . . . Mack . . . my heart—"

She smacked me in the chest while Matt stayed behind and tried to calm the angry model, who probably just needed a piece of bread.

I made a mental note to send her cookies with an apology that said *This dick is owned*, or something like that.

Hell, let Matt deal with it.

"I'm sorry," I said once we were back in my dressing room. "I hated that. I hated every part of it. I won't do ads anymore, Mack. I swear, I don't—"

Her mouth collided with mine.

I stumbled backward against the rack of clothes, then righted myself with one of the hangers before nearly falling on my ass. She shoved me onto the couch and unbuttoned my pants.

"Um, Mack?"

"Shut up." She tugged the pants down and then laughed out loud. "I've never seen so much sweat on another human being, and yet I still want to have sex with you . . ."

"Um, thank you?" I offered. "And the lights were hot, and I was panicking that she was going to cop a feel or just tug one of my nuts off and show it off like a prize to her friends."

Mack laughed even harder. "Careful, she can still barge in here, steal one of your nuts, and make a nut shrine out of it."

I shuddered. "Never say *nut shrine* again. I mean it. It makes me lose my erection and my pride all at once."

Mack ran her hands down my stomach, then grabbed the leather pants and peeled them even farther past my knees and my ankles. "We don't want that."

"Me to lose my pride?" I rasped as she leaned over my body, her hair creating a curtain across half her face.

"Your pride could take a few hits—I was talking about this." She lowered her head.

"Slade!" Matt knocked on the door.

"Open that door and I'm killing you!" I roared.

Mack's breath was hot against my burning skin, my dick strained toward her mouth in a painful way that had me lifting my hips toward her.

"Seriously, Slade?" Matt hissed.

"Matt . . . I just need some privacy."

"Yeah, yeah, I bet you do . . ."

Mack snorted out another laugh while I was in serious pain. "It's not funny, I need you. I don't know what good deed I did in this lifetime to deserve your mouth on my cock but   I'll take it. I'll take it every damn day."

Her smile lit up the room as I gripped her by the shoulders, tugged her forward, and kissed her soundly, making sure she knew without a doubt that I was hers—she was mine.

Mack broke away. "Did you mean it?"

"That I was going to lose my erection? Yes. Every word."

She rolled her eyes and then looked away from me. "You said you loved me."

"Love," I corrected. "Present tense. Not past." I cupped her face between my hands and forced her to look at me. "I meant it. And I'm sorry that you had to see me with another woman. I'm sorry that my hands were on her even though they wanted to be on you. I'm sorry that I'm the guy that used to feed off the attention—which just proves how wrong my ex was for me, because I didn't care when she was standing there watching, I didn't care that women threw themselves

245

at me. But with you? I would have walked away from this job and not looked back. I would burn every fucking bridge in this industry for you. I hope you know that."

Tears filled her eyes. Mack gave a jerky nod then pressed another kiss to my lips. It was softer this time, it tasted right. It tasted perfect. I never wanted to stop exploring her. There was always new skin to taste, new angles to try, new ways to make her cry out with pleasure.

And the more she gave.

The more addicted I became.

The more I needed.

I shoved her leggings down at about the same time she positioned herself over me.

"Look at me." I held her face again. "Only me."

She slid down my length, her lips parting with each inch. Filling her was a new experience each time—along with a feeling of coming home.

Mack braced her hand against my shoulder as I tugged her leggings the rest of the way to the floor, sat up, and picked her up by the ass, making it so either leg straddled me on the couch. I took her deeper.

A look of vulnerability crossed her features as she wrapped her arms around my neck, seeking another kiss. One I was more than happy to give her.

I ached for her in a way that bordered on painful.

And she was the only cure for it.

I felt my body throb inside hers, felt every breath she took like it was my own, experienced each wave as she rolled her hips.

Her lips trembled when I kissed her again, an ethereal feeling soared through me when it was me she clung to, when it was me she trusted with everything.

When I had no right for it to be me.

I dug my hands into her backside as her body started to shake.

No words.

I didn't want words between us.

Words you could misunderstand.

But this?

Our bodies joined together?

No misunderstanding. Just trust. Love. And completion. I withdrew from her then welcomed another open-mouth kiss as I drove home.

I felt her whisper my name across her tongue.

I smiled when she came apart all over me.

Body limp, she collapsed against my chest. "Now we're both sweaty."

I ducked my head against her perfumed neck, a mixture of sweat and the lavender body wash she kept at my house.

"Mack?"

"Slade?"

"Don't ever give up on me."

She probably didn't realize how hard that was to say out loud.

Or how much I needed her to replace the one person in my world who had promised to always have my back.

"Promise," she whispered. "As long as you never wear leather pants again."

"I'm burning them later, thought we could celebrate with some wine—since you go back to your old job tomorrow."

Her face fell.

"Hey." I took her chin between my fingers. "None of that, you love your job, just think, we'll both be at work, then we can come home and have food, wine, all the sex, never in that order since sex always comes first, but same idea." I winked.

"Sounds good." And yet again her smile felt forced.

"Are you okay?" I found myself being that guy, the one that was so stupid he couldn't tell what was bothering the woman in his life.

"Slade!" Matt pounded on the door. "I gave you eight minutes. Time to open up."

"Was it eight minutes, though?" I called back. "Could have sworn it was at least twelve . . . eight . . . eight, my ass."

"Weird, I thought it was five?" Mack said with a straight face.

I smacked her on the ass. "Careful there . . ."

She grinned just as Matt hit the door again, with what sounded like both hands.

"Fine, fine, give me a few minutes."

Chapter Forty-Eight

I wasn't being fair to him.

He said he loved me.

Loves me.

And I still had doubts.

Not because of the photo shoot but because of what Jagger said. I wanted to ask him if he took Jagger's girlfriend out from underneath him. I wanted to ask about the pregnancy.

But I felt trapped with knowledge I shouldn't have, all because I wanted to clear things up with Jagger—my fault.

And bringing up something painful that could create a chasm in our new relationship—also my fault.

My time was up, though.

It was the first day I was expected back at my family's winery, and while I was excited to be there at my old job doing what I loved . . .

It also meant I was going to see less of Slade.

What if things changed?

What if he suddenly realized that I wasn't what he wanted?

Or worse, what if I started to turn into one of those jealous girlfriends and pushed him away like his ex had?

I was ready to rip that model's hair from her skull, and the worst part? Every few minutes she'd look over at me with this knowing, manipulative little witch look that had me ready to slap her across the face.

She knew exactly what she was doing.

I was just thankful that Slade wasn't stupid enough to fall for it.

But what about next time?

What about the next photo shoot?

And the next?

What about when the season started up again in a few months?

Agh!

I was going to drive myself crazy.

I needed wine.

Good thing I was walking into a winery!

Slade: Kill it today.

I smiled down at my phone.

Me: I get to drink wine all day—I'll be just fine, but if I need you to pick me up later . . .

Slade: I would love to pick up my drunk girlfriend—only if that means she comes with a brand new bottle of that pinot noir.

Me: Did you just . . . are you talking dirty to me?

Slade: With its effervescent spice, and did I taste a hint of raspberry?

Me: I want you naked. On the bed. With two glasses of wine when I get home . . .

Slade: I'll bring some chocolate for that palate of yours—and Mack?

I was grinning so hard.

Me: Yes?

Slade: I love that you called my house home.

I sucked in a breath. Little prickly tears stung the backs of my eyes as I texted back.

Me: Home is where you are.

Slade: Love you, Mack. Try to stay sober.

I hadn't said it yet.
I hadn't told him I loved him.
And he didn't care.
He just kept telling me he loved me over and over again, and he never hesitated, he never waited for me to say it back.
It was like he couldn't help but love me.
And the very idea of that terrified me.
Because it was the first time in my life that I felt like maybe I was enough—even though it happened to be with a guy who Jagger said not to trust, who'd already proven himself once to be the kind to just leave.
It wasn't fair to hold his past over his head.
I dropped my phone back in my purse with purpose. No more. I wasn't going to do that anymore. It wasn't fair.
"Mackenzie!" Dad stood in the main lobby, his arms opened wide. The room had exposed beams above, with floor-to-ceiling windows on the north end. The patio boasted several outdoor fireplaces. It was both cozy and modern at the same time. And the tasting room? It had leather couches, snacks, and my favorite desk, where I sat and played chemist. "I'm so happy you're home."

He hugged me.

There it was. Home.

Funny how home used to mean my father's arms—it used to mean this winery.

And now? Now it meant Slade.

"I missed this place," I said honestly as Dad weaved us through a small crowd of people. I did a double take when I saw my face briefly on the flat-screen TV. But it was so fast that I told myself I was imagining things.

With a shrug, I followed him through the back to the tasting room, set my purse down, and got to work.

A few hours later my phone went off. I was so immersed in the tasting and feeling this rightness in the world that I ignored it.

It went off again.

Frowning, I looked at the screen.

Slade: Whatever you do, do not turn on the TV.

Slade: It's all just BS.

Slade: I have no idea how they have this information, but I'll get to the bottom of it, I swear. Matt is working on it for us.

Jagger: Are you okay?

My heart sank, I stopped reading texts and just called Slade. His phone went straight to voice mail.

Matt's went straight to voice mail.

So did Jagger's.

Slade: Sorry, was on the phone with Matt. We're fixing this. It looks bad, fuck I don't know how the press knows these things, I don't even know how they know where I live, let alone anything else. Text me when you get off work.

I was shaking by the time I put my phone back in my purse. Tempted to look at the TV or at least search Slade's name on the internet and see what was going on.

But I trusted him.

And if he told me not to look.

I wasn't going to look.

Not until he had time to explain to me why he was freaking out and why, an hour later, his phone still went straight to voice mail.

Chapter Forty-Nine

SLADE

"It's going to be fine," Matt said smoothly as he sat in my kitchen with a cup of coffee. Paparazzi lined up outside the gate.

And words were getting thrown around that made me want to puke. And her name. Her name was everywhere.

Britney Townsend.

And in every fucking article, every newspaper, all I saw was her teary-eyed confession that even though she cheated on me the baby was mine, which was a lie. The baby was Hawk's, but now the press was also under the impression that while she was still engaged to Jagger, I'd swept in and basically stolen her out from under him. Jagger and I had sworn not to discuss her publicly. It wasn't worth the drama or media firestorm that would follow—besides, it had been water under the bridge, they were broken up. Why would someone leak such lies now?

"She's on her way." Matt sighed. "How do you want to handle this?"

"We can sue her for breach of contract. She signed an NDA." I took a sip of the whiskey he'd put in front of me. Damn it, did it always come back to the NDA? "She has pictures of us, man, intimate pictures. Pictures of me naked in bed with her, pictures of Jagger naked with her. It looks bad. She has pictures of my dad she's trying to sell, my family in intimate settings—she's—" I growled low in my throat.

"None of what she's saying is true. She didn't cheat on Jagger with me. That's bullshit. They were completely broken up by then!"

Matt sighed. "Does it matter anymore? She's pregnant, she paints a damning story basically making you look like the guy who steals another guy's fiancée, gets her pregnant, then abandons her in order to get a bigger contract. And your old teammate, Hawk, isn't helping things. He's claiming that the breakup was all a publicity stunt you created to get more money and marketing campaigns."

I swiped my hand across the flowers Mack had put in the middle of the table. They went crashing to the hard tile floor. The sound of glass breaking was almost as piercing as the buzz of the gates as they opened.

I squeezed my eyes shut.

Jagger was the first to walk in the room five minutes later.

Followed by Britney.

She was still beautiful, with long, pitch-black hair, blue eyes, a wide smile, and a dusting of freckles across her nose. She was at least seven months pregnant, but I wanted to throw her out of my house the minute she smiled in my direction.

"Hey, baby." She grinned and rubbed her swollen belly.

"No." I held up my hand. "Hell. No."

Jagger actually coughed behind his hand like he was covering a laugh, which couldn't be right.

Matt flipped over his phone to record, and pointed to the seats.

"Britney, you're aware you aren't allowed to speak to the press about Slade in any way, shape, or form, correct?" Matt asked in a dry tone.

She reached for my hand.

I jerked it back.

Jagger stared straight ahead like he'd rather be burning in hell than sitting in my house. Get in fucking line.

She tilted her head and gave Matt a soft, conniving smile. "I would never go to the press about Slade. I signed an NDA."

NDA—I hated that term.

255

"Besides," she added, "doesn't he have other things to worry about, like Jagger stealing his new girlfriend?"

Jagger crossed his arms. "What the hell happened to you?"

"She's always been like this," Matt ground out. "You two were just thinking with your dicks."

Britney glared. "Shut up, Matt. You're just jealous because you never went pro like they did."

"No, I just think before I stick my prick into a conniving, money-hungry witch. Take that to the press, you psycho."

Jagger ran his hands down his face.

I rubbed my temples with my hands. "If you didn't say anything to the press about us, if you didn't give them those pictures that have been leaked all over the universe, who did?" I wondered out loud. "And why the hell would you say the pregnancy and cheating scandal was a publicity stunt? Cheating should never be a publicity stunt, and you know none of it's true. Matt's right, you've lost it."

She just grinned. "Hawk's out of the picture, I'm your ex-girlfriend. It's the best story ever, you take me back, we raise our baby, and we all live happily ever after."

"Should we invite Jagger in on that too? Maybe let Matt play godfather?" I narrowed my eyes at her. How could I have ever thought she was anything but a vapid, insecure girl with dollar signs in her eyes? She didn't even blink, just lifted her chin like she somehow deserved to be sitting at that table when she'd done nothing but try to break it apart with her bare hands.

The sound of the gate buzzing open alerted me to another visitor. Great.

I groaned into my hands.

Again.

"It's Mack," Matt said in a low voice.

Jagger stood so fast his chair flipped backward.

I stared up at him. I felt my entire face pale. I was bringing her into this, my fault. She wanted out of the press and now they were painting her as the woman who came between me and my pregnant ex-fiancée.

Fantastic.

It wasn't true. But the media didn't care. It sold stories, it got ratings, and right now the fact that Mack was left at the altar only to run away with soccer's newest bad boy . . . the entire story was like an expensive all-you-can-eat buffet.

"Let her in," I whispered.

Matt hit the comm.

I counted the seconds until she parked.

Until she was walking up the stairs like she used to.

Alfie ran to the door.

She greeted him first.

"I always knew I liked that dog," Jagger said to no one in particular.

I gave him a look of disgust.

He gave me a look of pity.

I hung my head in my hands as Mack rounded the corner. "Hey, guys, what's—"

Her eyes fell to Britney.

She would recognize her from the pictures.

And if her face didn't give it away, the belly sure would.

"What's going on?" Her voice shook.

I wanted to wrap her in my arms and tell her everything was going to be okay. I stood, ready to do exactly that, when Britney piped up. "She signed an NDA, like everyone in your circle, right?"

"What?" Mack's voice was small. "What are you talking about? Why does it matter?"

My gut twisted as I looked between Britney and Mack.

Britney looked triumphant.

Mack looked ready to hurl.

"Look," Britney said in an innocent voice, "all I'm saying is Matt and I have ironclad NDAs, Jagger has an ironclad NDA—and this bitch—"

"Watch it," I growled.

"This strange woman"—Britney rolled her eyes—"better have an NDA too. Otherwise, she's the one that leaked something to the press. Easy. She wants attention."

"Easy?" Mack repeated. "How the hell is that easy? I would never do that to Slade, and why would I? I don't need the money, unlike some people!" Mack countered the attack without hesitation.

Attagirl.

I almost cheered for her out loud.

Britney leaned back. "I'm not saying you did anything for money, it just seems suspicious. I mean your motives are your own . . . right, Matt?"

Matt bit out a curse. "Slade, did Mack ever sign anything in reference to Mexico or . . . personal matters?"

"No." I licked my lips. "But I never even told her about me and Britney, about the whole fucked-up love triangle with Jagger. I haven't said a word. I should have." Mack was white as a ghost. "I should have but—"

She shook her head and looked straight at Jagger, who looked equally shocked.

Jagger swallowed and looked away, guilt dripping off every feature. "I may have told her a few days ago."

"What!" I roared. "That wasn't your business to tell!"

"She asked, man!" He jumped to his feet. "I was trying to warn her away from you the same way I warned Britney away, and now look what happened!"

I clenched my fists. "You had no right."

"Neither did I," Mack said in a small voice. "I should have asked you, not Jagger . . ."

I squeezed my eyes shut and faced Mack. "I need you to be honest, Mack. Did you go to the press? I want to believe you. I want to believe this is all just a nightmare."

Her crestfallen expression should have been my answer, but she wasn't saying anything, she just stared right through me like she was paralyzed. "Mack, I need you to talk to me, I need you to tell me."

"It doesn't matter, does it?" she rasped. "I didn't go to the press, Slade. I love you. I would never hurt you. The fact that you even asked . . ." Tears dripped down her cheeks.

"Mack, wait!" She was out the door before I could stop her. Alfie tried running after her, tripping me in the process.

She made it all the way to her car and started it.

I banged on the car window with my palm. "Mack!"

She didn't look at me, just peeled out of my driveway and out the iron gate that she used to drive through with such care.

Cameras flashed.

Paparazzi yelled.

I felt nothing.

I heard nothing.

I walked back inside the house, grabbed the glass of whiskey, and drank the entire thing.

"So . . ." Britney grinned. "Now that *that's* settled . . . I was thinking, we can do a quick press conference, right, Matt? We'll tell everyone we're back together, Mack takes the fall, and Jagger can tell the truth—that he introduced me and Slade and we just hit things off."

"Truth." Jagger snorted out a laugh. "The truth is, you were fucking us at the same time!"

I blinked at him, then at her. "What the hell!"

Britney shrugged. "I wasn't sure Slade was a sure thing, plus he was a player. When I actually got to know him—" She turned to me. "To know you, it was different, so much deeper than what I had with Jagger."

"What bullshit," Jagger said under his breath. "You're lucky you're pregnant, Brit, otherwise I'd be chasing you with my car right about now."

Matt cleared his throat. "Mack wouldn't leak this. She has no motive, nothing to gain. So I'm going to ask you again, Britney . . ."

259

She shook her head. "No, it's her, it has to be her. This will work. The press will forget about it, everything is going to be fine."

"Brit," Jagger asked softly. "Where's Hawk?"

She bit down on her lower lip and looked away. "Gone."

"I see."

"Britney, I can understand you being scared," Matt said in his empathetic voice he used to calm people down. "But pulling people's names through the mud—that's not how we do things."

"No, we just sleep with the help, right, Slade? And punch people at restaurants."

I frowned. "What was that?"

She paled. "I said sleep with the help."

"The other part." I licked my lips. "About punching people at restaurants."

"It was on the news."

"Not the international news," Matt said quickly.

"I follow CNN."

"You don't follow shit." I laughed. "Britney, I'm going to ask you just this once . . . who the hell did you talk to?"

She stared at her hands.

I looked to Matt for help.

He drummed his fingers against the countertop. "How much did you get for the story?"

"A million," she said blatantly. "And another two for the cover of *People*—with Slade. They didn't want Hawk."

I eyed her cell.

The one she'd been gripping like a lifeline.

"Well." I gave her my hand. "I guess that's it. Two million . . ."

Jagger's eyes were bugging out of his head as I stood and helped her to her feet.

"Baby, it's going to be great!" She was practically dancing.

"Yeah, perfect, just one thing. Don't you think we should take a selfie? Like old times? For the Insta feed?"

Vain, crazy woman.

"Yes!"

"My phone's dead. Let's use yours."

She was too busy primping to realize what I was doing. I took the phone, typed in her password, and tapped on texts.

A: I have everything you need but I need my cut too.

A: She was at Jagger's house for two hours.

A: I can't get any good pictures of them in the stadium, too dark. He has a blanket.

A. I want more money. Leave my name out of this. She wouldn't sign an NDA. I know her, she's stubborn.

A: I want half a mil for the information.

B: how do I even know you have it? I want proof.

A· I have the iPad linked to her cell—trust me, I have screen shots and records of everything, and I followed her twice to the stadium. If we both combine the information we have, it will look like she's guilty and we may just get lucky.

B: Agreed. But only one payment.

A: Sure.

I'd seen enough. She was smart enough to at least not charge toward me in an effort to get her phone.

I handed it over to Matt. "Read the texts with her and A."

I turned to Britney. "Who's A?"

Tears filled her eyes. "He said it would be easy!"

"I'm sure he did." I rolled my eyes. "Who's A?"

"I don't know!" she cried. "Alright, he said his name was Alton! That's all I know!"

"Fuck, you should have killed him when you had the chance, Slade," said Jagger, glaring at Britney. "Matt, sorry, man, you're going to have to bail us both out of prison."

Matt shook his head slowly, then glared up at Britney. "Let me deal with this one first, and I'll be right there."

Tears spilled onto her cheeks. "Slade! You don't understand. We were perfect. I messed up. I get that. But Hawk, he's not even in the picture anymore. We can fix this! Just think of the possibilities!"

"Oh, I have," I said with heavy sarcasm. "And it sounds like my version of hell, been there, done that. I'm sorry, and I hope you have a safe pregnancy. But I need you to get the fuck off my property. Now."

"But where will I go?"

"Looks like you got half a mil, Britney, I don't know, stay at a hotel. Better yet, wait for some rich old guy you can sink your talons into, he probably won't even care that you're a lying, cheating whore."

"Watch it!" she seethed.

"Out. Of. My. House."

Matt stood and held out his hand for her to leave. Head high, she said through clenched teeth, "You'll regret this."

The minute the door slammed, Jagger grabbed the whiskey bottle, tilted it back, winced, and said hoarsely, "No regrets."

He handed me the bottle.

I took it without hesitation. "I messed up."

"Yeah."

Another swig.

"Mack hates me."

"Probably."

"I need to grovel."

"Yup."

I narrowed my eyes at him. "You aren't helping."

"I'm sorry," he blurted. "For not telling you that Brit was cheating on both of us. Honestly I hated you at the time, I didn't think you'd even believe me."

I snorted. "I probably wouldn't have."

He sighed. "So what are you going to do?"

"Chase."

Chapter Fifty

MACKENZIE

I couldn't see straight as I drove back to my house. And when I opened a bottle of wine and sat in front of the TV, I realized how bad the situation really was.

The picture they were painting of me wasn't good.

Apparently, I'd known Slade all this time.

They showed old pictures of me and Alton with Jagger, which linked me to Slade since Jagger had introduced Slade to Britney.

They were calling him a serial girlfriend stealer.

Me a cheater.

Alton a hero.

How the hell did Alton come out looking good?

Britney was a total victim.

And Jagger? Well, they just made him look stupid.

The more I watched, the more angry I got.

I dried my tears.

And stared at the reporters, who didn't give a flying rat's ass who they hurt or how long it took to get over the poisonous words they tossed around like candy.

With shaking hands I sent Matt a text from my own phone, not the one I'd been given.

Me: I didn't out them.

Matt: I know that.

Me: I want to do a press conference.

Matt: Um, what?

Me: At the winery. I want to tell my side of the story. We can control the location, we can control everything.

Matt: Are you sure you don't just want me and Slade to take care of this?

I grinned down at the phone, heart still a little bit broken, exhausted, but ready to fight.

I would never have fought for Alton.

And even though I was petrified of the power Slade held over me, I decided I would not be powerless again.

I wouldn't be the girl who would marry just because it made business sense. That girl was gone.

I wasn't going to sit back.

Old Mackenzie would have smiled through her teeth while people hurled insults.

But Slade had changed that.

And I loved him for it.

I loved the Slade that jumped off that cliff with me.

And I loved the Slade that joked with me—that used his anger as a shield and his grief as a weapon.

I loved every part of him.
I loved him more than I loved me.

Me: Tomorrow evening. Don't tell Slade.

Matt: If you guys could please stop telling me not to tell what you're all doing, that would be fantastic. It's hard to keep everything straight. For the record, Alton is the one that outed everyone. He had the password to your old iPad so he could see your emails and texts. Alton got ahold of Britney after stalking Slade online and seeing her picture. They both wanted money—and she wanted Slade back. The plan was to use you as the fall guy and make it look like you were the reason for everything that happened back in Europe. I'm sorry.

I gulped.

Me: And what did Slade say?

Matt: Oh sorry, Slade's in prison with Jagger right now—they went after Alton, more details on that soon!

Me: WHAT?

Matt: Don't worry, they'll get roughed up, I'm sure, but they're fine! Are you sure you really want to do this?

Me: Yes.

Matt: Alright . . . I trust you.

Me: And Slade? What about his trust?

Matt: He let his fear speak for him. I would extend a bit of grace to the guy.

I smiled down at my phone.

Me: I'll be set up at seven p.m. We'll have wine for the press.

Matt: Oh good, drunk paparazzi. Great idea. Bring a Taser!

Chapter Fifty-One

I didn't sleep.

Slade didn't text.

I tried not to be heartbroken.

I ignored everything and everyone and powered through my day, and when my dad approached me with arms wide—that was when I almost lost it.

I held on by a thread.

And by the time I made it to the press conference, I was a giant ball of nerves and stress.

Matt waved me over to the stage. He'd been talking to my dad for what felt like hours as the press made their way in, enjoying free wine and appetizers.

I slid my hands down my white skirt and adjusted the collar to my black blouse. The idea was to go for classy, not home wrecker, not the sort of girl that would just sleep with a soccer star in order to make a name for herself outside of her father's business. I was my own woman. I had no reason to go after him, no reason to take what wasn't mine.

I reminded myself that it didn't matter. I had money and my family's backing. I hadn't needed to expose him or anyone, and Britney was the one to blame for all of this—well, she and Alton, may he rot in whatever hole he was hiding in. On top of it all, they needed to know that I never knew Slade. I wasn't the one who came between them. I was the one who hopefully saved him—just like he saved me.

"Ladies and gentlemen, we'd like to start," Matt said into the microphone. I wiped my hands on my skirt again and exhaled slowly.

I felt the sting of tears.

And hated it.

Hated that the one man I wanted to see.

Hadn't so much as texted me.

Had broken all contact with me.

I squeezed my eyes shut, opened them, then slowly made my way to the front of the room. I hated the public eye. Hated it. They had thrown me to the wolves after my failed wedding.

I wanted vengeance against Alton.

For myself. For our reputations.

But now that I had Slade? If I even had him?

I wanted peace more.

I wanted to prove to him that I wasn't going to walk away, that even if he did, I'd fight for him, for us.

"Hi, everyone," I said into the microphone. "It's safe to say you probably all know who I am by now."

The audience chuckled.

"I met Slade Rodriguez—"

"On a plane," came a loud voice from the back of the room.

My eyes roamed the strange faces until they fell to his.

The one I loved most.

He stood, and beside him was a beautiful woman with silver hair and kind eyes I recognized from family photos, who patted him on the hand and winked at me—his mom.

He was wearing a three-piece suit, and his golden eyes were locked on me with such warmth I almost burst into tears.

"Yeah," I said, voice shaky. "A plane."

He made his way up to the stage. He stood next to me and held my hand. He squeezed it tight, and he leaned in and kissed my cheek in front of everyone, like he was claiming me.

And then he whispered just so I could hear, "Partners jump together."

I hugged him.

I couldn't help myself.

He held me so tight it was hard to breathe. "I love you."

"I know." He chuckled.

"No, I really, really love you. I think I fell in love with you the minute we jumped."

"Really?" He grinned. "Because I fell in love with you the minute you lectured me on wine."

The crowd laughed.

I pulled away from him and heat bloomed across my cheeks.

"As you were saying, Mack . . ." He winked.

I smiled so bright, on cloud nine as I explained. "The plane lost an engine. I was terrified I was going to die. I may have shaken Slade awake. I honestly had no idea who he was, just that he was nice to look at."

"Gee, thanks." He laughed, making me feel warm all over, it was so easy for him, wasn't it? And yet, I realized at his side, it felt easy for me too.

Everyone in the crowd was grinning so wide it was almost comical.

"I asked him one thing . . ." I whispered.

Slade tucked my hair behind my ear. "She asked me what I would do differently, just one thing."

"And then I kissed him."

"I kissed her back." He smiled. "And for the first time since my ex-fiancée cheated on me—I felt something other than anger."

"And I felt something other than fear," I added.

Slade turned to the cameras. "We spent the day together. Those memories are some of the best of my life, only to be topped when

Mack came back to the States. I was a complete ass to her after my father's death, blaming her presence for the reason I didn't answer his phone call . . . and she just . . . supported me."

A tear slid down my cheek, then another.

He continued. "She fought back, she told me what a jackass I was, she let me feel my pain, and she fed me . . ." Everyone burst out laughing. "I'm serious! She fed me casseroles, brought me coffee. She took care of my dog, but really, she was helping me heal bit by bit, until I finally pulled my head out of my ass and realized that this woman, this beautiful, talented, amazing woman was right in front of me . . . all I had to do was reach out." He cupped my chin. "She was the partner my father always promised I'd find."

"And Slade was the adventure I always wanted," I said with a shaky breath.

He didn't turn away from me. "There's been a lot said about me, about Mack—but this is our truth. I love her. I love her so much that I would quit soccer if she asked, I'd walk away from my life's greatest joy. Because without her, there is no joy. Because somehow I was lucky enough to get her, and she fulfills me in ways soccer never will. She's everything."

I wiped the tears from my cheeks.

"Mack . . ." He knelt down on one knee. "Marry me."

"What!" I exploded.

"Marry me." He smiled so bright, then dug into his pocket and pulled out a five-karat solitaire that looked like it had its own zip code. "Marry me in Mexico, let me take you back to the vacation we should have had together—marry me on our cliff. Be by my side . . . and forgive me for ever doubting your love and trust."

It was too soon. Logic told me this. My own stupid rationale told me this.

But it felt right.

I'd known Alton my whole life. And it had been wrong.

I'd known Slade for weeks—and it was so right my heart came alive in my chest.

"YES!" I shouted as he jumped into the air and twirled me around, kissing me soundly in front of all the cameras as they snapped our picture.

Matt whistled from his spot in the room.

And right next to him. Holding Alfie.

Was Jagger.

With a smile on his face.

Epilogue

MACKENZIE

Waves crashed against the rocky cliff. The salty warm breeze wrapped itself around me and then strong arms were pulling me back against an even stronger chest. Slade's mouth pressed kisses down my neck. "Was it everything you wanted?"

I smiled and let out a satisfied sigh. "Well, the groom didn't bail and I only cried happy tears, so what do you think?"

"Sorry that Alfie went the wrong way down the aisle."

I burst out laughing.

"And"—his voice cracked with amusement—"sorry that Jagger felt the need to stand up in the middle of the ceremony just because he wanted to freak you out."

I laughed even harder and turned in his arms. "I've never seen you look so angry."

"Bastard's still upset about shaving some of his hair."

I shrugged. "It just makes him look more mysterious."

He narrowed his eyes. "Second thoughts?"

"Nope." I wrapped my arms around his neck. "In fact, my only thought right now is how in the heck I managed to jump off this cliff in the first place without freaking out."

"I'd like to point out I was the one swearing and freaking out." Slade pulled away then shrugged out of his white linen shirt. "Ready?"

I bit down on my lower lip. "Is this a bad idea?"

"Now you ask?" He grinned, his golden eyes heating every inch of my body as that grin spread over his face like I was the most perfect thing he'd ever seen. "Correct me if I'm wrong, but weren't you the one that said, 'Hey, Slade, you know what would be great? An epic wedding picture of us jumping off that cliff.' To which I replied, 'Never again, no.' To which Matt said, 'Just think of the publicity.'"

"I was wrong." Matt came up behind us and peered over the cliff. "A man can admit when he's wrong. This wasn't a smart decision. In fact, I think we should all go back to the hotel and drink."

"Scared?" Jagger joined us, already shirtless with nothing on but his linen pants and bare feet. "Think of it as an adventure, Matty." He slapped him on the back. "Plus, nobody likes a guy that colors inside the lines. Live a little."

"Oh, I live a lot," Matt grumbled. "At least when I'm not babysitting." He grinned at both of them, then gave them a pointed stare for good measure just to make sure they understood who he meant.

"Ready?" I asked Slade in a nervous voice.

He interlaced his fingers through mine and then kissed the back of my hand. "Name one thing you would have done differently."

"One thing," I repeated with a grin.

"Just one."

"I already did it—I kissed you." I leaned up on my tiptoes and pressed a kiss to his lips. "And then I jumped."

"And then we jumped," he corrected as we both leaped off the cliff amidst screaming, followed by our friends.

When the cold water hit me all I heard was swearing from Matt and Jagger, but all I saw was my husband's face as he pulled me close and wrapped his arms around me and whispered, "I've never been so thankful for engine failure in my entire life."

Acknowledgments

First off, I have to thank God.

Oh man, this book was one of those books for me, one of those books that I wanted to be epic and romantic and just a wonderful joyride for my readers, and I remember just staring at the cursor going, *Where is this going? What's the story?* I had the first part of Puerto Vallarta written, but then I realized I can't just make this about soccer, I have to make this more . . . and the story was born. The minute Slade's father dies and we get into his head I saw that this guy needs help, he needs to heal, but I don't want Mack to be weak and put aside her needs for his. She has to be her own woman. You see, here's a secret: female characters can be really challenging to write because they can come out as damsels or whiny or just plain irritating, and that's such a misrepresentation of all the strong women I've been blessed to know in my life. But how do you create a strong female character without making her come across almost too harsh? It's such a difficult balance! I truly feel like Mackenzie is the perfect female representation of what to do when life gives you lemons. I look up to her so much, and it was such an honor to write her story. Thank you so much for joining me on their journey, guys! And thank goodness for answered prayers!

Thank you to my husband and son for all the time they let me have with my computer while I agonized over this story. To my family for their constant support. To the best publisher around—Amazon

Publishing knows how to treat their authors. I always feel like I'm part of the family, and I love writing for you guys! Melody and Maria, thank you so much for your support with this project. And to the marketing and merchandising team, thank you for helping me name this book, hah-hah! It was a struggle, I know! It took a village for this one, didn't it?

To Erica, the best agent in the world (no, seriously, she really is), thank you for supporting me, thank you for all of your encouragement.

To Nina, Becca, Jill, Angie, and the rest of my admins, you guys are a big part of making it so that I can write. I'm so thankful to have such an incredible team behind me. You do all the things I can't do, and I would be lost without you guys! Social Butterfly PR, thank you for another successful launch and for taking me on when I was desperate! Nina, you are more than my publicist. Thank you for always being available to me.

To the bloggers and readers, it never gets old. I'm so thankful for you guys, for the shares, the reviews, the comments. Thank you for caring and thank you for always being so supportive. I truly believe this community is one of the best around, and I'm so thankful to be a part of it. To my Rockin' Readers, I kind of feel like we're our own mafia now, hah-hah. Blood in, no out, RRR family ;)

Readers, if you want to connect with me, join the happiest group on Facebook: Rachel's New Rockin' Readers. We're big but we're a family, and we really care about each other. Everyone is welcome!

Thank you for reading!

Until next time.

HUGS, RVD